PORTRAIT OF VENGEANCE

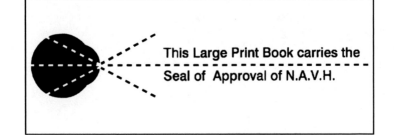

This Large Print Book carries the
Seal of Approval of N.A.V.H.

A GWEN MARCEY NOVEL, BOOK 4

PORTRAIT OF VENGEANCE

CARRIE STUART PARKS

THORNDIKE PRESS
A part of Gale, a Cengage Company

Farmington Hills, Mich • San Francisco • New York • Waterville, Maine
Meriden, Conn • Mason, Ohio • Chicago

LIBRARY OF CONGRESS CIP DATA ON FILE.
CATALOGUING IN PUBLICATION FOR THIS BOOK
IS AVAILABLE FROM THE LIBRARY OF CONGRESS

ISBN-13: 978-1-4328-4673-2 (hardcover)
ISBN-10: 1-4328-4673-6 (hardcover)

Published in 2018 by arrangement with Thomas Nelson, Inc., a division of HarperCollins Christian Publishing, Inc.

Printed in the United States of America
1 2 3 4 5 6 7 22 21 20 19 18

*To Rick, who brings me
story ideas and inspiration daily.
Along with hockey scores. Sigh.*

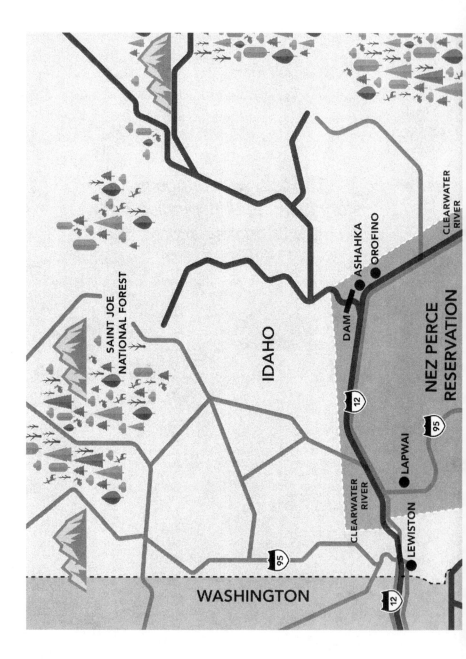

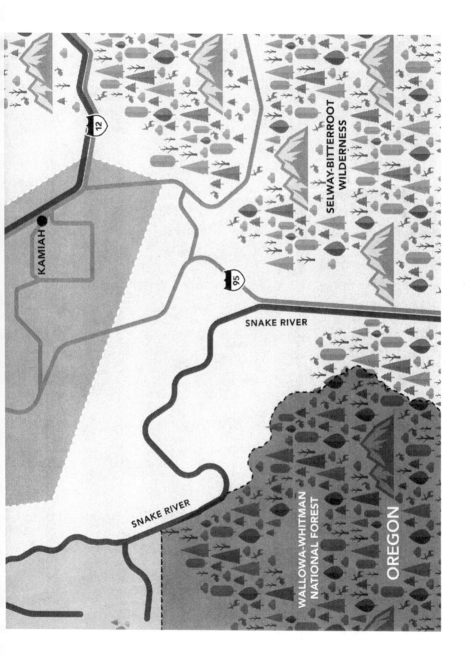

PROLOGUE

Kamiah, Idaho
June 1994

Someone had left the front door open.

I stopped abruptly on the front walk. I *knew* I'd closed and locked the door when I left to get the groceries, just like my mom, Holly, told me to.

Holly will be in a fearful mood if she finds out. When she finds out.

In spite of the heat beating on my back from the midday June sunshine, I shivered.

Jacob probably forgot. He was only four years old. He didn't understand Holly's . . . problems.

I would claim to be the culprit. At fourteen, I was better able to withstand Holly's raging storms. Lately I'd had lots of practice.

Slowly I approached the porch, climbed the few steps, and pulled open the screen door.

The rank stench of copper, body fluids, and sweat hit me like a locomotive.

I gagged.

Blood splattered the walls and floor. An overturned coffee table lay on a broken vase.

Holly's voice screeched in my brain. *Run, Gwen! If ever you find us dead, it means he found us!*

The sack of groceries and gallon of milk slipped from my numb hands, crashing to the floor. Spilled milk mixed with blood, making pink swirls on the floor.

My feet seemed rooted to the ground.

A hatchet was embedded in the center of the room, smeared blackish-red.

Run!

Jacob's favorite toy, a genuine Shari Lewis Lamb Chop puppet I'd given him for Christmas, was ripped apart.

Dead. They're both dead.

I turned and ran.

CHAPTER ONE

Present Day

Commander Gary James, my boss, looked around the room. Five of us had gathered around the "conference table," which was more accurately the dining room table of an old house outside of downtown Missoula, Montana. The government grant that funded us didn't stretch as far as a chrome-and-glass office overlooking the mountains.

I was just happy to be on a regular forensic art job. I had a new identity card with my name printed on it — *Gwen Marcey, Forensic Artist* — and the unit's seal. A new gun, a set of flex-cuffs, and the use of a car rounded out my perks. I straightened the shiny gold badge mounted on a leather holder and hanging by a chain around my neck. Even though I was still on probation, I was ridiculously proud to wear it.

The Interagency Major Crimes Unit had been in the works for years, the brainchild

11

of two police chiefs who'd been on the painful end of major crime waves. They'd been overwhelmed, understaffed, and underfunded. They pitched the idea of a group of individuals with various specialty backgrounds who could be available on an as-needed basis should a smaller agency get hit with a major crime. In addition to a government grant, the IMCU received an annual fee from the agencies that used it. This concept kept the local agencies in charge of their cases, an idea they relished.

Commander James pointed to the projected image on the screen behind him. "Turning to the last box on the W307 form, this space is for the narrative . . ."

I stifled my yawn and peeked again at my watch. This mind-numbing lecture on filling out paperwork had to have gone on for hours. Blake Adkin's plane should have landed by now. He'd be on his way to pick me up. I hadn't seen him since I returned from the case in Kentucky six months ago. I smiled.

"Do you think it's funny when you misspell words on an official form, Gwen?" Commander James asked.

"Oh no, sir. Misspelled words are a serious crime —"

Someone kicked me under the table.

"Ump!" I looked around the table but no one would meet my gaze. "I'm just excited about the new cases that came in." I waved at the perfectly aligned stack of files resting in front of him.

He glanced down and I again checked my watch.

"All right." He turned off the projector and picked up the files.

I let out a sigh.

"Four agencies have contacted us in the past day requesting our services." Commander James made sure we were all paying attention. "I've already assigned staff to each of them."

Picking up my mug of stone-cold coffee, I nodded and gave him a slight smile.

He gave me a frosty stare and opened the first file.

I wanted to throw a pencil at his head for being such a boring grumpbox, but if I missed, it would shatter the graphite of a perfectly good pencil.

"Anaconda has a convenience-store robbery with a homicide." Commander James closed the file. "It's the second in three weeks. Jennifer, I'm sending you." He handed the file over to our crime-scene specialist, Jennifer Bailey.

"You men" — James nodded at the two

officers on his right — "will be working an accident reconstruction outside Mills, Wyoming. The highway patrol is involved and wants outside assistance."

"Gwen." He turned to me. "Kodiak, Alaska, needs forensic art help on a cold case."

"Pun intended?" I grinned at being sent somewhere besides Mills or Anaconda.

"I don't understand." He frowned.

"You know . . . cold? Alaska? Um . . ." I gripped my coffee to keep from throwing a pencil anyway. "What's the last case?"

"From the Nez Perce Tribal Police, in Lapwai, Idaho. Double homicide, missing four-year-old child. Killer used a hatchet."

I sloshed the coffee over my hand and onto the table. Jennifer helped me mop up. When I knew my voice would be somewhat steady, I asked, "Where exactly is Lapwai located?"

"North Central Idaho, near Lewiston."

Lewiston? Where my parents had been murdered.

"Are you okay, Gwen?" Jennifer asked. "You're as white as a sheet."

I gave her a trembling smile. "The case just reminds me of an old . . . case I was once involved with. What kind of specialist did they ask for?"

14

"General help in interviewing." Commander James glared at the mess I'd made. "Maybe some crime-scene help. I've assigned it to Kirt."

"No." I took the file before Kirt had a chance to grab it. "They need a forensic artist."

"They didn't ask for one." Kirt reached for the materials I held.

"They've probably never even heard of forensic art." I moved the folder out of range. "Listen, with a missing child, time is critical. By the time someone figures out they saw something, it could be too late. And I . . . kinda know the area."

"It's my case." Kirt's voice went up a notch.

Commander James tapped his lower lip. "I don't know —"

"Please." I leaned forward. "You said Kodiak was a cold case. There's no rush. And you know I'm a trained interviewer. And I've worked crime scenes. I'm already packed." *To go on a trip to Glacier Park with Blake.* I held my breath.

"Okay. I'll call them and say you're coming —"

"Today. I'll be there as fast as I can drive over."

Everyone at the table was staring at me. I

15

didn't care. I ran away from a scene like that once. I wouldn't run again.

CHAPTER TWO

I didn't wait for commander James to change his mind. Grabbing the case files, I dodged into the restroom and looked at my watch.

Blake is probably waiting outside. What are you going to say to him?

"He'll understand," I whispered. "I hope." A swift phone call to my best friend, Beth, alerted her to my immediate departure. She agreed to take care of my Great Pyrenees, Winston.

Blake was leaning against his rental car holding a bouquet of coral-colored roses. He wore a low-brimmed, black Stetson over sun-bleached hair, a Pendleton jacket, jeans, and alligator boots. He grinned at my appearance, his manganese-blue eyes crinkling.

Throwing all dignity aside, I flew down the steps and into his arms. He engulfed me in a bear hug, making breathing difficult on several levels. After a few moments I extracted myself and stepped away. "Blake! I'm so happy you're here."

"Ready to go? I've booked two rooms —"

"Wait. There's been a slight change of plans."

The boyish grin on his face turned to a frown. "Your daughter's birthday? Did you decide to be with her today after all? I understand —"

"Not quite. Aynslee's staying with her dad." Neither my daughter nor my ex-husband had bothered to tell me when, or if, they were having a birthday celebration.

"What, then?"

"There's been a homicide, actually, two homicides, and a little girl is missing."

Blake straightened. "That's terrible, but what does it have to do with you? With us?"

"I need to go. It's only for a few days."

His gaze sharpened. "Why you? Aren't there other members of your team who could take care of it?"

I placed my hand on his arm. "No one has my particular skills. Listen, you could come with me. I'd be gone during the day, but we could spend the evenings —"

"I didn't fly all the way here from Kentucky to have a few evenings with you."

"If you can wait, I'll be back in a couple

of days —"

"I won't be here in a couple of days." He stepped away.

"I'm sorry, Blake, it's just bad timing. I wanted to see you, I *want* to see you —"

"Obviously not enough to change your plans." Blake shook his head. He was even more handsome than I remembered.

"Blake, this is important —"

"Important enough that I may not be waiting for you when you're done?"

I searched his face. "If there's anything between us, it can't be this fragile. You'll have to trust me."

He took another step back and stared at me a moment. "Let me think about it." He turned and got into his car.

I should stop him. Someone else could work on the homicide. Commander James wasn't even going to give me the case.

Don't bother. The voice of my ex-husband, Robert, echoed in my brain. *You might as well break up with him now, before he has a chance to find out you're damaged goods.*

"Shut up, Robert."

You're toxic to men.

"Get out of my head!"

"Are you feeling okay?" Commander James stood behind me as I watched Blake drive off.

"I . . . um . . . a gnat flew in my ear and . . . um, I'm leaving." *A gnat?* I sounded like a raging idiot.

It was a four-hour drive from Missoula to Lapwai, Idaho. I spent the time trying not to think about the upcoming case. I didn't want to form an opinion without the facts. I wondered instead if Robert was right. Maybe I *was* toxic to men.

The route took me past the small town of Kamiah. I hadn't been back to this area in more than twenty years.

My sweaty hands slipped on the steering wheel and I grew light-headed. I'd never wanted to return.

How strange that there would be two different ax murders involving four-year-old children. Especially just over sixty miles apart. And within a few miles of where my own biological parents had been slaughtered before I went to live with Holly.

It's just a strange coincidence.

But I didn't believe in coincidences.

The house where the most recent double murder had occurred was easy enough to find. Lapwai's population was just a bit over eleven hundred souls in the rolling hills of the Palouse farming region. Police and emergency vehicles clogged the streets nearby, and I had to park several blocks away.

An attractive female deputy with the name badge of "K. LoneBear" stopped me as I passed under the yellow crime-scene tape. "You can't go in there. It's a crime scene. The chief will give a statement to the press later this afternoon."

"I'm not the press. I'm with the Interagency Major Crimes Unit." I held up my badge. "Your chief requested me."

"Credentials." She held out her hand and tapped her foot while I rummaged in my purse for the identification card and handed it over. She took her time reading it and comparing my face to the photo. "I don't know why we need an outsider like you."

I smiled without showing my teeth.

She pointed outside the crime-scene tape. "Wait there." Not waiting for me to agree, she spun around and headed to the house.

I stayed where I was.

LoneBear returned shortly and signaled for me to enter the house.

The house reeked with the stench of death. I'd never seen so much blood, not even when Holly and Jacob died.

The room reminded me of a painting by Jackson Pollock, monochromatically spattered with perylene maroon. Matching smears of blood tinted the oyster-colored carpet. I gripped the purse strap slung over my shoulder and carefully picked my way through the crimson splashes. Black fingerprint powder created abstract smudges on the different surfaces.

Overturned and broken furniture looked like a herd of buffalo had stampeded through the living room of the single-story ranch.

Several police officers conferred in the dining room straight ahead. The medical examiner must have already removed the bodies, but it was easy to see where one victim had died. The coppery smell permeating the air made me queasy.

LoneBear watched my face intently for a reaction. She looked disappointed when I gave her a slight, dismissive smile. When she turned her head, I swallowed hard and bit my lip.

"The lady from Montana is here," she announced to the room.

My body chose that moment for a massive hot flash, a reminder of the lasting effects of my battle with breast cancer and antihormonal therapy. Lava-hot burning started in my chest, raced up my neck, and slammed into my cheeks. Sweat dampened the back of my cerulean-blue uniform blouse, and air seemed to be at a premium. I knew my face would be flushed red with beads of moisture on my upper lip, hardly a professional presentation to a room full of police officers.

I pivoted and studied the blood spatter to my left as if I were at an exhibit at a modern art museum. I hoped by the time anyone came over to greet me my face wouldn't be flushed and sweaty.

Someone on my right cleared his throat, then coughed gently.

I'm just going to have to meet him looking like this. I turned and held out my hand. "Hi. I'm Gwen Marcey, the forensic artist from the Interagency Major Crimes Unit."

The man took my hand as if uncertain whether my hot flash was contagious. "Are you okay?"

"Mmmm."

"Ah, welcome, then, to Lapwai. I'm Seth Kus, chief of the Nez Perce Tribal Police."

I blinked several times. Chief Seth Kus of the Nez Perce Tribal Police was bodice-ripping-cover-of-a-romance-novel handsome. His caramel-colored skin didn't seem to sport pores. Blue-black hair, combed back off a high forehead, gleamed in the overhead light. His black eyes, under level eyebrows, had a slight tilt to the outside corners. A few radiating wrinkles around his eyes spoke of spending time outdoors and squinting at the sun. Midthirties, I'd say. His lips were full, cheeks prominent, and jaw chiseled. I mentally pulled out a stick of charcoal and started drawing him.

"Are you sure you're okay?" he asked again, his right eye narrowing.

I reluctantly dropped my imaginary sketchpad. "Yes. I'm sorry. I came as fast as I could, but it was a long, winding drive from Missoula."

"Well, Mrs. Marcey —"

"Call me Gwen."

"Okay, Gwen, Commander James called and told us you were on your way. He said you were a forensic artist. I'm not sure exactly what it is you do."

"I can do your interviews, of course, and watch subjects for signs of deception. If you have a description from a witness, I can sketch it. I can photograph your scene, scale out and draw it, work on surveillance photos, image modification —"

"Whoa, I'm sold. Everyone in this department is artistically challenged." He started to turn toward the dining room when his attention shifted to my right. "Officer Lone-Bear, shouldn't you be on patrol now?"

"Of course, *Chief.*" Her gaze held his for

a long moment before sliding down his body. "Will you be coming to the casino tonight?"

Chief Kus clenched his jaw. "I might. I'm sure Gwen here" — his gaze slid to my ring finger — "wouldn't mind joining me for a good dinner."

LoneBear looked like she was ready to claw out my eyes.

Chief Kus took my elbow and moved me toward the area of drying blood near the dining room table. "I'm sorry about that. LoneBear . . . well, I'm sorry if I put you on the spot."

I waved away his apology.

He nodded his relief. "I've formed a task force. I'm heading up the investigation. You'll be reporting directly to me." He looked around, then pulled me slightly aside and said in a soft voice, "Feelings are running high about these murders. They're our own people, brutally murdered, with a missing child. You may get some pushback for being an outsider."

"Thank you for sharing that. I can handle it. I'll try to ruffle as few feathers as possible."

The chief nodded, then indicated a pool of blood. "The victims' names are Adam

Sinopa and his wife, Alice. Adam was found here."

I looked from the floor to the walls in the living room. "The weapon was an ax?"

"Possibly some kind of a small ax or hatchet. We think Adam was struck on the head first with something else."

I knew by now my face wouldn't be flushed. I just hoped it wouldn't go pale. "Okay. So he fled from his attackers but didn't make it. I'm not a blood spatter —"

"The IMCU is sending someone. I just want you to have the background before you meet with the possible witnesses. Alice was in here." He again took my elbow.

Although his fingers only lightly touched my arm, it felt like an electric current. *This is ridiculous.* I just blew my relationship with Blake. I didn't need to start another that I could wreck as well. Without appearing to do so, I extracted my arm from his grasp. We arrived at the bedroom and the second crime scene was abundantly apparent.

"We think the murders occurred after midnight but before 0800 this morning." He didn't seem to notice my actions. "Alice was still in bed."

The bed in question had been stripped of bedding, but the mattress and walls told the story. Some blood showed on the right side of the mattress, but the left side was drenched. "She was found on the far left side." He moved in that direction. "On the floor between the bed and wall."

"So she rolled away from her killer."

Chief Kus's eyebrows rose. "I thought you weren't a blood spatter expert."

"I'm not."

The man stared at me a moment. "Must be that artistic eye."

"Something like that."

He moved away from the bed and waved me toward the door. This time he didn't take my arm. "The phone lines were cut. The daughter's room is over here."

Sucking in a deep breath, I walked to the little girl's room, which opened off the kitchen. The walls were painted azo green with stenciled ballerina teddy bears. Lettered over the bed was a poem:

The teddy bear dances
In the gentle moonlight.
She twirls and she prances,
Her dreams taking flight.

A shelf circled the room near the ceiling with a large collection of stuffed animals, mostly teddy bears. No blood, but the bed was unmade and a few toys were scattered on the floor. A white rocking chair sat in the corner of the room. Sitting in the middle was a lamb puppet.

A Shari Lewis Lamb Chop puppet.

My legs grew rubbery. I grasped the doorknob to stay upright.

"Are you all right?" The chief's buzzing voice was distant and faint. "Mrs. Marcey? Gwen?"

I couldn't hold on. Blackness lapped around my eyesight before closing in.

CHAPTER THREE

I inhaled the aroma of newly cut grass and opened my eyes. The sky overhead was a cloudless rich blue. Not just blue, most definitely Winsor blue. I had a tube of it somewhere. Such a lovely color —

A face intruded on my view. He looked familiar. Quite handsome. A striking resemblance to . . . Chief Kus of the Nez Perce Tribal Police.

And I had fainted at a crime scene.

"Mrs. Marcey, Gwen, are you okay?"

Heat rushed across my cheeks. I put my hands over my face and curled up on my side.

"Mrs. Marcey?"

"Go away," I said through my fingers. "I'm waiting for the earth to swallow me up."

Chief Kus cleared his throat. "We've called the paramedics —"

"Oh no!" I sat up quickly, then clutched

the ground to keep it from rolling any more. "I'm fine. Really. Please don't make a fuss. I . . . I . . ."

A number of law-enforcement officers, the same group that had been discussing the homicide in the dining room, now stood around me.

"Rookie," someone muttered.

"Amateur outsider," someone else whispered.

Wailing sirens grew louder, then stopped.

I groaned. My first official job for the Interagency Major Crimes Unit was turning into a goat rodeo. "I appreciate the concern, Chief, but really, I'm fine."

Chief Kus's right eye narrowed and he stepped away. A paramedic took his place. "What's your name?" he asked, taking my pulse.

"Gwen Marcey. What's yours? Never mind. Please, this isn't necessary. I'm fine, just embarrassed."

"What happened?"

"I guess I fainted. I had a long trip, didn't eat . . . Please don't make a fuss." After a lot of convincing, the paramedic glanced at the chief, gave a slight shrug, and moved away.

Glancing around, I found I'd been carried to the front lawn of the murder house. Most of the other officers had moved to the front door and were whispering to each other. Standing, I looked around for my purse, finally spotting it lying some distance away. I retrieved it and returned to the chief. I could still barely look him in the eye. "I'm sorry about that. I'm ready to work. Did you . . . get the pdf files on our services?"

"Yes." A flick of his hand summoned an officer with a three-ring binder. "The names, addresses, and phone numbers of the witnesses we'd like you to interview are in here." He was all business. "Since you do those sketches, maybe if someone saw something . . . ?"

"Of course."

"You'll find the homicide report in there as well. You're booked into the Clearwater River Lodge." He handed me the binder and a business card.

I took all the material from him and quickly reviewed the contents. "Are there photographs?"

The chief pulled out a small notebook and jotted something. "I'll send them over. Would you also do a rough sketch of the crime scene? That is, if you promise you won't faint." He didn't smile, but his lips twitched slightly.

"Promise. Um, my kit's in the car. I'll

31

need to get my tape measure and compass
—"

"We have those here. There's graph paper
in the back of the binder. Officer Attao" —
he signaled to a patrol officer standing
nearby — "can help you."

Officer Attao proved to be a Native American with a roundish face, black hair, and
tanned skin.

"Steve, this is Gwen Marcey, the forensic
artist," Chief Kus said. "Please assist her
while she sketches the scene."

Officer Attao nodded a greeting. "Gwen?
Is that short for Gwendolyn?"

"No. Just Gwen."

Kus gave a small signal to his officers.
They parted as I approached, maybe to give
me room to faint again, should I need it. Or
maybe to make it clear how unwanted I was.

Once more in the living room, I placed
the binder on an end table and opened it to
the graph paper in the back. While I roughed
out the room, Attao brought me a compass
and tape measure. I dated the paper, re-
corded the reading on the compass, and
handed Attao the stupid end of the tape
measure.

He looked at it a moment. "Your agency
didn't have any regular investigators available? Just an artist?"

I gritted my teeth for a moment. "Just me. But I do have the ability to draw my own conclusions." I checked to see if he got my humor.

He didn't.

Moving around the room, I jotted down the measurements and locations of windows, doors, furniture, and a freestanding pellet stove. The dining room was next. The dining room and kitchen were connected with off-white ceramic tile flooring. The blood had soaked into the grout. "I don't suppose anyone measured the location of the body before you moved it?"

Attao just looked at me.

I measured one of the tiles. It was 24 × 24 with a quarter-inch grout in between.

"What are you doing?" Attao asked.

"I can get the approximate location of the body from the crime-scene photos by counting how many tiles over it was from the different walls."

Chief Kus approached. "How's it going?"

"Almost done in here. I still have the two bedrooms. Did you want any of the other rooms measured?"

"No. That's great." He spotted someone outside and headed off.

The master bedroom didn't have any other furniture in it beyond the bed, dresser, and two small tables.

Attao's phone rang. "Attao. Yeah. Okay. Be right there." He hung up and looked at me. "I'll be back in a few minutes. You okay?"

"Yes. Just the one remaining room."

After he left, I tugged a small sketchpad out of my purse along with a lead holder. I wrote *Known* on the left side of the paper and *Unknown* on the other, then drew a line between them. Under *Known* I wrote *identity of victims, location of murders, approximate time, hit with something first, ax.*

I wandered out of the master bedroom, still writing. Under *Unknown* I wrote *daughter alive/target? number of assailants, know victims? why killed?* Avoiding the large bloodstain on the floor, I strolled to the kitchen and opened the refrigerator. The sparse contents — milk, beer, bread — each rested on its own shelf. The freezer was stuffed with microwavable meals. The cupboards were loaded with Hamburger Helper, mac and cheese, and cans of SpaghettiOs and applesauce.

Mrs. Sinopa appeared to be of the same caliber of cook that I was.

In the child's bedroom the Lamb Chop puppet stared at me from the rocking chair. *Lots of children have puppets. I'm sure this is readily available on the Internet. Just because it was Jacob's favorite toy . . . And the blood . . . And the age of the child . . . And . . .*

I'd ask Chief Kus.

I reluctantly turned my back on it. The fingerprint-powder-smudged dresser held a framed photograph of a beautiful little girl. I crossed to the bed and pulled the covers back. The sheet was urine soaked. I pulled up the corner. The mattress pad underneath wasn't waterproof.

"Her name was Beatrice."

I turned to find Chief Kus leaning against the door.

"Was?" I asked.

"Is? We don't know. She's been gone for maybe sixteen hours. Roughly 89 percent of kids abducted are murdered within the first twenty-four."

"Then she has a slim chance." I held up the photo of the little girl. "Could you send me a copy of this?"

"Take that one. Just bring it back."

I tucked the framed image into my purse, then picked up a teddy bear from the floor and hugged it. "She was terrified."

"I'm sure she was, but how —"

"She wet the bed, but she's not a bed wetter or she'd be sleeping on a waterproof mattress liner." I held up the bear. "May I?"

35

Chief Kus's right eye narrowed. "If you feel you need it."

I smiled at him. "For Beatrice. She'll want to have something familiar to hold when we find her." I turned to the puppet. "Do you . . . does anyone know if this is her toy?"

Kus looked at the puppet. "I'll ask around. Why?"

"Well, um, she collects teddy bears and it just seems out of place. Can it be finger-printed?"

Kus raised his eyebrows at me. "Everything that could hold a fingerprint has already been checked."

"In that case, can I take it with me too?"

The chief nodded, but his eyes clearly expressed his doubts about my professionalism.

Officer Attao returned. Once again I handed him one end of the tape measure and we finished the child's room. I went over my notes to be sure I hadn't missed something. Officer Attao shifted from one foot to the other. I finally looked up. "Done." I reached into my purse and pulled out a business card with my cell number. "Thank you for your help. If I can do anything for you, please call."

Attao's eyes opened wide, but he took my card and tucked it into his wallet.

Gathering up the binder, teddy, puppet, and sketchpad, I left the house. I didn't want to think about the fate of that little girl, but I also wanted to keep in mind the stakes if I failed to do my best work.

The town of Lapwai, the seat of the Nez Perce tribal government, was less than a square mile in size. I headed for where I'd parked the IMCU car, a 1995 burgundy Honda Accord with over two hundred thousand miles on it, a couple of blocks away. When the unit promised an agency car, I'd somehow thought I'd get an official black SUV with tinted windows. Or at least a Ford Police Interceptor.

My car was gone.

CHAPTER FOUR

I glanced up and down the street, sure I'd parked there, in front of a mass of blooming lilac bushes and across the street from the gold-and-white mobile home. Every house had a large number of vehicles parked in front, on the side, and sometimes on the lawn, as it seemed everyone was having a neighborhood party. It had been tricky to find a spot to park without blocking someone's driveway. I thought the lilacs were a good marker, albeit not my favorite fragrance anymore.

This is ridiculous. The town isn't that big. I could see the emerald-green rolling hills marking the outside of town. How many oversized lilac bushes and mobile homes could there be in this place? I walked around the block, then the next one. Lots of mobile homes. Lots of lilacs. No sign of my car.

A warm wind smelling of fresh earth and

fragrant syringa restlessly tossed my hair. Curious faces peered at me from the houses I passed. A dark-haired woman stepped onto her porch, stared at me intently, then called her two children inside. Other children rode bicycles at the end of the street.

A patrol SUV pulled up next to me and parked, and an officer stepped out. "Can I help — Oh, it's you." Officer Attao didn't look happy to see me again.

"Someone stole my car."

"But not your teddy bear or stuffed lamb?"

I'd forgotten I was still carrying Beatrice's bear and the puppet. I tucked them under my arm. "This is serious."

"Are you *sure* you parked it here?" He shaded his eyes with one hand and looked around with an exaggerated gesture. "Such a big city and all."

A cow mooed in the distance.

He dropped his hand. "And you think you can help us find a killer when you can't even find your own car?"

I gritted my teeth. "It was a 1995 burgundy Honda Accord."

"And you think someone would have stolen *that* car? Did you leave your keys in it?"

"Of course not." I swung my purse off my

shoulder and rummaged around inside. "My keys are . . . Just a minute . . . They're in here somewhere."

The keys were missing.

I slumped against the patrol SUV. Could I possibly have been so focused on getting to the crime scene that I left the keys in the ignition? Of the agency's car?

Shaking my head, I turned. "Officer Attao, the keys are missing from my purse, maybe removed when I fainted." *Yeah, right, someone takes keys for a beater car and leaves my wallet and brand-new Glock 42 pistol.*

"Get in." Officer Attao barely waited until I jumped into the front seat before he drove us the short distance to the Nez Perce Tribal Police Department.

I was glad he was driving. I never would have found the department on my own. The only clue was the chain-link-enclosed parking area for police vehicles. The department was a pale-yellow building with the main door recessed between a single-wide mobile home and two other structures. It was accessed by a long cement ramp leading to a door with a computer-generated sign on paper stating Main Lobby. Once inside, we turned left, opened another door, and entered the lobby, about the size of a large walk-in closet. A woman behind the glassed-in reception waved us through a secure door. Chief Kus was walking toward us. He paused, folded his arms, and raised his eyebrows at me.

"Stolen vehicle," the patrolman said to the chief.

For the second time that day I hoped the earth would open up and swallow me. "I think someone took the keys out of my purse while I was unconscious —"

The chief's cheeks reddened slightly. "The only people around at that time were my officers."

"I'm not accusing your staff —"

"From where I'm standing, it looks that way." He glanced at the patrol officer. "Get the paperwork filled out and drive her to the lodge." He stared at me. "I'm short-handed as it is and don't have an extra officer to cart you around. You're supposed to be assisting us here, so I assume you can get other transportation. You can start your interviews at the lodge." He turned and moved away, then stopped and said over his shoulder, "The task force will be assembling here at 0800 tomorrow. I need results on finding that little girl."

My face burned and I looked down. Someone shoved a police-report form at me. I took it and followed the retreating patrol officer's heels to a small interview room with a table and two chairs. He nodded at one, then left, leaving the door open behind him. The jaundiced fluorescent light buzzed and flickered overhead, and the room reeked of sweat, disinfectants, and a hint of burned coffee. I rummaged in my purse and found a pen and my cell phone. My best friend, Beth, was on speed dial. "Hi, Beth —"

"Gwen! You must have just arrived in Lapwai." The background music of a forensic television show stopped. "What's wrong? Is it true a little girl is missing? And you have a double homicide? It's in all the papers. Can I help? All you have to do is ask."

"Yes. A lot. Yes. Yes. I'm not surprised. Yes. I'm asking."

Beth was silent for a moment. "I hate it when you do — Really? You need my help?"

"More than you know. It's not just this double homicide." I took a deep breath. "What I'm going to tell you I've not shared with anyone else. Except Robert."

Beth snorted.

"When I was fourteen, I came home from the store and found the front door open, the house trashed, and blood everywhere. I knew that Holly, who was sort of my mom,

42

was dead, along with her four-year-old son."

"What's a sorta-mom?"

"I'll explain it all later." I took another deep breath. "There are elements to this double homicide that are strikingly similar to that murder. It may be nothing, but I just have this hinky feeling. I need to concentrate on finding the killer and little Beatrice, but I need you to do the research on the earlier murders."

"You know I'll be there and help you."

"There's more." I explained the stolen car. "So here's my problem. All my clothes, my forensic drawing kit, and my newer laptop were also stolen. I can do a few interviews and hope they find my car, but if they don't find it right away, I'm dead in the water."

"Let me know what to bring and I'll be there as fast as possible."

"Thanks, girlfriend." I explained what I needed and where to find it. "Drive my car over. I'm staying at the Clearwater River Lodge just outside of Lewiston. You'll find a spare set of keys in the kitchen drawer on the left of the sink, and I'll get you a flight from Lewiston to Missoula —"

"Hold on to your deerstalker, Sherlock! Your faithful Watson is sticking around to help you through the case."

I rubbed my forehead. "What about your

husband? Won't he miss you?"

"After April fifteenth, Norman can only think about his yearly fishing trip. He won't notice I'm gone."

"But you're dog-sitting Winston. I'm sure this lodge won't appreciate a 165-pound Great Pyrenees, albeit well behaved."

"Let that be the least of your problems. I'll find a dog-friendly place and we'll make that headquarters. I'll drive my car because it's bigger. With fewer dents. I commend you on your foudroyant insight, will pack up your schmatte, and see you soon!"

"Did you just —"

"Yes. Got two words of the day into one sentence. Bye."

I clutched the phone after Beth disconnected, reluctant to let go of her caring voice. *That's not surprising, she's your best friend.*

Your only friend, Robert chimed in.

"Not true, Robert," I whispered. "There's Dave —"

His family raised you since you were fourteen. He just feels responsible.

I squeezed the phone tighter. "Again, not true —"

Name one other friend, let alone a boyfriend. You can't. You're so selfish and self-centered that no one can get close to you.

"Shut up!" I slammed down my phone before Robert could intrude on my thoughts any more.

I filled out the paperwork. Officer Attao was speaking with a coworker when I emerged. He took the report, handed it to a secretary, and jerked his head for me to follow. The drive from Lapwai to the hotel at Lewiston took us down the Lapwai Valley. Though I had vague memories of Kamiah, I'd forgotten so much of that time, for obvious reasons. Officer Attao thawed enough to inform me the Nez Perce named the region Thlap-Thlap, referring to the sound of butterfly wings.

"Are there a lot of butterflies now?" I asked.

"No."

Shortly he jerked his thumb right. "Spalding."

Hoping to show at least a particle of knowledge of the area, I said, "I did read that Lillian Disney, the wife of Walt Disney, was born here and grew up in Lapwai. I didn't realize she was Nez Perce."

"She wasn't."

Okay, then, so much for small talk.

"You've heard of Spalding and Whitman?" Attao finally asked.

"Um . . ."

"Reverend Henry Spalding and his wife were missionaries to our tribe. This was the first white settlement. Eighteen thirty-six."

"And Whitman?"

"He and his wife, Narcissa, had a mission near Walla Walla, with the Cayuse tribe. Exposure to the white man brought measles that wiped out nearly half the tribe. As a result —"

"I have heard of him. The Whitman Massacre."

"Yep. They were both killed, along with eleven other settlers. The start of the Cayuse War." He glanced at me, then focused on his driving.

"I'm afraid about all I remember of Northwest history is Lewis and Clark."

"And Sacagawea, a Lemhi Shoshone woman who spoke three languages and did the entire journey carrying her infant son."

I can't even drive over from Montana and walk into a house without fainting. "Impressive."

He snorted.

We were now driving along the Clearwater River, the largest tributary of the Snake River, to the edge of the city of Lewiston, the farthest inland seaport in the western United States. Overlooking the river, the casino and lodge were housed in an imposing wood-and-log structure.

The teddy bear and Lamb Chop puppet under my arm and lack of luggage raised the clerk's eyebrows, but the presence of Officer Attao must have reassured her. She handed me a key card, pointed right, and fluttered her eyelashes at the officer.

My room was decorated in warm tones with two queen beds and a desk. I locked the door behind me, placed my few belongings on the desk, sat, and closed my eyes. Two bloody crime scenes. Two hatchet murder weapons. Two of the same toy. Both Beatrice and Jacob were four. The murder locations were within an hour of each other.

I opened my sketchpad to a clean sheet. Nothing cleared my mind more than visualizing a case. At the top of the page, I wrote *Similarities.* Underneath I drew a line forming two columns. I wrote *Holly murders* on one side, *Sinopa murders* on the other.

On the next page I did the same, but changed *Similarities* to *Differences.*

I'd already identified the similarities: bloody scene, age of children, location, murder weapon, toy. I'd record the differences as I worked the Sinopa case. That would settle the uneasiness I felt.

I picked up the teddy bear. One eye was missing, and a small tear along a side seam allowed a puff of stuffing to seep out. "Finding your mom and dad's killer will lead me to you, Beatrice. And I *will* find you."

CHAPTER FIVE

Opening the binder on the desk in front of me, I read the case file.

Bob Williams, the principal of the Lapwai Elementary School, called dispatch at 0817 about a body at the home of Adam and Alice Sinopa. He said he went to the home when Alice, a second-grade teacher, hadn't shown up for work or answered repeated phone calls. He saw Adam's body through the living room window. He sat on the porch and waited until police arrived.

The report went on to say that Alice wasn't discovered for over an hour after the police entered the home because her body was concealed between the bed and wall. Beatrice's absence, however, was immediately noticed and an Amber Alert went out. *Good.*

I removed Beatrice's photo from my purse. Her shoulder-length dark hair was held back by a beaded headpiece. She was wearing a heavily adorned, white buckskin jingle dress. Her skin was quinacridone deep gold, with a slight coral blush on her cheeks. With a heart-shaped face, huge black eyes, and infectious grin, she was adorable.

The slain man, Adam, was the manager of the Clearwater Casino. A quick peek at my list showed several employees of the casino in need of interviewing.

I wouldn't need a car for the casino employees, but if any of them had seen someone I should sketch, I'd have to reschedule for a composite until Beth arrived with my materials.

My laptop was in the trunk of the missing car. Beth was bringing my old one, barely working, but buying a new computer would be a painful replacement. The money I received from my last job in Kentucky hadn't gone as far as I'd hoped. A down payment on a new house, Aynslee's college fund, and the move emptied the account pretty fast. I had four weeks of probation — unpaid, of course — before a salary kicked in.

I scheduled an interview with the casino's assistant manager. I also left a message with Andi Tubbs, a home health nurse who'd been visiting the family next door to the Sinopas the day before the murders.

Before I left the room, Andi returned my call. She *had* seen someone at the Sinopas' house. I asked her the critical question — would you recognize him again if you saw him? If the answer was yes, we could attempt a drawing. We never ask witnesses if they think they could do a composite. It's too easy to say no. If they feel they would recognize someone, however, that means enough memory is present for a skillful interviewer to retrieve that memory.

We agreed to a meeting time the next day at eleven. That would give me time to meet with Chief Kus's task force.

I got directions and disconnected. After checking my watch, I headed next door to the casino to interview Peter S. Otskai, the assistant manager of the casino and lodge. Adam Sinopa had been his boss.

Glass display cases of traditional Nez Perce clothing lined the walls of the main hallway leading from the lodge to the casino. A huge bronze of Chief Joseph, easily the most famous tribal member, stood in front of the gift shop. Entering the gambling section, I peeked into the Qeqiit Lounge.

Chief Kus and Officer LoneBear, who'd announced my arrival at the murder scene, were sitting at a table, heads together in intense conversation.

51

Not wanting to be seen spying, I ducked behind the menu board.

LoneBear shook her head, then glanced around the lounge. She spotted me.

Straightening, I brushed off my slacks as if they were covered in dog hair, then studied the daily specials as if that were my reason for lurking.

LoneBear smiled and placed her hand on the chief's arm.

I quickly moved away before she could see me blush. Continuing forward, I was soon enveloped in a haze of cigarette smoke and a cacophony of pinging, beeping, dinging slot machines. The room was dim, but the machines, placed back-to-back in rows, flashed splashy lights and dazzling images.

Peter had told me on the phone that his office was on the right side of the room as I approached the casino from the hall. I entered the door marked Employees Only. A surprisingly young man in an open-collared light-gray dress shirt glanced up from behind a messy desk. His long black hair was parted in the middle and pulled into a loose ponytail at his neck, making his face appear quite round. "Can I help you?" he asked.

I offered my hand. "I'm Gwen Marcey and I have —"

"Yes. You're from the sheriff's department. I'm Peter Otskai." He shook my hand. "Please have a seat. I see the tribal police checked you into the hotel."

Taking the chair opposite him, I sat and pulled out my sketchpad. "Yes, though I'll probably have to find someplace else. My friend is bringing my dog later —"

"We don't allow —"

"I know. He'll sleep in the car tonight." I smiled at him.

He jotted something on the yellow legal pad in front of him. "I see. Well, if you're checking out tomorrow, could you let me know where you'll be staying? Just in case someone is looking for you." He handed me his business card.

I tucked it into my purse. "Sure. Not a problem. Before we begin this interview, let me offer my condolences —"

He snorted. "Don't bother. The guy was a jerk." At my expression he held up his hands. "Don't get me wrong. I didn't kill him. But I can't say I'm sorry he's dead."

"I see." I took out a pencil and twirled it in my fingers. "Why was he a jerk?"

"Micromanaged everything. Rude. Obnoxious. Always looking for ways to put people down. And he was a Blackfeet." Peter punctuated his last statement by tapping the desk with a finger.

"And that's important because . . . ?"

"His job should have gone to a Nez Perce. Just saying."

"So." I thought for a moment. "The rest of the staff?"

"Also hated him."

"I see." I doodled a face. "Did anyone threaten him, or were there —"

Peter looked down at his desk and shifted a pencil. "No. No. Not really." He shook his head. "Not that I know of. We all wanted to keep our jobs."

Breaking eye contact, multiple denials, change of behavior. Peter had just lied. I made a note of his deception on my sketch-pad and added horns to the face. "When was the last time you saw him?"

The man leaned back in his chair and closed his eyes. "I guess it would be the Easter egg hunt at Clearwater Park. I saw him with his wife and little girl." He opened his eyes and straightened. "Any word on her?"

"Not yet. The Easter egg hunt was on what day?"

"Sunday."

I sketched an egg. "Tell me more about it."

"It's an annual event. Very popular. My

54

wife and I took our two kids."

"Were there a lot of people there?"

Peter nodded. "The place was packed."

"But you noticed Adam's family. Tell me about that."

The man leaned back in his chair again. "Beatrice — I heard Adam calling her Busy Bee — is a beautiful little girl. And she was wearing a pink dress, you know, the fluffy kind that costs an arm and a leg at Nordstrom. I mean, all the kids were dressed up, but Bea looked like a . . . a kid movie star. Everybody would turn and look at her when she walked by." His face flushed and lips thinned. "Do you think someone killed the Sinopas just to get Bea?"

"I want to look at all possibilities. How do you think they found the Sinopas' home? Lapwai is about fourteen miles from the Lewiston Easter egg hunt."

Peter opened a desk drawer and rummaged around for a moment before pulling out a flyer and handing it to me. The cover featured a large Easter bunny. "You had to register in advance."

"May I keep this?" I held up the flyer.

He nodded, then grabbed a computer printout of the local news and dropped it in front of me. "The press had the same idea, though." The headline screamed, "Couple

Slain, Child Missing!" Under that it said, "Lethal Easter Egg Hunt?"

"You can keep that," he said.

I placed the printout under my sketchpad. "You said you last saw Adam on Sunday. He wasn't at work on Monday?"

"He takes . . . took Mondays off." He stared at my hand.

I stopped twirling my pencil. "Where were you Monday night?"

Peter grimaced. "The million-dollar question. I was at home. With my wife and kids." He grabbed a business card from a holder in front of him and wrote on the back. "Here's my home number. Call my wife. Her name's Michelle." He handed me a second card.

"I'll do that." I stood. "Where's Adam's office?"

He jerked his thumb toward a door on my left. "Through there, up the stairs. The police released his office about noon." He fiddled with a letter opener on his desk. "I guess I need to go up there. But it's kind of creepy." He remained seated as I went out.

I entered a small foyer with a door on my left leading to the casino and stairs straight ahead. Interesting. Someone could go up to Adam's office without going past Peter. At the top of the stairs was a large, richly carpeted room with a wall of one-way glass overlooking the casino floor. Pendleton wool upholstery with Native American prints covered the rustic furniture, and fingerprint powder overlaid most of the surfaces. Moving to the center of the room, I slowly turned in a circle. I have a photographic memory when it comes to faces. With a bit of effort, I can do the same with a scene. The cherrywood desk was void of papers, the matching bookshelves contained three-ring binders of manuals and a few books, and the four-drawer filing cabinet held a single dying plant on the top.

After one last look around, I left Adam's office and found my way to the business center, where I used their computer to compose a report on the interview. I'd have to discover if the chief wanted me to pursue leads, such as the Easter egg hunt. After sending off the report, I stared at the blank wall, then checked my watch. Every minute Bea was in the hands of a stranger, the possibility of her survival dimmed.

I placed calls to the remaining staff members on my list of people to interview. None of them were working at the casino tonight.

Great. I'd be showing up at the task force meeting tomorrow with a big, fat goose egg.

CHAPTER SIX

After dinner at the Qeqiit Bar and Grill, I wandered through the hotel, ending back on the second floor. My room overlooked a parking lot and, beyond that, a large RV park. Farther still, the grass-covered, steep hills rose to the Columbia Plateau, broken by jagged outcroppings of basalt. Night had fallen and few lights illuminated the lot. I pulled the drapes against the darkness outside. I'd left a message for Beth at the front desk along with an extra key card.

Settling at the desk, I read the printout Peter gave me. The article mentioned Adam was the manager of the casino and speculated his murder was work related or somehow connected to the Easter egg hunt.

Each presented a challenge. The Easter egg hunt involved hundreds of young children and could have been a hunting ground for pedophiles. But pedophiles don't usually brutally murder the parents. The child is their target.

On the other hand, if someone who knew the Sinopas — a disgruntled worker, a family member, a neighbor — hated them with enough passion to slaughter them with a hatchet, why take the little girl? The crime didn't make a lot of sense.

A *click* and *thump* in the hall announced Beth's arrival. Opening the door, I found her with a cart loaded with luggage. She was wearing a striking houndstooth jersey jacket and matching ankle pants with a cream blouse. Her hair was casually clipped up and her porcelain complexion held just a whisper of makeup. She looked like a Paris runway model.

I ran my fingers through my hair and straightened my crumpled blouse. "You look nice."

"Thanks. Dog-fur-resistant clothing. You look . . . professional. And tired. Can I come in?"

Opening the door wider, I helped her maneuver the cart into the room.

"I can't believe I'm working with you on a homicide." She shoved the key into her purse. "This is so exciting! Just wait until my cousins in Oconomowoc hear about this."

"Are you moving in?"

"Oh no. You said we had to find a dog-friendly place, so I only brought a few things. The rest of the stuff's in the car. Along with Winston."

"Unfortunately, my poor dog'll have to sleep out there." I pulled some suitcases from the cart.

"He seems happy. We stopped at a rest area on the way and he took care of things, ate, and drank water. He has a bone to work on —"

"You're spoiling him."

"He deserves some spoiling." She pulled the remaining bags off the cart. "At the gas station, a couple of unsavory individuals came around the car. Winston warned them off."

"He knows when folks are up to no good."

"Look at you." Beth stepped back and examined me from head to foot. "I haven't seen you in 'uniform.' " Her fingers made air quotations. "They gave you a badge! Did you get a gun and handcuffs?"

I opened my purse, which was sitting on the dresser. "Glock. Handcuffs." I lofted both items.

"Those don't look like handcuffs. More like plastic twist ties."

"Flex-cuffs. Disposable restraints. Ten to a package. Cheap. But it's not as if I'll be handcuffing any of my witnesses or victims." I returned them to my purse. "I'll take the cart to the lobby and check on my dog. Where did you park?"

She gave me directions, then handed me the car keys. Opening my suitcase, I found a jacket and pulled it on. Beth's SUV was in the far corner of the lot, with no other vehicles nearby. Traffic noises in the distance from Highway 95 gave a slight feeling of civilization, but an ax-wielding murderer was still on the loose. I pulled my jacket tighter and broke into a trot.

Winston stretched across the rear seat, a hairy, snow-white mound of Great Pyrenees. He greeted me with a juicy burp and sloppy kiss, then politely waited for me to snap on his leash.

Baaa baaa baaa . . . ! A fire alarm sounded from the hotel.

I jumped. Winston leaped from the car and spun toward the sound.

Hotel guests, some in nightclothes, poured out of the exit doors.

A prickly feeling danced across my shoulders. *False alarm.*

Winston and I raced toward the exit nearest to our room. I searched for smoke or signs of fire that I knew wouldn't be there.

Beth emerged from the building and

glanced around. She quickly spotted us. We met up halfway across the parking lot just as sirens from fire engines howled in the distance.

"Did you smell any smoke?" I continued to check the building.

"No." She held up her computer and purse. "But I'm not taking any chances." I noted she hadn't brought mine.

Before Winston could attract attention, I steered him toward a patch of grass and low plantings near the RV park. Beth followed. "This is quite an exciting place. Homicides, car theft, fire."

"Don't forget the missing girl."

"I can't." Beth rubbed her arms. "What are you looking at?"

I stopped staring at the hotel and looked at my friend. "Listen, Beth, stay here with Winston. I think something hinky is going on. When the firefighters say it's clear, put Winston up and meet me in the room —"

"Waaait a minute. Where are you going?"

"I need to check this out."

"I'm not going to sit in the room and twiddle my thumbs while you have an adventure."

Taking a deep breath, I nodded. "Okay. I'm heading to the manager's office. He's the guy who got killed. You can access it off the casino on the far side of this structure. Put Winston up and meet me there. Stay clear of the firefighters because they'll just send you outside until everything is clear."

"That's better."

Leaving Beth, I strolled to the end of the building. The door was locked, but my key-card opened it. I plotted my path to the casino. Racing down the hallway, I made it almost to the lobby before the sounds of the firemen's voices shouting evacuation orders sent me skittering into the ladies' room. I ducked into a stall but left the door ajar and climbed on top of the commode. The room smelled faintly of bleach.

Bang! The door slammed against the wall. "Anyone in here?" a man asked.

I held my breath.

The door swished closed.

Jumping off my perch, I ran to the door and peeked out. Ahead was the empty lobby and beyond that, the casino. I flew into the casino, not worried that my passing would draw attention with all the pinging and chortling of the slot machines.

Across the room was the casino access to Adam Sinopa's office. It was open a crack.

Someone grabbed my arm.

I spun and caught myself before punching Beth.

"I come in peace." Beth held up both hands.

"Sorry." I pointed toward the open access. "I thought the alarm might have something to do with the Sinopas. I closed that door behind me when I checked out his office earlier." With Beth in tow, I raced across the casino but paused before stepping through.

"What?" Beth asked.

"Checking the location of security cameras. See if you can spot any aimed at this door." I nodded at a camera in the corner of the room.

Beth moved away from the door and turned in a circle. "I count five, but only that one" — she pointed — "would give the right angle."

"And it rotates. So someone would just need to time it. Probably no surveillance image to look at. Let's go up." Beth and I moved through the door and up the stairs to Adam's office.

The lights were on. The top two drawers of the filing cabinet were open, and several books lay on the floor by the bookshelves.

"Was Sinopa . . . was he killed here?" Beth asked.

"No. But it looks like someone was looking for something —"

"What are you doing here?" Peter entered

the room behind Beth.

"I saw the open door." I waved at Beth. "This is my . . . associate, Beth Noble. Beth, this is Peter Otskai, the assistant manager —"

"Yeah, yeah. Did you leave the door to the casino open?" Peter asked.

"No one got up here because of me. How about you? Did you leave your office unlocked?" I shot back. "There are two ways to get into Sinopa's office, as you well know."

Peter wouldn't meet my gaze. "Whatever. Someone must have used the fire alarm to gain access to here. Is this how the police left it?"

"No. And the fire alarm is far too convenient timing. I'd bet our burglar was the one to set it." I pulled out my cell and dialed Chief Kus's number.

He answered on the first ring. "Seth Kus."

I explained what I thought had happened. "On my way." He disconnected.

I gave Peter a quick nod, then moved to the center of the room and slowly pivoted. Something nagged at the back of my mind. Every item in the room had been moved, yet there was no destruction. The invasion looked deliberately staged. The most noticeable item was the top drawer of the filing cabinet. I strolled over and used my pencil to pull the drawer completely open.

"Shouldn't you wait for the police?" Peter asked.

"I am the police. Sort of." The files were neatly labeled, color coded, and in alphabetical order.

"Very nice." Beth peered over my shoulder. "Organized, efficient —"

"OCD." As I slid the drawer closed, it made a *shhhhhh* sound. I opened it, reached in and upward. My fingers encountered a thick piece of paper. I gave a gentle tug and pulled out a large, gold-colored envelope.

"You really need to be called Sherlock Bones," Beth whispered. "That was awesome."

"Mm," I grunted. After placing the envelope on the desk, I again used my pencil to nudge the flap open and slid out two pieces of paper. Each one bore a sentence assembled from newspaper or magazine cutouts. The first one said, *I warned you. your a dead man.* The second said, *Im comming for you and your family.*

"Terrible speller," Beth said.

Peter came over and read the notes. "Why would Adam hide those?" He reached for them.

I grabbed his arm before he could touch

66

them. "Don't. Fingerprints." Pulling out my cell, I stared at the blank screen. "Beth, I don't know how —"

My friend took the cell from me, fiddled with it for a moment, then snapped photos of the notes. "Did you want anything else photographed?"

"Yeah. Just get a picture of everything."

She'd just completed a circuit of the room when Chief Kus arrived. "Who are you?" he asked Beth.

"Beth Noble." I stepped forward. "My associate and transportation, at least until you find my car."

He touched the brim of his baseball hat. "Ma'am." He turned to me. "We found it."

"You found my car? That's great —"

"In the middle of the Clearwater River."

CHAPTER SEVEN

I stared at him. "You're kidding."

"Nope. Someone drove it into the water at a boat launch downriver from Fir Island. About halfway between Lapwai and Lenore." He nodded at Beth. "Looks like your friend will have to continue to be your driver."

Beth tried to hide her grin.

The chief strolled over to the notes spread out on the desk. "Where did you find these?"

"Hidden on the underside of the filing cabinet. But . . ." My gaze flickered to Peter, then back to the chief.

"Mr. Otskai, I wonder if you could wait for me in your office?" Chief Kus jerked his head slightly toward the door. Peter looked like he wanted to argue but left without saying anything, closing the door behind him. "What is it, Gwen?"

The way he said my name made my brain

go blank for a moment. "I . . . ah . . ." *Oh, for crying in a bucket, Gwen.* "Yes. Um. I don't think your detectives missed that envelope when they searched this office."

"Go on."

"And I don't think the fire alarm was pulled so someone could get in here and look for those letters."

The chief sat on one of the colorful chairs. Beth took another. "I'm listening," he said.

"I think someone wants you to think a disgruntled employee murdered the Sinopas."

"Why an employee?"

"Possibly because that's what the newspaper suggested. I read the online article. I'd bet by now the evening edition has hit the stand."

"Do *you* think that's a possibility?"

"I think there's a lot about this case that doesn't add up."

Beth leaned forward, her gaze alternating between the chief and me.

I picked up the pencil I'd left on the desk and used it to punctuate the air. "Let's say you're the killer. You see Beatrice at the Easter egg hunt. Maybe you have access to the registrations and know where she lives, or you follow the family home. You kill the parents and grab the child."

69

"Somehow I don't think you're buying that. Are you leaning toward someone with a grudge against the Sinopas? Or maybe even a random killing?"

"Let's just say I have more questions than answers." I licked my lips. "I am inclined to think the killer pulled the fire alarm, emptied the building, and planted the letters that point to someone at the casino. He would want the letters well hidden, yet easily found. He would leave the door open a crack and stage the room so it looked like someone was searching for these letters."

"So now we're back to the Easter egg hunt?" Chief Kus's right eye narrowed, then he grinned. He had a beautiful smile with snow-white teeth and a small dimple on the left side. His perfect skin —

"I said" — Chief Kus waved his hand to get my attention — "your sheriff was right about you."

"You talked to Dave Moore?"

"We go way back. I called Dave after you fainted at the scene, figuring he would know you. He recommended you. And he sent me a glowing report from a Sheriff Colton out in Summer Harbor, Maine."

"You fainted?" Beth sat up straighter. "And *you* tell me not to barf at a crime —"

"Not now, Beth."

70

Chief Kus stood. "I'll get my crime-scene folks back over here and have them recheck the room and get on those notes." He headed for the door, then turned and looked at me. "See you at the task force meeting tomorrow." He left.

I followed him out of the office with Beth trailing behind, making sure the access doors locked behind us. We headed for our room.

"That is one good-looking man," Beth said.

"Really? I didn't notice."

The next morning Beth and I loaded up and headed to the task force meeting. Beth would explore Lapwai with Winston until I called.

Although I arrived early at the police department, I was the last one to enter the conference room. One wall had a map pinned to it, a white board took up another wall, and 8 × 10 photos of the crime scene finished off the third side.

The haggard faces around me answered the question of whether they'd found the little girl.

No one looked overjoyed at my being there.

Each member took turns reporting their

progress. I gave my verbal report, then turned in the written printout on the interview and how the letters were found at Sinopa's office.

The elderly woman next to me took my materials. "Can you e-mail this all to me so I can enter it into the case file?" She handed me a card.

I nodded.

She looked around the table. "Chief Kus had me do a check to see if there were any similar cases anywhere around here. I found nothing."

"Excuse me, but did you go back far enough?"

"What do you mean by far enough? I was very thorough." Her voice was frosty.

"I'm sorry." I gave her an apologetic smile. "I didn't mean to imply —"

"I went back over twenty-five years."

"Well then." I looked around the table. All eyes were on me. "You should have found a double homicide involving a hatchet in Kamiah. Twenty-three years ago. June twelfth. And there was a four-year-old boy involved."

She sniffed, glanced at the chief, then typed on her computer for a few moments. After reading the results, she turned the screen toward me.

The screen showed types of crime, location, and the year. In that particular year, only a single homicide-suicide appeared. A husband shot his wife, then himself.

My mouth dried. I stared at the results until she turned the computer toward herself.

"Did you have something to report, Gwen?" Chief Kus asked me.

My ears buzzed. The room seemed overly bright. *I am not going to faint.* "Nothing to report. I'll . . . I'll need to do some investigating."

The meeting continued.

I folded my hands and pretended to listen. *What is going on? Did I mistake the year? The location?* I didn't want any further attention from the task force. I'd have Beth look it up.

The meeting ended and I headed for the door. Chief Kus stopped me. "Something's going on with you. Did you have some information to share? Something you're holding back?"

I chewed my lip. "I'm . . . not sure. Something's not right, but I need more . . . research. I'll let you know if I come up with anything."

"Please do."

Beth answered the phone promptly and picked me up in her car. Winston puffed in my hair from the back seat. "What's the matter?"

"I think I'm losing it."

"I doubt that. What happened in there?"

"Remember I asked you to look into the murder of my sorta-mom, Holly, and her son?"

Beth glanced at me and nodded. "I haven't had time to start on that, but I'll get right on it. And, to remind you, you said you'd explain what you meant by 'sorta-mom.' "

"I will, but I have something more pressing. I may be mistaken about the year of the murders. Or possibly the location."

"Okay."

"If there's any way possible, see what you can find out about Holly herself."

"Last name?" Beth asked.

"She changed it a lot, but I remember what her name was from when I first knew her because I thought her name sounded like Christmas. Holly Green. Maybe with an *e* at the end."

"Okay."

"Her son was named Jacob. He'd be about nine years younger than me. And I think . . . maybe part Native American."

"Husband?"

"No. Holly never married."

"So. Research a Holly Green, maybe with

an *e*, unmarried, son Jacob, both murdered somewhere around North Central Idaho between twenty and twenty-five years ago. When I do all that, will you tell me what on earth is going on?"

"Yeah."

The morning air was fragrant with all the blooming trees and bushes in well-tended yards. We passed by downtown Lewiston, hugging the banks of the Snake and Clearwater Rivers, and climbed up a bluff where the bulk of the population resided. Beth drove, weaving by a number of stately older homes on our way to my witness, Andi Tubbs. Up ahead, a driveway looked familiar. "Beth, slow down."

"I thought you said she lives —"

"Stop the car!"

She slammed on the brakes, sending Winston sliding off the rear seat. "What's wrong?"

"That house." A soaring Victorian home rested behind a row of older trees. A discreet red-and-white sign noted this was the Two Rivers Bed-and-Breakfast.

"Have you stayed there before?" Beth asked.

"No. To the best of my knowledge, I've never been to this part of Lewiston before. But I've dreamed about that house."

CHAPTER EIGHT

"You've never mentioned dreaming about an old house." Beth pulled the car next to the curb and put it into park.

"It's been years, but I used to have this strange dream . . ." My stomach fluttered. "It's nothing. I probably saw a photo of it somewhere." I checked my watch. "Let's go. I don't want to be late."

Beth stared at me a moment longer, then shifted into drive. We didn't speak until we reached Andi Tubbs's house, a modest ranch. "I'll call you when I'm about done. Okay? Find us a good place to stay." Giving Winston a quick scratch, I pulled my forensic kit from the back seat and headed for the house.

An older woman with short gray hair, thick glasses, and porcelain skin answered the door. "Are you the artist?"

"Yes. Gwen Marcey. Call me Gwen." I offered my hand and she took it.

"I'm Andi." She directed me to her dining room and a round antique oak table. "I thought you might need a good surface."

"How thoughtful of you." While I pulled my drawing materials from the case, Andi brought me a steaming mug of coffee. I elevated her to my favorite witness of all time. "I understand you were checking on a neighbor when you saw someone at the Sinopa home."

"Yes. I was late, about eight in the evening on Monday, when I saw a man standing on the porch. He rang the bell, then glanced at me."

"What were the lighting conditions?"

"A porch light was on and I could see him pretty well."

I tried not to stare at her thick lenses. "What was your overall impression of him?"

"I guess I'd say that he was young and out of place."

"Young?"

"Twenties."

"Why out of place?"

Andi fiddled with her coffee cup. "Lapwai is a small, close community made up of mostly Nez Perce. This guy was white and . . . I don't know, just looked wrong."

"How did he make you feel?"

"Uneasy."

Glancing down at my interview form, I marked the boxes on age, race, and sex. As much as possible, I wanted her to do the talking during the interview. "Okay, let's start at the beginning and don't leave anything out, even if you think it's unimportant."

"Like I said, it was late to be checking on someone, and as I hurried up the walk, I saw the man. He had brown hair and wore a sweatshirt and jeans."

I wrote down her scanty description. "You mentioned he rang the doorbell. Which hand did he use?"

She thought for a moment. "Left."

"What about his right hand?"

"It was . . . He had a small duffel bag! I just remembered."

"Tell me about that."

She took a sip of coffee. "Black, or dark colored. That's why I didn't really pay attention. About this big." She held her hands about eighteen inches apart.

I wrote as fast as I could. "Let's back up even more. You parked where?"

"On the street, like always. I grabbed my bag from the seat beside me, then got out of the car and hurried up to the house." Her eyes grew wide. "No cars."

I thought of all the vehicles I'd seen in the

small community. "No cars?"

She grinned. "I mean, no cars or trucks that I wasn't familiar with. There were the standard three to five cars per house. Maybe that's what made me uneasy. I must have wondered where this guy came from."

After a bit more conversation, it was clear she had nothing more to offer in terms of verbal descriptions. I handed her my facial-identification book. "Go through this book and look for anyone that reminds you of the man you saw. I very much doubt he'd be in here, so you're not looking for him. Once we find similar faces, I'll put them together and you'll make changes to bring the sketch as close to your memory as possible. It won't end up being a portrait, just a likeness. At the very worst, it will help us to eliminate anyone not similar. Okay?"

She took the book and started paging through. I tugged out a piece of bristol paper and drew my facial grid. Unfortunately my "cheat ruler" now sat at the bottom of the Clearwater River. The ruler made it easy to lay out the face. Without it, I'd have to measure, but fortunately the average Caucasian male face was easy to put together. The width of the eye was the same as the width between the eyes. Depending on the head shape, the width of the eye is usually the distance from the outside corner of the eye to the outside of the face. The nose is about an eye and a half long, and the mouth is located one-third of the distance between the nose and chin.

As Andi selected each feature, I jotted the number on the interview form. My heart sank at the selections. Average. Average. Average. I mentally groaned. Give me bulging red eyes, eyebrows long enough to braid, skin pocked like the moon's surface. Anything but average.

The drawing developed swiftly, with Andi making few changes. That was never good. I needed a picky witness, someone who made me use the eraser more than my pencil. Few changes meant one of three things — the witness was lying, I was a brilliant artist, or the witness didn't see or remember the face that well. In this case I doubted the first two.

Forty-five minutes later, the drawing was complete. Average. Andi was thrilled with the likeness, rating it a 9.5 on a 1-to-10 scale. I gave Beth a quick call to pick me up, then collected the clutter of art materials that covered the tabletop. "Thank you again, Andi. You've been a great help."

"I just keep thinking about that poor little girl. Any word?"

"Not that I know of." We moved toward the door.

"I can't help but think about another case like this."

My mouth suddenly dried. "Oh?"

"A couple of years ago I was living in The Dalles, Oregon. A father and mother were killed, I think, and a child, a little girl, was missing or taken."

"Oh really?" I licked my lips. "Do you remember if anyone was ever arrested or the child recovered?"

"I don't. I moved here shortly after."

A car horn beeped.

"That's my ride." I hoped my hand wasn't quivering as I shook hands with Andi. "Here's my card. Call me if you think of anything else."

Trying hard not to run, I made it to Beth's SUV, slamming the door too hard. From the back seat, Winston greeted me by sticking his muzzle in my hair and blowing nose-kisses.

"Are you all right?" Beth asked. "You look like you've seen a ghost."

"I have."

CHAPTER NINE

Beth drove, sending me worried glances every few moments. "Can I ask —"

"Not just yet. Did you find a place to stay?"

We pulled up in front of the Two Rivers Bed-and-Breakfast. "Ta-da!"

"What are we doing here?"

"I booked us a couple of rooms. Since you're already dreaming about this place, you might as well stay here." She turned into a short driveway that ended in a small paved parking lot. "I hope you don't mind. I've already unpacked."

Slowly I got out of the car and stared up at the impressive Victorian entrance. "This doesn't look like a place that would be dog friendly."

"They're not. Or they weren't. The manager, a nice guy named Eric, originally said no, but I explained you were working on the homicide and missing child and guess what?"

"What?"

"No, you have to guess."

I would have thrown a pencil at her head, but I was currently unarmed. "He said he'd let us stay here with Winston."

Beth looked down and frowned. "You guessed."

"You already said you'd booked a room and unpacked." I opened the back door and let Winston out.

"So I did. So I did. I thought a bed-and-breakfast would redintegrate you."

"That sounds painful." Winston thoughtfully inspected a nearby tree before watering it.

"Word of the day. It means 'make whole' or 'renew.' I'm trying to keep your mind sharp."

"I keep my pencils sharp."

Beth shook her head. "That's not the same thing."

"You're not an artist."

"Anyway." She pulled her purse from the car and locked the doors. "There's more. He gave us a discount on the rooms and then threw in a meeting area for free!"

"Why?"

"He wanted to help, and he said he

couldn't get away from work to help look for Beatrice. Anyway, you know the saying about looking a gift horse in the mouth and all. Come on." I followed her up a set of stairs leading to a wide porch with wicker furniture on my right. The unlocked door led to a hall with an open door on one side and stairs going down on the other. A solidly built man in his twenties with thick, unruly light-brown hair stepped out.

"You must be Mrs. Marcey." He eyed my dog. "I'm Eric Winchester."

I recognized the look on his face. He was afraid of dogs. Or at least dogs the size of Shetland ponies. "Thank you for letting us stay here." I tightened Winston's leash so he wouldn't give his usual greeting of plowing his head between Eric's legs. "You're the . . . owner of this place?"

Eric laughed. "No, not at all. I moved from Minneapolis and started working here about, oh, ten years ago. Worked my way up to manager. Lila also works here. You'll meet her later. Let me show you to your rooms." We traipsed behind him across a striking parlor that raised goose pimples up my spine. Antique chairs, tables, and sofas formed conversation areas. The huge fireplace mantel of deeply carved, dark wood was just as I remembered it.

84

I must have been here before.

I even knew what was ahead. Through the double doors would be a grand hallway with a massive stairway leading up. The carpet would be a floral pattern on a black background. Neither Eric nor Beth noticed me slowing down.

Eric pointed left. "Coffee and tea over there." He reached the double doors, passed through, and waved his hand. "This is actually —"

"The front entrance," I finished for him.

"Ah, yes," Eric said. They both turned and stared at me a moment before moving on. Another set of double doors opened to a comfortable game room with a big-screen television, microwave, small refrigerator, and table in the center. The room was smaller than I remembered and had been remodeled, but I knew it.

"You can use this area for your, what would you call it? Investigations? Strategy room? Your bedrooms are on either side, and these doors lock." He pointed. "If you enter and leave through the front doors, most of the other guests won't even know you're here with a dog, unless they see him outside."

"Thank you," I said through stiff lips. "I'm sure we'll be very comfortable."

"Well then, breakfast between seven thirty and nine thirty. Go down the stairs over there." He backed out, closing the doors behind him.

"You're acting very strange." Beth took Winston's leash from my freezing hand. "I went ahead and took the room on the right. They are almost the same, but the one on the right is —"

"Smaller. And overlooks a fountain with three fish, no, make that dolphins, in the center." I slowly turned in the center of the room, staring at each item of furniture. The only piece I recognized was a Victorian mahogany rolltop desk. "BA plus FP," I said. I got on my hands and knees and crawled under the desk, then lay on my back. Winston rose, then wandered over and stood near my feet.

"Okay, Gwen, you are really scaring me now." Beth's voice quivered. "Even your dog is concerned."

"Come here."

Beth bent down and peeked at me.

"No. Lay here beside me."

She opened her mouth to say something, then joined me on the floor. "Gwen, if we need to call someone —"

"Look." I pointed up.

She looked in the direction I pointed.

Written in smudged white were the letters *BA* plus *FP* with a heart drawn around them.

CHAPTER TEN

"I don't understand." Beth crawled from under the desk and sat on the mint-green and peach floral-patterned sofa. Winston left my side and promptly jumped up and joined her. "No, Winston, down." The dog slunk from the sofa and lay on the floor, staring at me to be sure I knew he felt abused.

I sat up and crossed my legs. "Before I tell you, if you don't mind, would you do some additional research for me?"

"You know I will. I wasn't a researcher for Microsoft for nothing." She stood, disappeared into her room, then returned with a computer case and leather notebook. After opening the notebook and finding a pen, she looked up at me. "I've already started working on Holly Green, maybe with an *e,* not married as of the time you left, Jacob, murders in North Central Idaho roughly twenty to twenty-five years ago. This is so interesting! Is the new research about you not being here before, but for some reason you were? Does it have anything to do with the missing child? I do have a —"

"Beth —"

"— way to access —"

"Beth!"

"Oh. Sorry. Go ahead."

"I need you to look for similar cases of parents murdered and a child killed or missing. Go back twenty — no, make that thirty-two years."

Beth's eyes widened. "You found out about another one?"

"Andi mentioned a case in The Dalles, Oregon. We'll look at that soon enough. I want you to look specifically at thirty-two years ago."

"Okay. That's easy. Nationwide?"

"No. Not to start. Go with the Pacific Northwest. Washington, Oregon, Idaho, and Montana. I may expand that later. While you're doing that, can I borrow your car? I need to get this composite to the chief."

"Absolutely. But speaking of Chief Kus, you might want to . . . um, tidy up first."

I glanced down at my rumpled clothing dusted with Pyrenees fur and graphite.

"And you have a smudge of pencil lead on your nose." Beth pointed to a spot on her face. "I didn't notice a wedding ring on his finger, by the way."

"You just never give up, m'friend."

"Waaait a minute." Beth put up a hand. "In the excitement of joining you on this case, I didn't think about it, but weren't you supposed to drive to Glacier Park with Blake?"

"Change of plans."

"And he was okay with you working on this homicide?"

"Mmm."

"Which means no and I should mind my own business."

I ducked my head and moved to my room where I discovered Beth had hung up all my clothes by color, arranged my makeup and hair products in the bathroom, and set up Winston's nylon-mesh kennel. My old laptop rested on the Queen Anne coffee table in front of the small sofa in the bay window. The dresser drawer held my underwear and a second set of breast prosthetics. I hadn't made up my mind about reconstructive surgery following my double mastectomy, so they were a necessary evil. The insurance company insisted I buy backups after I lost the first pair of breast forms, named Lucy and Ethel, in Utah, and the second set, Thelma and Louise, in

Kentucky. I'd dubbed this pair Laverne and Shirley. I was wearing Ginger and Mary Ann.

The Gideon Bible was next to the bed with a new devotional booklet on top. I checked to see if she'd given me any reading assignments.

I washed my face, applied fresh makeup, and ran a comb through my hair. Clean khaki slacks, a blouse, and a coral cotton sweater finished the outfit.

Beth looked up from her laptop and gave me a nod of approval as I headed out the door. "Thank you for unpacking for me."

"Just trying to help."

"You're the best sidekick!"

"Better than Watson was to Sherlock?"

"Yup."

"Kato to the Green Hornet?"

"As long as you're not Cato to the Pink Panther." I smiled at her.

"Just so you know, I'm not giving up on the subject of Blake and your love life."

"Why am I not surprised?" I picked up the car keys. "Oh, if you get a chance, see if Eric has any suggestions for good places to eat. And if you could call this number" — I handed her Peter Otskai's business card — "and tell him where we are. He said if something comes in for me at the Clearwater Lodge, he'd make sure to get it to me. Also, I have some more interviews later this afternoon, but I'll check in with you first. And one final thing. I had you bring a sheet of foam board." Foam board was a lightweight, rigid surface used for a variety of art and display projects.

"Yes. It's in my room."

"Prop it up on the easel you packed. We'll be using it to visualize the current crime."

"Oh boy." Beth beamed. "Just like they do on television."

"Yeah. And let the director know I need to see him about the script."

"Sure, I'll . . . You're joking with me, right?"

I chuckled all the way to the car. Once I reached the driver's-side door, I called Chief Kus. "Andi Tubbs's composite is done."

"Could you drive it to the department? I have some new names for you to interview."

Just as I hung up, the phone rang again. It was my ex-husband, Robert. "Yes?"

"The court date is set. May nineteenth."

My stomach clenched. "I don't see why this needs to go to court. I'm sure we can work out something with my daughter —"

"*Our* daughter. And I told you if you put her in any further danger I'd petition for a change in the parenting plan. She almost

92

died the last time she was with you. You're an unfit mother."

"I'm not —"

"You missed her sixteenth birthday party yesterday!"

"You didn't invite me or tell me where it was! I called, sent a gift —"

"Good thing you sent the receipt. The sweater didn't fit."

I tried to loosen my grip on the phone. "Look, Robert, in another year she'll be off to college. She'll be leaving home —"

"And I'm going to keep her safely with me until then." In the background I could hear Caroline's voice. His new wife. "You have to tell her, Robert."

"Tell me what?" I asked.

Robert must have put his hand over the phone. Muffled conversation continued for a moment, then his voice cleared again. "Caroline's pregnant."

Slumping against the car, I tried to say *Congratulations, Wonderful news . . .* something. My mouth refused to work and my eyes burned.

"Did you hear me?" Robert asked.

"Um," was all I could manage before disconnecting. I wanted to go back to the room, tell Beth, maybe hug Winston and let him blow nose-kisses into my hair. I wanted to cry until it made me sick and gave me the hiccups. Instead, I got into Beth's car and headed to Lapwai.

I'd spent a lifetime pushing away black thoughts, but they reared up despite my best efforts.

You're jealous, Robert whispered in my head.

"I'm not. I'm genuinely happy for Caroline. I was just . . . surprised. You told me you never wanted another child."

With you, Gwen, with you.

"Won't you be too busy with the new baby to want Aynslee around?"

It's best this way. If your past is catching up with you, you may not survive this time.

"I don't want to talk about it, Robert. Just be quiet." I turned on the radio to still the voices.

The newscaster was in midbroadcast. ". . . no further word on the missing four-year-old, Beatrice Sinopa, taken from her home in Lapwai sometime Monday night. Nez Perce Tribal Police will be releasing a composite sketch later today of a person of interest in the case . . ."

I turned off the radio. I didn't need another reminder of how high the stakes were in solving this case.

The parking lot of the police department

94

was completely full, with cars spilling out onto the street. I finally found a spot several blocks away, this time making sure the car was securely locked.

"Marcey!" a woman's voice called from behind me.

Turning, I saw Officer LoneBear barreling down on me. "Yes?"

"I heard your car was dumped in the river." She was out of uniform, wearing jeans so tight there'd be no way she could breathe, let alone sit, red spiky heels, and a blouse low enough to leave little doubt of her cup size. Her lips were coral, setting off her tanned skin. Placing her hands on her hips, she moved her gaze from my flat leather shoes, up my khaki slacks, to my blouse, which I'd buttoned to the top.

I felt . . . practical. I wanted to point out that low-cut shirts were out of the question when your breasts were silicone inserts. When you bent forward, the heavy inserts would flop forward into the bra, and someone could look down your front and see the gap between flat chest and bra.

I shook my head. *Why do you need to explain yourself to her?* Instead, I said, "Just now you used passive language, usually the choice of someone who wants to conceal the identity of the perpetrator."

"What?"

"I'm just wondering if you know more about my stolen car."

"No, no, of course not." She shook her head. "Lots of people don't want an outsider like you getting involved in tribal issues. You might want to take the hint."

"Multiple denials." I folded my arms. "More signs of deception. Better watch yourself, LoneBear. Car theft is against the law, even on the reservation. I may be forced to tell your *boss* of my suspicions."

Her eyes narrowed. "He's more than my boss, so just keep your eyes and hands off of him."

Is she actually jealous of me? "You're kidding."

She muttered something, then turned and stomped off. I was pretty sure I'd just heard my first Nez Perce cuss word.

"Soggy wooker," I called after her. *Oh, that was mature.*

Men, women, and children spilled from the department onto the ramp and gathered in small groups in the parking lot. I plowed through the throng of citizens, feeling very blonde, and finally edged through to the lobby. A man in a blue flannel shirt and jeans pounded the tiny counter in front of the glassed-in reception area. The woman behind him added her voice to his. "He's out there! None of our children are safe!"

The officer on duty spotted me and pointed to the door. The room grew silent as I pushed forward. Whispers followed me. "She's that artist."

"They know what he looks like!"

"Finally something will be done."

With a buzz, the door opened and the officer ushered me into the hall. Chief Kus waited just inside. "Sorry about that. Ever since that article came out suggesting the killer found Beatrice through the Easter egg hunt, everyone's been on edge. Seems most of the tribe who have young children were at the event." He showed me into the task force conference room where several other officers were manning phones. Three more were bent over a map and marking locations. Pulling out the composite, I lifted the tracing paper I'd used to protect the sketch and held it up. "Unfortunately, the witness —"

"That's an awesome drawing." The chief took it from me.

"Yes, well, the thing is, the witness didn't —"

"It's like a portrait," one of the men said.

"That's amazing," another said.

"He looks pretty average," Chief Kus said.

"True. The good news is that it will eliminate a lot of people not similar."

"Meaning," Chief Kus said, "all I have to do is arrest a third of the population of Idaho." He taped the sketch to the wall with the crime-scene photos. "Hopefully we're not back to where we started."

CHAPTER ELEVEN

Several of the officers slumped in their seats. The chief indicated a chair for me and sat at the end of the table. "So do you think we should release the drawing?" he asked.

"It's really your decision," I said. "You'll get a ton of calls you'll have to wade through, but at least the public will be reminded there's a missing child. Who knows?" I pointed at the sketch. "This guy may have been selling magazine subscriptions or, um, Avon or something door-to-door. He might recognize himself in the composite and come forward. You'll be able to eliminate him as a suspect."

Chief Kus studied me for a moment. I tried not to stare back. He was definitely a good-looking — make that an amazingly handsome man. *Almost as good looking as Blake.* I closed my eyes for a moment.

He lifted a set of papers, stood, and distributed them around the room to the different officers before placing a set in front of me. "All right. We'll get the composite into the newspapers and online. Here is your next set of witnesses to interview. We're going to follow up on the Easter-egg-hunt angle. Gwen, I gave you the people who claim they saw someone at the hunt paying too much attention to Bea. Find out if any of them could provide a composite sketch. Jonah here" — he nodded at a man on his right — "will be collecting surveillance tapes from nearby businesses. We'll also be asking the public to bring us any video or photos they may have taken that day of Beatrice. We'll have you look at everything to see if anyone was hanging around her or paying particular attention to the little girl."

The paper Chief Kus handed me bore my name at the top and five names, addresses, and phone numbers. The witnesses lived from Clarkston, Washington, to Kamiah, Idaho, sixty-eight miles upriver from Lewiston. I wouldn't exactly be sitting around twiddling my thumbs waiting for the photos and videos. At the bottom of the paperwork were the same crime-scene photos and a copy of the autopsy reports.

As the officers stood and collected their assignments, the chief motioned for me to stay. "I'll e-mail you a copy of the photos as soon as you have a computer."

"You can send them here." I wrote down Beth's e-mail address.

"Your car, I'm afraid, can't be recovered just yet. The river's too high with the spring runoff. My diver did get a chance to look inside. The keys were in the ignition."

Either I forgot to take the keys, or someone at the Sinopa crime scene took them from my purse. I bet that someone wears low-cut blouses and has a jealous streak a mile wide. "My friend's providing the car, but we did have to move out of the lodge. We're staying at the Two Rivers Bed-and-Breakfast in Lewiston. Any recommendations for good places to eat?"

"I like the Qeqiit Lounge, but then again, the profits from the casino and lodge go to the tribe. I often eat there."

"I know —" I clamped my mouth shut.

His eyebrows rose. "And how did you know?"

My cheeks burned. "I, um, saw you in there with Officer LoneBear . . ."

He bit the inside corner of his mouth. "That explains it."

Whatever *it* was, he didn't explain it to me. "And . . . um . . . speaking of Lone-Bear, we had a bit of a run-in outside. She mentioned that my stolen car might be a message that I'm not wanted here. And she seems to be . . . possessive of you."

"Really." He rubbed his chin. "What else did she say?"

I repeated the word she'd said, pronouncing it the best I could.

He straightened. "Do you know what that means?"

"No. Probably something bad. I called her a soggy wooker."

"Soggy —"

"Wooker. A wad of hair caught in a sink drain and named after the Wookiee in *Star Wars . . .*" Heat rushed to my face at his expression. I sounded like my sixteen-year-old daughter. I held up the list of names. "I'll get on this." I stood and reached for the door.

"Mrs. Marcey . . . Gwen. Just for the record, there's nothing between Kelli Lone-Bear and myself."

I didn't look at him. "Thank you, but it's none of my business."

On the drive back to Lewiston, I batted away the things I didn't want to think about: Blake, the upcoming custody battle over my daughter, Caroline's pregnancy, how frightened a missing four-year-old child would be, that these murders could be related to me somehow . . .

In our B and B meeting room, Beth had completely covered the table with her laptop, books, pads of paper, a stack of lavender Post-it notes, and a collection of pens in various shades of purple. The 30 × 40 piece of white foam board was on the easel. "Almost done. I would have had this information a lot sooner, but the Internet is slow and spotty. Old houses." She snorted in disgust.

"I'll take Winston out for a walk." The dog stood at hearing his name, then stretched, flopping a luxuriously plumed tail across Beth's computer.

"Please do." She spit out a dog hair.

After snapping on a leash, I led Winston outside. We hadn't gone far when Eric caught up with us, stopping well short of Winston. "Ah, Mrs. Marcey —"

"Call me Gwen."

He was wearing gardening gloves and carried a rake and small shovel. "Okay, Gwen." He had the most extraordinary green eyes. "Have you stayed with us before? You seem to know the place."

"No. I . . . must have read about it. How well do you know its history?"

"Pretty well, but if you want to know more, there's a three-ring binder in the parlor that talks about the past. It's sitting next to the guest book on the sideboard."

"Thanks."

He turned to leave, then stopped. "Almost forgot. Your friend, Beth, asked about places to eat." He reached into his back pocket and handed me a brochure. "We made this up for our guests. Our recommendations." He gave a quick wave of his hand and strolled off.

"Thank you," I called after his retreating back.

The parlor was empty when Winston and I passed through. The binder and guest book were where Eric mentioned. I grabbed them up and returned to the game room. Winston trotted into my bedroom, undoubtedly to sneak up onto the bed.

I moved to the foam board and taped the photos around the outside edge. They proved to be not only of the crime scene but close-ups of the Sinopas' fearsome injuries. I found the printout from Peter and attached it to the bottom. The crime-scene sketches were in my binder. I winced at the drawings. I needed to redraw and clean them up before turning them over to the task force. Taping these to the board for now, I stepped back and took in the effect. The photos were extremely graphic. "Beth, we'll need to keep this turned to the wall when we're not here. I don't want a guest walking by and seeing the gore."

Beth glanced up from her work. Her face drained of blood, but she didn't comment, just nodded.

I read the autopsy reports before attaching them to the foam board. Mr. Sinopa was struck on the head with a blunt object. He must have been unconscious when his body had received such awful wounds. That was a blessing. Mrs. Sinopa wasn't so lucky. There was a lot of anger in that attack. *Personal?*

I settled across from Beth and pulled out a large sketchpad, a T-square, and a ruler. I redrew the rooms of the house, making the measurements neater. Using the crime-scene photos, I placed Adam Sinopa's body along with his wife's. After I finished, I glanced at Beth. "Well?"

"You believed you were mistaken about the timing and location of Holly's and Jacob's murders. You also wanted me to look at murders with a child missing sometime in the last thirty-two years."

"Right."

"So I made the original search parameters the Pacific Northwest, last thirty-two years, and murders involving a child. That took me to a couple of years ago in The Dalles,

Oregon."

"Wait! You should have found Holly's and Jacob's murders!"

"No. Not anything even similar. Not to be insensitive, but when you came home that day at fourteen and saw all the blood, did you . . . um . . . see any bodies?"

"Nooo."

"Where do you think all that blood came from?"

I closed my eyes and thought about that day. The sky was clear, the day hot —

"Are you going to sleep?"

"Um, no. I was giving myself a cognitive interview."

"Ohhh." Beth nodded knowingly. "They talk about that all the time on the television show *Criminal Minds.*"

I grimaced. "And they always act like it's a terrible ordeal, something to be avoided, terrifying even. It's just a way to help someone concentrate by using memory techniques."

"Would you consider teaching me how to do it?"

"Sure. You can help me." I found a blank piece of paper and wrote for a few minutes, then handed her the notes. "Just ask these questions. Speak slowly and wait for an answer."

Beth took the outline and read, "Close your eyes and relax. I want you to think about that day. Start at the beginning and tell me everything that happened, even if you think it's unimportant."

"Okay." I closed my eyes. The old house creaked and moaned around us. The light fragrance of Beth's perfume mingled with the smell of bread.

"Tell me about the kind of day it was."

I took a deep breath. "The sky was clear, phthalo blue, with a hint of yellow . . . from a forest fire somewhere. The day hot. June, a hot June day. I was . . . outside. Walking up a hill. With a . . . paper sack. Heavy paper sack, and I'm sweating and thirsty." I shifted in my seat, the room suddenly warm.

"How do you feel?"

"Confused. Holly sent me to the store for . . . soup. Tomato soup, which I loathe. And macaroni and cheese. And milk. A gallon of milk. But . . ." I chewed my lip, thinking. "But we had just gone to the store, so why did I have to? It was a long walk. And I couldn't see the rabbits in the hutch. Maybe they were all lying down because it was too hot."

"Tell me about the rabbits."

"Jacob loved them. He'd sneak in the house with one when Holly was gone. Holly said we couldn't have an inside pet."

"Now, Gwen, you're a camera on the inside of the house, recording everything. The camera picks you up at the front door. What does the camera see next?"

"I reach for the screen door, but I don't want to open it. Because . . . it's too quiet. But I open the door and step into the room." I turned my head, looking at that long-ago scene. "Everything is red. Carpet, sofa, walls. Furniture . . . the coffee table is overturned . . . a chair tipped over, broken vase . . ." My voice caught. "Smells like copper. And . . . guts. And stinks like an outhouse."

Breathing hard, I spread my arms. "He found us! Like Holly said! I dropped the groceries. The milk spilled on the blood . . . and . . . and I turned to run . . . and I stopped . . . then I ran as fast as I could." I opened my eyes and jumped to my feet. Sweat dampened my shirt. "I'm done."

"What made you stop?" Beth asked.

"What?"

"Before you ran, what made you stop?"

"Because I saw . . . because I saw something. In the corner of the room."

Beth waited.

"It was brown. Small. One of the rabbits." I looked at Beth. "Holly must have found

Jacob with one of the rabbits in the house and killed it. From the amount of blood, she must have killed all of them." I picked up a pencil and tapped the surface of the table. "Jacob was only four. Could Holly and Jacob still be alive?"

"I'll start looking for an alive Holly and Jacob next. After The Dalles."

My heart thundered in my chest. "No. Wait. What about earlier?"

"Nothing. At least in that time period."

"That can't be!"

Beth stared at me, mouth open.

"There has to be a murder, a bloody murder of two people thirty-two years ago. The child, a girl, went missing."

"Gwen, you're as white as a sheet. Why are you so convinced this happened?"

"Because the two people killed were my parents. And the child who disappeared is me."

CHAPTER TWELVE

"What?" Beth asked.

Taking a deep, shuddering breath, I sat and made an effort to relax. "When I was four or so, a man broke into our home and murdered my parents."

"Oh, Gwen! Were you there?"

"No. I was with Holly. She was the sitter, the one who found the bodies. She described the blood, the carnage, so many times. She said the killer was after me. She said she would hide me, keep me safe, but I could never tell anyone who I was or he'd find me." My armpits were damp and my stomach hurt.

"Are you telling me your babysitter took you from your parents?"

I stared at her, drumming my pencil against the table. "I . . . I never thought to question her. She loved me. Cared for me. That's why I called her my sorta-mom. Until the day I came home and found her dead . . . or at least I thought she'd been killed."

Beth reached over and took the pencil out of my hand. "You're going to scar the table." She set the pencil down. "You made a big assumption that Holly was murdered. Considering I found no evidence that your parents were killed, you might want to think about Holly kidnapping and brainwashing you."

Blinking rapidly, I wiped my palms on my slacks. "No. It wasn't like that. We were always on the move, town to town, state to state. She was always afraid, always watching out for someone to take too much notice —"

"Of course she would be — if she'd kidnapped you." Beth reached over and touched my arm.

I jerked away. "No! She told me if anything happened to her that I must run. Change my name. Never tell anyone because *he'd* found her. When I came home that day, I believed it all. I would be next unless I ran. So I did. Hitched a ride to Montana and hid out at Dave's dad's place. When they found me, I didn't say a word."

Beth got up and started to pace. "Dave's dad was the sheriff. He would have looked for your folks —"

"He did, but he didn't know where to look. Like I said, Holly moved us around a lot, and I was homeschooled."

"He should have been able to track you through one of the homeschool organizations."

I gave her a wry smile. "Not officially homeschooled. Dave's dad actively searched for any records for almost two years, hired a private investigator, contacted different agencies —"

"You *knew* he was doing all this and didn't tell him the truth?"

"I didn't know at the time. Dave told me much later, after his dad died. He told me his dad wanted to adopt me, but officially I didn't exist, so he simply raised me like a daughter. Dave became my big brother."

"Gwen, this doesn't make sense. I found no record of your parents' murders. And even if they were murdered, your family, friends, neighbors . . . people would have gone crazy looking for you." Beth stopped pacing. "Didn't you wonder?"

"No!" I said with more force than I meant to. "Holly wouldn't have lied to me about my parents' deaths."

My friend slowly lowered herself to a chair. The silence stretched between us.

Surely she could see why I'd never looked

into my childhood. It was bracketed by murder. The murder of my parents at the beginning and of Holly at the end. I put that time of my life in a box and vowed never to open it. But now the facts were staring me in the face. Holly *had* lied to me. Everything I knew, everything I believed for those many years, needed to be pulled from the box, researched, and reassembled.

I reached out to grab the armrest and knocked against a glass vase on the side table. The vase fell on the floor and shattered, the sound abnormally loud in the quiet room.

We both leaped up. Winston charged from the bedroom. I caught his ruff before he could walk in the glass and led him to his mesh kennel. The dog slunk inside, making sure I was aware of his displeasure. By the time I'd returned to the living area, Beth had brought the waste bin from the corner of the room and was gingerly picking up the pieces. When we'd removed all the larger shards, Beth said, "I'll borrow a vacuum cleaner." She stood. "Have faith, m'friend. We'll get to the bottom of what happened to you as a child."

"Why can't my life be easy and straightforward for a change?" I threw my arms in the air. "Cancer, divorce . . . now this . . ."

"Whoa, there. Since when have you started looking at a glass half full?" She studied my face for a moment, then squeezed my shoulder. "I've told you often enough that I believe everything happens for a reason. I also believe that we go through seasons in our lives, some good, some bad."

"And this season?"

"Maybe it's your time to search."

"And after that?" I asked softly.

"I'd say a time to mend. I don't know what God's plans are for you, but I do know all the trials you're going through are molding you into an amazing person." She left, closing the door behind her.

I curled up on the sofa and thought about her words. Beth returned shortly with a vacuum cleaner, plugged it in, and cleaned up the last of the glass. "There now, good as new."

"Thank you, Beth."

"For vacuuming? Not a problem."

"For your friendship. And your wisdom."

Beth's cheeks turned pink. "Ahhh. I'm not so wise. I just have a good source."

A whine from my bedroom reminded me I'd evicted Winston until after the glass cleanup. I strolled to the bedroom and released the dog from his kennel, then returned to the living area we shared.

"Now." Beth glanced at her stack of research covering the table. "Back to your parents. I guess I have to ask you . . . do you want to know the truth? Do you want to find out what happened?"

I wandered across the room. *Did* I want to know? What if . . . ? Sinking onto the sofa, I curled my legs under me. Winston jumped up next to me, but I didn't correct him. I wrapped my arms around his furry ruff and gave him a hug. "Yes. I need to know. As soon as possible."

"And your work on this case?"

"Don't worry. The case has priority —"

My cell phone rang. The caller ID said *Seth Kus.* "Hello?"

"Just got a call from the casino. You had an appointment for an interview —"

"Doggone it!" I looked at my watch. "I was doing some . . . um . . . background research and the time got away from me. I'm on my way." I disconnected and looked at my friend. "I am so in trouble. I have to run. See if you can find *anything* that happened to a family with a child thirty-two years ago." I dashed for the door. "And check the history of this house and the guest book for a murder, or anyone named Gwen."

115

"Wait! Was your name always Gwen?"

I paused and thought for a moment. "Yes."

Assistant manager Peter Otskai let me use his office for the interviews of his staff. The first was the head of housekeeping, a pretty, slender woman of about forty named Kim.

"Please be comfortable." I pointed to a chair. "May I get you something to drink?"

"I'd love a Coke." She sat and crossed her legs.

"A Coke." I stared at her blankly.

She smiled. "In the casino, to your left."

Grabbing my purse, I stepped from the room and looked around the pinging-ringing casino. I spotted the soft drink machine and walked over. Two men stood in front of me, deciding on a drink. While I waited, I thought about what Beth and I discussed. *Did Holly kidnap me and lie to me for ten years? Could my parents still be alive?*

"Are you going to make a selection?" a woman asked.

The men had left. *Why am I here?* I started walking back to Peter's office. *Did my folks look for me, miss me? Or was Holly telling the truth? Is there a connection between the current murders and the murders of my parents so long ago? But why couldn't Beth find out about it?*

116

Coke.

Turning, I rushed over to the machine and bought the soda.

The interviews dragged on, with a maintenance worker pointing out he'd given me the same information three times in a row. The final scheduled interview ended and I glanced at my sparse notes. I'd learned nothing new. The staff hated Adam. No one sent the threatening letters. No one saw anything. They all felt bad about Beatrice.

I drove as fast as I could back to the bed-and-breakfast. I didn't want to call Beth about her results. I wanted to hear them in person, but the closer I got, the more my heart pounded.

Beth was outside with Winston when I arrived. I wanted to ask her then and there, but several people were wandering around the grounds and I needed privacy. After my dog inspected and watered several trees and one car tire, we moved to the game room and I shut the door. "Well?"

"How'd the interviews go? Did anyone lie? I love it when you can figure out when someone is lying."

"Lie? No . . . I mean, I don't know."

Beth slowly sat at the table. "Well. That's a first."

"Let it go, Beth. I . . . just . . . I need to

know what you found out."

Her eyebrows furrowed, but she didn't speak and instead pulled a lavender-tinted notebook in front of her. "My research work with Microsoft gave me access to a lot of different . . . people with . . . skills . . . um . . . Just don't ask about my sources."

"My lips are sealed."

"Knowing the year made a huge difference. I'm not surprised that neither the private investigator nor Dave's dad found the information. With a ten-year gap between events, they probably didn't look far enough back."

"And Holly was very good at hiding by then."

"I looked at every event that happened to a family in the year you said you . . . um . . . left with your sitter. I stayed within the Northwest. I found two car accidents, one murder-suicide, and a plane crash." She glanced at her writing. "I focused on the plane crash. Four people died, a man, a woman, the pilot, and a four-year-old child."

"That can't be it —"

"I'm not done. The plane went down in the wilderness area southeast of here in the Clearwater National Forest. It took them a bit to find the wreckage and recover the bodies. All but the little girl. They never found her body. They assumed . . . well, there are cougars, grizzlies, wolves, you get the picture."

My legs felt like cooked noodles. I sat before I fell down.

Beth folded her arms and looked down for a moment as if praying. "One final thing. The girl's name was Gwen."

CHAPTER THIRTEEN

"A plane crash." My mind went blank. A Steller's jay scolded from the white pine outside. Faint voices came from another part of the house. Dust motes floated in the light pouring in from the window. Winston shifted and sighed in his sleep. The odor of baking bread drifted up from the kitchen below us.

Beth cleared her throat.

I looked at her. "I have to start over."

"What do you mean?"

"My life — from when I was four to when I ran away at fourteen — was a lie. Everything was a lie. I have to find the truth about those ten years. And what really happened to my parents. And to Holly and Jacob."

Beth tapped her pad of paper with a manicured nail. "You are right in the middle of a homicide investigation."

"Yes." Standing, I retrieved my notes from the interviews and the redrawn crime scene.

"I'll get these off to the chief." I placed the notes on the table. "How strange is it that my decision to take the Sinopa case led me to search, and discover, my own history — or should I say, personal mystery? If it hadn't been for that silly Lamb Chop."

"Lamb chop? Something you ate?"

"No." I strolled into the bedroom, grabbed the puppet and the sketchpad with the comparisons between the Sinopas' case and my own, then returned. "Lamb Chop puppet. It was in Beatrice's room." I opened the sketchpad. "I was struck by the similarities between the crime scene at the Sinopas' house and the one I *thought* I saw the day I ran."

Beth read down the list. "It does seem strange. I mean, bloody crime scene and the proximity of the locations don't jump out at me, but the hatchet, puppet, and age of the child involved do seem to stretch coincidence to the limit."

"Do you think . . . Is it possible . . . that someone could be behind both events?"

Beth scrunched up her face. "You mean, like Holly?"

"Or Jacob."

"He was just four —"

"Okay, maybe I should use a different word. Not so much *behind*, but . . . aware.

The slaughter of the rabbits would have strongly impacted his young mind. He'd be in his twenties now."

"Looks like I'd better find both Holly and Jacob as soon as possible."

"Right, and see if you can order another sheet of foam board, a really big one. And some pushpins in different colors."

After typing up my notes from the interviews, I e-mailed them to the chief, then dialed his number.

He answered almost before the phone rang. "Kus."

"Hi. This is Gwen."

"Gwen." His voice warmed considerably. "I was just going to call you. We found a child's body."

I sucked in a deep breath and looked over at the teddy bear propped on the desk. "You found Beatrice?"

Beth put her hand over her mouth.

"No. This one's been dead for a long time. Years."

I shook my head at Beth. "Where are you?"

"About three miles upriver from Spalding, right alongside the road. Couple of kids saw a rolled-up tarp and checked it out."

"I'm on my way." I disconnected and told Beth what Chief Kus said. "Car?"

Beth nodded. "Of course. When do you think you'll return?"

"I don't know."

"Have you eaten anything since breakfast?"

I paused in packing my forensic kit. "Now that you mention it, no."

She stood and went to her room, returning with a banana, an apple, and a bottle of water. "Thank you again, Beth. I don't know what I'd do without you."

The corner of her mouth curled up. "Where would Ben be without Jerry, peanut butter without jelly, macaroni without cheese?"

"Now I'm starving." I grabbed up Beth's car keys, patted Winston, and headed to the car.

Stowing my kit in the back seat, I slid in and headed to the scene, eating my impromptu meal on the way. I soon reached the site — a wide spot in the road next to a bridge crossing the Clearwater. Behind a line of Jersey barriers, parked tribal police cars blocked the view from Highway 12. An officer impatiently motioned rubbernecking motorists to keep moving.

The sun had drifted behind a line of storm clouds, casting dark cerulean-blue shadows on the rolling mountains. The tiny body had been left on a cracked and grimy stretch of asphalt, rolled in an incongruously cheerful blue tarp.

Chief Kus motioned me over.

I pulled my kit from the back seat, took a deep breath of ozone- and petrichor-scented air, and walked to where the officers stood. My footsteps slowed as I approached. It was always like this, the moment when I'd first see a body before my professional side could take over.

The men parted as I approached. The tarp had been pulled open and very little was left of the body — bones held together by tattered remnants of clothing, tangled brown hair with a pink plastic clip.

Feeling the officers' gazes on me, I made sure my voice wouldn't come out all wimpy. "A girl. Any idea who she is?"

"We're checking." Seth Kus rubbed his chin. "He dug her up and put her here, making sure we'd find her."

"Interesting."

Seth gave a tiny jerk of his head, then moved away from earshot. I followed.

"You have something?" he asked.

"Two things." Overhead a magpie chattered his *wock, wock, wock.* A raindrop splashed on my arm. *Great.* I'd forgotten to ask Beth to pack a raincoat. "After the forensic anthropologist finishes up, if you don't have an identification, I can do a skull reconstruction."

"Okay. But I could see you were struck by something."

I looked over at the remains. "I'm not a profiler —"

Seth waved his hand.

"That body was dug up and left for you to find. Why?" I bit my lip and thought for a moment. "Part of his signature changed."

"So you think this is a serial killer."

"I think it's too much of a coincidence for a body to show up roughly the same age and sex of the missing Beatrice."

A few more drops of rain hit my head.

"Do you have a raincoat or umbrella?" the chief asked.

"No."

He jerked his head for me to follow him to his car. Opening the rear door, he took out a navy-blue raincoat with *Nez Perce Tribal Police* printed across the back. "Here."

"I can't take your coat."

The corner of his mouth twitched and he tugged out a second identical jacket. "Part of my emergency supplies."

The slight sprinkle became a steady rain just as I slipped into the coat and pulled up the hood. The jacket was enormous, with

125

the sleeves hanging completely over my hands and the hood drooping to my nose. I tilted my head backward to see.

The chief quickly yanked on his jacket and bent closer to be heard over the steady patter of the rain. "What did you mean by 'part of his signature changed'?"

Heat radiated from him. I wanted to step away. Or move closer. I remembered Blake's embrace, and I cleared my throat before continuing. "Stop me if you already know this . . ."

Seth gave me an encouraging nod.

"Modus operandi and signature are different. Modus operandi refers to the actions someone takes to commit a crime. These actions follow a learning curve as the killer hones his craft. If something works, great. If he makes a mistake, he'll change to become more successful. The signature is *why* — the psychological motive for the crime. What fantasy was he playing out? You could think of it as his calling card. The third part of this triad is the choice of victim."

"Okay."

"MO can change, but the signature usually remains the same. Usually, though not always, the choice of victims doesn't change. Displaying a past victim is a signature, and this hasn't happened before — at least not that you know of, right?"

"Right. So what do you think it means?"

"It means he knows his attempt to throw off the case by staging those notes didn't work. Now he's introducing himself to us. He wants us to know he's the killer."

CHAPTER FOURTEEN

All of the officers now wore matching navy raincoats and, with the hoods up, looked identical. Someone had pulled the tarp back over the body. The van from the coroner's office arrived and parked nearby. A man got out, opened an umbrella, briefly examined the remains, then had the officers load her onto a stretcher. After shutting the doors, he approached the chief. "Seth. Good to see you. Sorry it took so long."

"Not a problem. This is Gwen Marcey, a forensic artist from the Interagency Major Crimes Unit out of Missoula."

"Ma'am."

"If you can't get an ID right away," Seth said, "she can help with a facial reconstruction."

"I've read about those." The coroner stuffed his hand into his pocket. "I'll let you know."

"Anything you can tell me now?" Seth asked.

"Well, she's been in the ground for a few years. No obvious signs of trauma. That's about all I can say until the autopsy." He headed toward his van.

"Thanks," Seth called after him, then turned to leave.

"Chief Kus?" I didn't want to ask him, but I had no choice. "I . . . um . . . may have a lead on something."

"On something?"

"It's a long shot, but it has to do with a missing child a long time ago. A cold case. Maybe a kidnapping. I . . . um . . . think there may be a connection with other cases. I don't want to draw any conclusions just yet, not until I find out a few more things, but I wanted to give you a heads-up."

He didn't speak for a moment and I became aware the officers were leaving. All but one. From the body build I could tell it was a female officer. It wasn't until she lifted her head and I could see her face that I recognized Officer LoneBear. Her jaw clenched and she stared daggers at me.

I couldn't help it. I laid my hand on the chief's arm and gave her a slight smile.

LoneBear jumped into her car, slamming the door so hard I expected the windows to shatter, and spun away.

The chief looked after her retreating vehicle, frowned, then glanced down at my hand still resting on his arm. His right eye narrowed in what I had figured out was a concealed smile.

I snatched my hand away.

"Having a bit of a catfight?" he asked.

"Mm." My face burned and I suddenly found the tip of my shoe fascinating.

"So what is the connection you want to pursue?"

"I'm looking into two people who may have lived around here over twenty years ago. And there's a plane crash that occurred thirty-some years ago. I want to go there."

"Where did it crash?"

"The Clearwater National Forest." When he didn't respond, I gave up studying my shoe and looked at him.

He rubbed his chin. "You do know that the Nez Perce–Clearwater National Forest is four million acres, at least half of which is designated wilderness?"

I gave a half shrug, folded my arms, and waited. The rain slowed, then stopped.

He stopped rubbing his chin and squinted his eye. "What would your boss say?"

"Well. He'd . . . um . . ."

"That's what I thought. Since the things

you want to look into are in the past, and I have a missing child right now, you can do your chasing on your own time. I have some video in the car that my task force collected on the Easter egg hunt. I want you to look at it."

I slowly nodded. "Of course." Following him to the car, I tried to think of a way to convince him I had a possible lead. The problem was, I just didn't have enough evidence.

After handing me a white Walmart bag, he bent forward, pulled a notepad from his pocket, clicked a pen, and wrote something. "Here." He handed it to me.

He'd written a name, Dan Kus, and phone number. "*When* you're done helping me, if you're going to be fumbling about in the wilderness, you'll want to find a guide or an outfitter. Dan Kus volunteers at the Nez Perce National Historical Park. He's a virtual encyclopedia of the history and geography of this area. He can recommend someone or ask around for an expert to take you to the crash site. But remember, on your own time."

"Any relation?"

"Yeah. He's my dad. Retired."

"Should I tell him you sent me?"

Seth nodded and his right eye crinkled.

"And be sure to tell him you got LoneBear's goat."

Night had fallen, and the heavy rain had returned. My thoughts bounced from the present murders and abduction, to the upcoming change to the parenting plan for Aynslee, to my own checkered background. I was soon parked at the Two Rivers Bed-and-Breakfast. My cell rang.

"Mom, Dad just told me I was to, like, pack up my stuff from home and that, like, I'll be living here in Big Fork." Aynslee's voice was shrill. "Is that true?"

"Ah, no. I don't think so. Just wait until I get back. Put your father on."

"He's not here. He and Caroline have gone out."

"Don't worry, sweetheart, everything will be fine."

"When are you coming home?"

I hesitated, thinking about all the work I had to do for the police and how I would find time to pursue my own investigation. "Soon."

"Whatever." *Click.*

I sat in the car until my fingers relaxed from their claw shape. Running into the old house, I found Eric filling the coffee machine in the parlor.

He smiled a greeting. "Still raining?"

"Cats and dogs." Winston rose as I entered the game room and slammed his massive head against my leg to let me know he needed attention.

A fresh oversized sheet of foam board sat on the easel, blocking the photos from the murder scene. Beth still sat where I'd left her, now surrounded by white take-out boxes of food. The pungent odor of curry filled the air.

"Chinese?" I asked.

"Thai. Try that and that." She pointed at two boxes. "Do you like spicy? No. Don't answer that. The only two dishes I've ever seen prepared by you are frozen pizza and tuna noodle casserole."

"What's wrong with my casserole?"

"Ask anyone who's tried it." She pointed again. "Stay away from that one and probably that one."

I picked up a paper plate and loaded it with the remaining food items. "Whaja fin out?" I said around a mouthful of something with rice.

Beth tucked a wisp of hair behind her ear. "I did an Internet search for *Holly Greene* and *Idaho* to limit the search. Here's where it gets interesting. Or creepy. Six years ago, a Holly Greene started writing letters to the editor that would appear in Kamiah's local weekly paper."

The skin on my neck prickled. "So Holly's alive! No other information?"

"The dates of the letters varied, the last one written over a year ago, and the subject was usually pretty bland. The initials *SHN* appeared after her name."

"Maybe a clue to another name? Maybe Jacob's new name, or . . . I don't know."

Beth shrugged. "I tried *SHN* as an Internet search. It yielded almost eleven and a half million hits, so I needed to narrow it down more. I went back to the Kamiah area and kept digging. I typed *SHN* along with the names of the different towns around here."

"And?"

"One interesting hit came up when I typed in *SHN* and *Orofino,* a small town between here and Kamiah. Though Orofino has just over three thousand residents, it has several things that caught my attention. It's home to a prison and a mental hospital."

"Prison . . ."

"Specifically, a men's prison. But *SHN* might have referred to State Hospital North. It's the mental hospital."

I wiped my sweaty hands on my pants. "Go on."

"I took a chance, called the hospital, and asked to speak to Holly Greene. They said no one was there by that name. But" — Beth grinned — "just as I was about to hang up, they said they did have a Lucinda Holly Greene."

"So —"

"So your Holly Greene is not only alive, but living there."

CHAPTER FIFTEEN

As I strolled from one corner of the room to the other, my brain examined the news of Holly's whereabouts from every angle. Why was Holly committed to a mental hospital? How long had she been there? And where was Jacob?

"Gwen." Beth stood in front of me and grabbed me by the shoulders. "I know finding out about Holly is a shocker, but you're upsetting your dog again."

Sure enough, Winston was sitting up and panting with nervous, ropy drool hanging from his dewlaps. I sat on the floor beside him and gave him a hug. "I'm sorry, old boy."

Winston slimed my pants with his drool and gave me a juicy burp.

"By the way, did you hear from Aynslee?" Beth asked.

"Oh. Yes. How did you know?"

"She called me. She seemed upset."

"Why did she call you?"

Beth tilted her head. "She hoped I could give her a better idea of when you were coming home."

"I'm afraid I was rather vague with her." I rubbed my eyes, hoping a headache wasn't forming. *Do I have other family? Why didn't anyone look for me?*

"Maybe what you should do is treat your mysterious past like one of your cases." Beth moved to my forensic art kit and pulled out a sketchpad. "Write those known and unknown columns?"

"Of course! Why didn't I think of it?" I took the sketchpad from her.

"You have a bit on your mind right now. Double homicide, missing child, stolen car, not to mention this new job."

"And Aynslee's upcoming custody —" I clamped my mouth shut, but it was too late.

Beth spun in my direction. "What do you mean?"

"Nothing, nothing, just let it go."

"Is that why Aynslee called? There are days I'd just like to shoot Robert."

"That's why I didn't tell you."

Pulling out the DVDs from the Easter egg hunt, I settled down with my old computer. "I need to look at these, but in the meantime, could you start the second piece of foam board with all we've gathered so far on my past, Holly, Jacob, the plane crash, notes, and so on?"

The video was typical amateur filming, with the operator moving too fast and jerking up and down. After twenty minutes, I was seasick, my eyes gritty, and that headache was forming. The shots were probably taken by the parents or grandparents of three different sets of children, and the focus was on them. A beautiful Beatrice appeared in all three. In spite of myself, my eyes filled with tears over the priceless little girl. *Please, Lord, keep her safe.*

I looked at the faces of men, their body language, clothing, and shoes. Unlike composites, which are usually just the face, in video I could watch movement.

None of the brief appearances of Beatrice showed anyone paying her undue attention.

Finishing up the work, I wrote up a report and e-mailed it to Chief Kus. My morning meeting with the task force would prove to be another disappointing report.

Yanking out a sketchpad, I wrote *Known* on one side of the paper and *Unknown* on the other. Under *Known* I wrote *recognized Two Rivers house, locations where we moved and when we moved (roughly every year), Jacob, Holly.* I added *admitted to state mental hospital* after *Holly.* Under *Unknown* I wrote *Why taken? What happened to Holly and Jacob after I left? Any connection with me and current homicide?* I added *When Holly admitted to mental hospital?*

"What can I do to help?" Beth asked.

I tapped the paper with my pencil and thought for a moment. "Could you look up visiting hours at the mental hospital?"

"Are you going to see her? Will you recognize her after all these years? What do you think happened to her son? Do you think this house is somehow related to all that happened to you?"

"Mmm."

"Gwen, hello? Where are you? You usually answer me like, 'Yes, probably, I don't know, possibly.' "

"Well, see? You're learning something." I sounded lame.

Beth bent over her laptop for a moment. "They list visiting hours as 'reasonable.' "

Glancing outside at the thick blanket of darkness, I sighed. "I suppose —"

"Yes. It's too late. Get some rest."

Winston trailed me into the room and flopped on the floor. I pulled the curtains and undressed, pulling on a smoky-gray cotton lounge outfit. I didn't think sleep was possible as I slid between the crisp white sheets.

Winston erupted with frantic barking.

Adrenaline shot through me. I leaped from bed. The clock said two in the morning.

Winston was focused on the window. I patted him to quiet his barking, then peeked out the curtains. My room overlooked a lawn and a corner of the parking lot. A dim yellow streetlight illuminated small sections of asphalt wet by rain and cast deep pools of shadow. Grabbing a jacket, I snapped on Winston's leash, then stuffed my Glock in my pocket.

Beth was at the door to her room clutching a rose-patterned robe. "What?"

"I don't know. Stay here." Grabbing Beth's car keys, I allowed Winston to haul me through the game room, across the softly lit parlor, and to the back door. I hoped his barking didn't rouse the other guests.

No one appeared to challenge us as we scurried through the sleeping house. Winston came to a stop in the middle of the parking lot, head raised, ears alert, and tail stiffly curled over his back.

I pulled out my Glock.

He remained motionless for a moment, then tugged me to Beth's car. Returning the pistol to my pocket, I checked the ground around the car. Everything appeared undisturbed.

Reaching for the car door with the keys, I noticed I'd left the car unlocked. *Great. How about another stolen car?*

The overhead light came on as I opened the driver's-side door.

Sitting propped on the passenger seat was a white Shari Lewis Lamb Chop puppet.

My heart raced. I yanked out the Glock and spun around. Still no one in sight, but clouds hid the light of the moon.

I didn't want to touch the toy in case it held fingerprints. A quick check of the car showed nothing out of place and no bag to put the puppet in. I ran back into the house, and Beth was waiting in the parlor holding two steaming white mugs. "Chamomile tea? What's wrong?"

"I need a bag. Quickly."

Beth put the tea on the table, yanked the trash bag from the garbage container in the corner, then pulled out an unused bag underneath.

I snatched it from her, handed her Winston's lead, and returned to the car. After bagging the puppet, I locked the car and returned to the house.

Beth sat at the table, a cooling mug of tea in front of her, arms wrapped around her shoulders.

Winston had thumped to the floor, stretched out, and closed his eyes. Around us the old house sighed and creaked. A moth softly beat against the window.

After carefully placing the bag on the table, I walked to my room and returned with the puppet from the Sinopas' home. "Someone got into your car and left a matching Lamb Chop puppet on the seat."

"What does that mean?"

"That's the problem. It could mean several things. I seem to have made an enemy of LoneBear, and I think she's the one who took my car. She'd relish making me look like a fool. And another officer, Attao, isn't so crazy about my outsider status. He knows I have the puppet from the Sinopas' crime scene."

Beth glanced at the lamb. "I can tell that you don't really believe either of those things is the reason for this."

"You're right. I don't. With the placing of the child's body in plain sight today, I think the killer is no longer trying to cover up. He's providing a direct connection between himself, the Sinopas' murder, the bloody scene when I was fourteen, and me."

"What are you going to do?"

Taking a deep breath, I looked at her.

142

"Make my case to Chief Kus that I have a reason to search out my past."

Chapter Sixteen

Once again I didn't think I could sleep, but after what seemed like a minute, I awoke. I was freezing. Winston had sneaked up onto the bed and was hogging all the covers and two pillows. I was about to have a tug-of-war to retrieve a blanket when I spotted the clock.

Unless I hurried, I would be late for the task force meeting.

Overcast daylight glowed behind the curtains. I tore out of my room and tapped on Beth's door. "I'm late. Help me."

Beth appeared, grabbed a leash, and lured Winston off the bed and out for a walk.

I showered and swiftly dressed in a pair of black wool slacks and matching blazer with a beige shell underneath. My wardrobe came from a secondhand shop in Missoula where someone my size had dumped a boatload of designer clothes.

When I came out of my room, an attractive, auburn-haired woman was waiting in the hall holding a paper sack and a travel mug of coffee. "Beth said you were late. Here's something to tide you over. I'm Lila. I work with Eric."

"Thank you so much!" I gratefully took the sack and mug.

Beth already held my kit in one hand and the bag with the puppet in the other.

"Put that other puppet in the kit and follow me out." On the way to the car, I said, "Up for more research?"

"You know I am."

"See if you can locate Jacob Greene. Ask Eric or Lila if they have earlier records on who stayed at this house. See if you can find out about the plane that crashed — like who owned it, who the pilot was, what they were doing."

"Got it."

"I'll call if I have anything new to report. And I hope to stop by and talk to Holly."

Driving as fast as I dared to Lapwai, I bolted down the muffin Lila had so thoughtfully provided. I walked into the task force meeting seven minutes late.

Chief Kus was speaking. He stopped when I entered. Everyone else stared at me with varying degrees of hostility. "Nice of you to join us."

That stung. "I was up part of the night. Someone broke into Beth's car and left this." I upended the bag and dumped the puppet on the table.

Silence for a moment, then the room erupted in laughter.

My face burned. I reached down and pulled the other puppet from my kit. "This was found in Beatrice Sinopa's room." I put it on the table.

Officer Attao grabbed Bea's puppet and stuck it on his hand. "Hello." He worked the puppet's mouth. "I'm a lamb clue. I'm here for ewe, and ewe, and ewe." He poked the puppet at different officers. "That's spelled *e-w-e.*"

"Knock it off." Chief Kus glared at the man, then looked at me. "Please remain after the meeting."

I focused on the chief, avoiding the gaze of the members of the force. The map that the officers had been looking at the last time I was here had been mounted to one wall. Two enlarged driver's license photos of men of interest joined my composite sketch.

"We've received tips from the Amber Alert from as far away as Tucson and Colorado Springs. Lewiston police have almost finished contacting the last of their registered sex offenders. I've passed out the printout

146

of suspects to check out today. The last search party organized by the tribe goes out today and will cover this area." He strolled to the map and pointed. "You all have your assignments. Let's find Bea today."

I remained while the room emptied, using the time to remove the crime-scene diagrams from my kit and place them on the table.

Chief Kus sat across the table from me. "Your interviews produced no leads. Nothing in the tapes I sent you. So far, just a composite of an average man who may or may not be connected. And this." He picked up the puppet.

I explained my strange childhood and the similarities between the cases. The more I spoke, the weaker my evidence seemed that anything was related. I could see the doubt in the chief's eyes.

When I finished, he leaned back and drummed his fingers on the table. He took a breath. "I'll have the crime lab dust the puppet you found in the car for prints and any hairs or fibers, but I don't think we'll find anything. I'm inclined to think someone is pulling a bad joke on you."

"But —"

"Continue with the interviews I've given you. We have a ticking clock on finding

Beatrice."

"Could you do one thing for me?" I folded my hands to keep from making a pleading motion. "When you had your analyst look for similar cases, you looked in Idaho, right?"

He gave a half nod.

"Three years ago there was a case in The Dalles, Oregon, where the parents were killed and the child went missing."

Kus reached for a yellow pad and jotted some notes. "How do you know this?"

I wanted to say my researcher was better. "I'm supposed to be gathering information. That came up in the course of making the composite with Andi Tubbs. Anyway, could you have them send over their crime-scene photos?"

He wrote something else, then nodded. "I'll look into it, but I mean it about you staying on task."

"Thank you." I got up to leave.

"And I'll also look into whether someone on my staff is playing games with you."

I tried not to think about the officers' reaction to the puppet. I focused on the next project. I called my next witness, Randy Wait, and set up a composite session. He'd seen a man following Beatrice around the park on Easter Sunday.

The day was overcast and sultry as I drove toward Kamiah on Highway 12. The road hugged the winding Clearwater River, with blooming dogwood and wild cherry trees parading their glory. The hills rose above me in undulating waves of emerald green.

I slowed when I saw the sign for Orofino and the state mental hospital. If Beth was right and my parents died in a plane crash, today I could find out the truth of why I'd been whisked from town to town evading a fictional murderer. Resisting the urge to stop now rather than wait until I'd done the composite sketch, I continued the remaining miles, but my thoughts wouldn't let me take them captive.

From the day I fled the bloody house in Kamiah, I'd crushed the memories of living with Holly, not wanting to feel the pain of her death. Now, in such a short span of time, I'd learned that her murder, like my parents', was a work of fiction.

Neither Holly nor Jacob died in Kamiah, according to the records, and my parents perished in an accident, not at the hand of some crazy, vengeful killer.

My jaw ached, and I made an effort to relax. *Think about Beatrice.*

A devastating forest fire in 2015 had burned more than forty homes and destroyed over seventy thousand acres surrounding the small town of Kamiah. The evidence of this devastation clearly showed in the large strips of blackened earth and rust-colored trees. Patches of white smoke on the hillsides indicated where someone was burning slash piles of downed trees.

I turned off the highway to the main street of town. I'd scheduled the interview with Randy to take place at the library. For the composite artist, the easiest and best location of the drawing is the police department, but some witnesses aren't comfortable in a law-enforcement setting. Unless I had an officer with me and had no other choice, I seldom went to someone's home. Between curious children, ringing phones, snoopy neighbors, and almost always a dog with an overactive bladder, there were simply too many interruptions. Not to mention the safety issue.

The directions were simple and direct: Look for city hall, which would be on the left. The library was next to it. Both buildings had western-type facades that resembled stores, with an overhanging roof shading the sidewalk.

A young man waited by the checkout desk. "Mrs. Marcey?"

"Call me Gwen. You must be Randy Wait."

Randy was a twenty-something, oval-faced native wearing a red baseball hat, a green jacket, and jeans. His skin bore the memory of teenage acne, and a sparse mustache sprouted from his upper lip. His hand was sweaty as I shook it. Before I could ask about the meeting room, Randy moved into the library, around a corner, and through an open door. The space was big enough for a large table and several folding chairs.

I selected the area with the most light and indicated the chair to my left for Randy. In no time I'd covered the table with my art supplies. Randy selected a round face with a double chin, a large, bulbous nose, squinting eyes, and a pockmarked face. Clearly the man he'd seen following Beatrice in the park wasn't the same man Andi saw on the front steps of the Sinopa home. Finishing the drawing, I held it up for his final evaluation. "On a one-to-ten scale, with one being not at all similar and ten being perfect, how close does this come to your memory?"

"A ten. Will this be in the news?"

Slowly lowering the sketch, I leaned back in my chair. How stupid could I be? The signs were there: no changes to the drawing, a perfect score, asking about attention in the media, and making the suspect ugly — called the Quasimodo Effect. Randy was lying. Where were my warning bells? "Randy, you didn't see anyone following Beatrice in the park, did you?"

Randy took a deep breath, scratched his nose, and blinked rapidly at me. "Why are you asking? I mean, don't you believe me?"

"You gave me three signs — no, make that four signs you were lying to me just now."

Before I could continue, Randy bolted from the room.

I rubbed my forehead and sighed. I'd just wasted almost two hours drawing plus the drive. It would be up to Chief Kus to charge Randy for obstructing justice. Gathering my materials, I quickly left the library.

Deciding to eat lunch before leaving town, I found a small mom-and-pop café. Comfort food filled the menu — chicken-fried steak, meat loaf, spaghetti. I ordered a club sandwich, but when the waitress served it, I found I wasn't hungry. I stared at the dill pickle spear leaking juice over the handful of potato chips. *Can you think of any more delays? Time to face Holly.*

The closer I got to Orofino, the faster my heart beat. Different memories of the years I spent with her, the many moves we'd made, and the prevailing sense of fear that my parents' killer would catch up with me crowded my mind.

The state mental hospital, state prison, and high school all were located in the same area and offered breathtaking views of the Clearwater River and surrounding mountains. The grounds were beautifully landscaped with picnic benches under the flowering trees. I neared the edge of the lot, turned off the engine, and stared sightlessly ahead. Today I'd have the answers to questions I'd long since forgotten.

Rain thumped on the roof of the car and the windows soon steamed up, but I couldn't move, not yet. For years I'd stuffed the memories of my time with Holly into the dark recesses of my mind, but now I'd opened the door to those years and it wouldn't close.

I needed to document all that I remembered, capture the moments while they were fresh so I could study them later. Maybe get Beth to help me. Somewhere would be the clues to what happened to my parents, to me, those many years ago.

Picking up a pencil and sketchpad, I leaned my head back on the headrest. I'd assumed Jacob, Holly's son, was murdered at the same time Holly was. What had happened to him? I began sketching the young child. Soon I had a rough drawing of his four-year-old face.

I finally stepped from the car and pulled up the hood on the borrowed rain jacket. After locking my pistol in the glove box, I scurried through the rain, holding the hood of the jacket so I could see.

The building was made of reddish decorative blocks with a brown metal roof. Visitors could unload under the porte cochere leading to the main entrance. A slender woman with spiky, strawberry-blonde hair was reading behind the reception desk. She looked up as I approached. "May I help you?"

I licked my suddenly dry mouth. "I'm here to see Holly Greene."

"We don't have . . . Wait, did you mean Lucinda Greene?"

"Oh, right, sorry."

She stood. She wore pressed khaki scrubs and matching soft-soled shoes. "Follow me. Lucinda seldom gets visitors."

My legs felt weak and I wiped my damp hands on my pants. "Um . . . does her son come to visit?"

The woman glanced at me but continued to walk down a short hallway. "I don't think so."

We entered a spacious room painted buttercup yellow and smelling faintly of cleaning solution and floral air freshener. On my right, a man and woman chatted on a sofa. Two men in gray sweatpants played cards at a table while a third watched. A woman in a jade-green oversized sweater and black leggings looked up from the book she was reading. Slipping off my wet jacket, I followed the nurse across the room to a gray-haired woman, her back to us, slumped in a wheelchair.

"She has paranoid schizophrenia. Believes someone is trying to kill her. Hears voices. Classic."

I fought a sudden urge to bolt from the room.

The nurse walked around the chair until she was facing Holly. "Good day, Lucinda. Someone is here to see you. Isn't that nice?"

Sidling next to the nurse, I took a deep breath and held out my hand. "Hello, Holly. It's me. Gwen."

The woman didn't acknowledge me, didn't even look up. Her gray-white hair was pulled into a loose ponytail at her neck. Her sallow skin was deeply wrinkled and creased. Pale venetian-red pouches underscored her eyes.

I did quick calculations. If Holly had been in her mid-to-late twenties when she took me, she would only be in her late fifties. This woman looked to be in her eighties. I turned to the woman still standing beside me. "Are you sure —"

"Must save the child," the old woman muttered.

A chill raced up my spine. I swayed a moment and grabbed for a chair. I knew that voice, those words. Sitting before I collapsed, I tried to get Holly to look at me. "Holly? What happened when you took me from my parents? Where is Jacob? What happened in Kamiah when I came home and found all that blood? Was there anyone after me?" After each question I'd wait for an answer.

Holly looked down at her arthritic, gnarled hands and whispered something.

Leaning forward, I asked, "What did you just say?"

"Water . . ." Her voice trailed off.

I straightened. "You'd like a glass of water?" I hoped the nurse would get some but then noticed she'd moved to the card-playing table. I spotted a watercooler with Styrofoam cups on top. I hurried over and poured a cup, then brought it back to the woman.

Holly continued to stare at her hands.

I gently touched her shoulder. "Here's your water."

A male nurse sauntered through the door,

spotted me, and walked over. "Can I help you?"

"Jacob," Holly said.

I jerked, then focused on his face, looking for anything familiar. He was native, or part native, with thick black hair, overhanging eyelids with epicanthic eye folds, a full lower lip, and an oval face. "Are you her son?"

His brows drew together. "Who are you?"

"Gwen." I waited to see if he reacted. "Gwen Marcey."

His face remained blank. "Okay then, Gwen Marcey, why are you bothering Ms. Greene?"

"She asked me for water and I just brought it to her. You didn't answer my question. Are you Holly's son, Jacob?"

"That's none of your business." He took the water from my hand and handed it to Holly. The woman sipped, then held it cupped in her hands.

"The nurse told me she's a paranoid schizophrenic —"

The man's lips thinned. "What nurse? Medical conditions are strictly confidential."

I nodded at the nurse, then glanced back at the man. The name *J. Pender* was embroidered on his scrubs.

Pender smirked. "Are you talking about Amy? She's not a nurse. She's a patient.

157

I'm going to ask you to leave. Lucinda is due for her therapy session." He grabbed the push handles of Holly's wheelchair.

"Wait."

He paused.

"Can you at least tell me if she is ever lucid? Could she have written letters to the editor over the years? Is there a chance I might get through to her?"

"You said she asked for water. Did she say anything else?"

"She said 'Jacob' and 'must save the child.' "

"Well then. That's the most anyone's gotten out of her in years." He aimed Holly's chair for the exit.

I caught up with him and grabbed his arm. "This is important. You heard about the missing child? The double murder in Lapwai? Holly may have some critical piece of information. Is there anyone I can talk to about her history? How long she's been here? What happened to her son?"

"I told you. Confidentiality. If you want to get a court order, be my guest, but she's still not going to say anything useful." He pulled my hand from his arm in a practiced move.

"Could you please take my card and call me if she . . . says anything, or, um . . . if anything changes . . ." I held out a business card.

He took it and stuffed it into a pocket, then swiftly pushed the chair from the room.

I'd reached another dead end. I started to follow his retreating back.

"Pssssst."

I turned around.

Amy motioned me over to the card table.

Glancing around, I found no one was paying us any attention. "Yes?"

"Do you want the dirt on Holly or don't you?"

"Well . . ."

Amy looked up at me. "Look, I may be crazy, but I'm also a snoop. You'd be surprised what doctors say when they think the drugs have kicked in and we're too doped to listen."

What do I have to lose? "I'm listening."

"Holly's been here for over ten years. That's unusual 'cause they want to get us out and back into society as soon as possible." She jabbed me in the ribs with her elbow and grinned.

"Mm."

"You know they only lock you up if you're a threat to yourself or others. Rumor has it" — she dropped her voice to a whisper — "she'd been heading to la-la land for years,

159

but one day she took a hatchet and started chopping up pets in the neighborhood. That's it. Cuckoo for Cocoa Puffs."

The hairs on the back of my neck stood on end. "And her son?"

"You asked that one before. She didn't kill any person, least not that I heard, but anyone living with her, well, they'd be pretty twisted." She stared off into the distance, eyes unfocused. "Yeah."

Chapter Seventeen

Before I left I stopped in the ladies' room to wash my face. I looked pale and drawn. My next stop was the police department, and I looked like I wanted to be arrested for vagrancy. I combed my hair and reapplied makeup. *Better.*

The rain had lessened slightly but still fell in a steady drizzle as I left the hospital. The chill dampness pushed through the raincoat and into my body. I was shaking by the time I reached Beth's car.

The car's hood was ajar.

I spun around, but no vehicles were parked near me and no one was walking around. Moving to the front, I pushed the lever and opened the hood. The engine of a car was a vast mystery to me, and I wouldn't know the difference between a camshaft and an oil sump, nor would I care. A bomb, however, might be recognizable. I inspected the assembly of belts, pipes, round and square metal boxes, but nothing looked out of place. Closing the hood with a *bang,* I stepped on something.

Squatting down, I picked up a pebble. No. Not a pebble, a polished stone. A brown-and-gold tigereye.

Under the car, next to the tire, was a glint of metal.

I snagged one end and pulled out a long rod with a small hook at one end and a handle at the other. A long-reach tool. Used to open car doors without a key.

Shoving the hood of the raincoat off my face and head so I could see, I checked the parking lot for security cameras. Several appeared near the hospital, but none were aimed in my direction. I pulled the hood back up and reached for the driver's-side door. Unlocked, as I'd figured.

Someone had opened my car, or make that Beth's car, and got into the engine compartment but didn't touch anything. Maybe they were interrupted by someone.

The pelting rain intensified, forcing the hood of my raincoat even farther over my face. The drumming of the raindrops would cover the sound of anyone running up to me. I spun around, then jumped into the car and locked the door. The windows swiftly steamed up.

The inside of the car was dry. No one could have sat here without soaking the seat. *Unless they did so between rain showers.*

I took a deep breath and started the engine. The car roared to life and I remained in one piece. No bomb.

After checking the back seat for visitors, I placed a call to Chief Kus. He answered on the first ring. "Hi. I finished the composite sketch, but I'm afraid it won't be of any use. The so-called witness lied."

"We'll pick him up and discuss false statements and their consequences. Where are you now?"

"I just . . . um . . . stopped at Orofino. Do you have a lot of carjacking?"

"Why do you ask?"

"I found a long-reach tool under my SUV, the door unlocked, and the hood unlatched."

Seth was silent for a moment. "Can you stop by the department and drop off that tool? Also the composite."

"Sure."

"I'll meet you there. You're about forty-five minutes out."

I disconnected, then wiped the steamy windows and turned up the heat. No one was lurking around the parking lot as I left, and I tried to keep from thinking about the attempted break-in. With Holly unable to help me, I hoped Beth would have a lead on the plane crash that killed my parents. She might have even found out about my presence at the Two Rivers B and B thirty-two years ago.

And Jacob had moved to the top of my list of people I needed to find.

Then, of course, little Beatrice was still missing.

The squall passed during my drive to Lapwai, but dusk had fallen. I kept alert for deer or elk, or even moose that might stroll across the highway. Traffic was light, critters few, and I made it to Lapwai without incident. Chief Kus was waiting for me just inside the door leading to the lobby of the department. He waved through the window to show he saw me.

The parking lot was small, with a hill rising above me on the right, dumpsters straight ahead, and a line of vehicles on my left. I parked between a patrol SUV and pickup, then debated taking my purse with the Glock tucked inside. *Nah. I should be safe enough in a police lot.* I placed the composite drawing in a waterproof envelope and tucked it under my arm, then took the long-reach tool by the edges. Hopping out, I locked my purse in the glove box and dashed toward the station. As he opened the door for me, he looked even more strikingly handsome under the stark lighting.

I wished I'd taken a moment to fluff my hair and apply fresh lip gloss.

I handed the tool to the chief and followed him through the secured door into the inner reaches of the station. We moved to his office, a pleasant room decorated in earth-toned browns and deep greens. He closed the door behind us.

Placing the envelope on his desk with slightly trembling fingers, I started to pull off the wet jacket.

Chief Kus helped me, his fingers lightly brushing my neck as he took the jacket and hung it on a bentwood coat tree.

The air seemed to get thinner and I sat in the nearest chair to catch my breath. "Um . . . so . . . I . . ."

"You saw no one around your car in Orofino?" The chief placed the long-reach tool next to the composite and took a seat behind the desk.

"No. I'm wondering if he was interrupted, if someone came by before he could do . . . whatever he was going to do to the car."

"You do seem to be attracting interest in your rigs." He pulled the envelope closer, opened it, and studied the sketch. "Too bad it's a lie. This is a great composite." He placed the drawing on the side of his desk, then opened a drawer and pulled out some papers. "The autopsy on the body we found." He slid it across to me. "No sign of trauma, so not much help."

"Do you want me to do a reconstruction?"

"She was identified. Taken from Lacey, Washington, about seven years ago."

"How sad." I picked up the autopsy report and glanced at it. "Lacey's near Olympia, right?"

"Yes. That's your copy of the report. See if you have any ideas after reviewing it."

"Sure." I placed the paperwork into the envelope.

"How did the other interviews go?"

"Other . . . ah . . . interviews?"

"You had the names of two other people to interview in Kamiah."

I opened and closed my mouth. I probably looked like a gasping carp. How could I have not checked the list of names and assignments before driving all the way up to Kamiah?

"Hello." A deep male voice from behind me saved me from having to come up with a response. I turned, grateful for something to look at besides my hands, the tips of my shoes, or Chief Kus's frowning face. An

166

older man with the same striking features as Seth Kus stood in the doorway. His hair was black and worn in two long braids. He wore a plaid, western-cut shirt with a silver and turquoise bolo tie. A horsehair belt held up his crisp denim jeans.

"I'm sorry, son. I didn't know you were still working," the man said.

"Just finishing up. Dad, this is Gwen Marcey, the forensic artist I told you about from over in Montana. Gwen, this is my dad, Dan Kus."

I stood and offered my hand. "A pleasure to meet you, Mr. Kus."

Dan took my hand and gave it a slight squeeze. "Call me Dan. My son has spoken highly of you. He said you were able to get Kelli LoneBear riled."

My face burned and I swiftly let go of Dan's hand. "Well . . . I just sort of . . ."

Dan waved his hand and grinned. "Don't try to explain. Kelli's a tenacious woman who's been in hot pursuit of Seth here for some time —"

"Dad!"

Dan's grin grew wider. "Now I've got *your* goat, son." He took a chair and sat. "The sooner she's out of your life, the sooner you can marry and produce that grandson before I get too old to see him."

Seth's face was as red as mine had been. I moved toward the door. "Well, I have more work to do, so I'll leave you now —"

"Wait." Seth leaned forward. "You mentioned you were doing research on a plane crash. You can ask Dad for advice while he's here."

I turned to the older man. "I'm looking into a fatal plane crash in the Clearwater National Forest that occurred thirty-two years ago."

Dan straightened. "Thirty-two years ago? That's pretty ancient history."

"She thinks it has something to do with our current murders and kidnapping." Seth gave a slight shrug.

"Why would you want to look into a plane crash?" Dan asked.

"My parents died in it, and I believe I was supposed to have perished as well. It's a long story."

"And an even longer stretch of the imagination," Chief Kus said, "but I said you could recommend an outfitter to take her to the crash site and you'd probably know something about the accident."

Dan furrowed his brow and absently stroked his upper lip. "Sure. Glad to help. Why don't you drop by the museum sometime?"

I nodded.

"In the meantime, I'll look some things up and talk to Thomas Wolf, the young man I work with. He's the resident expert on who the best guide is for what you want."

"Thank you. Here's my cell if you find something sooner." I handed him a business card.

Dan stood. "I have to get going. Don't forget the poker game tonight, Seth." He left.

"Your dad seems nice."

"Yeah, a great dad. He taught me a lot."

"Was he a cop?"

"No. He taught me about our heritage." He looked down and smiled. "Dad decided he'd follow an old Nez Perce tradition of letting the spirit of the wind name me. When I was eight, he sent me alone into the mountains to discover my *Wy ya kin,* my spirit guide. I couldn't eat until an animal or bird spoke to me and gave me a name. I was to wear a symbol of the attending spirit throughout my life. Nothing could harm me if I did."

"And your spirit guide named you Seth?"

"My mom did. She didn't buy into the traditions. Anyway, Dad has studied the tribe's history, stories, and legends. Throw in a little reincarnation and some Protestant beliefs and you have my dad's philosophy of life."

Growing up with a dad would have been nice. "Thank you for sharing that. I should be going."

"I'll see you tomorrow at the meeting." He placed a gray plastic bag on his desk. "More videos."

I picked up the bag and headed to my car. The first splash of rain on my hair reminded me I'd forgotten the jacket in Seth's office. I spun around to retrieve it.

The truck window shattered next to me.

CHAPTER EIGHTEEN

I leaped to the front of the truck and dived to the wet pavement. Several more shots slammed into the back of the pickup. *Pop! Pop! Pop!*

My heart raced and I ducked down even farther. My Glock sat in my purse in the glove box of my car parked next to me, but it might as well have been on the moon.

Footsteps crashed through the underbrush on the hillside. I stayed hunkered down, my knees pulled to my chest. That could be the shooter. Or just someone running from the gunfire. The cold, wet pavement chilled my bottom, and more rain dripped on my head.

A door squeaked open and Seth's voice carried clearly over the slight rain. "I can't get hold of LoneBear, so —"

"Get down! Active shooter!" My voice was shrill.

A door slammed shut. In what seemed like seconds, the lot filled with police vehicles, lights flashing, sirens blaring. I remained where I was crouched until Officer Attao, gun drawn, ducked beside me. "Hurt?"

"No."

"Shooter?"

"Ten o'clock. I think."

The officer poked his head up, glanced in that direction, and dropped down. Another patrolman crouched behind a patrol SUV to our right. Officer Attao gave hand signals for *sniper* and the area to cover, then moved away.

I listened to running footsteps, crackling radios, then silence. A dog barked in the distance.

Seth appeared beside me. "Looks like whoever did the shooting is gone now." He offered his hand to help me up, holding on a second longer than needed.

"Someone ran through the underbrush up on the hill just before you opened the door. That must have been the shooter." A cold breeze swirled around me. I shivered. "They would have hit me, but I forgot the jacket you gave me and turned to come in and get it."

"Why didn't I hear anything?"

Leaning against the pickup, I wrapped my arms around myself to ward off the chill. "M-maybe they had a silencer. The gunfire was more of a popping sound."

Seth wrapped an arm around my shoulders and pulled me close. "Come back into the station and get your jacket. You're freezing."

His arm and body radiated heat like a furnace. *Jacket? I don't need no stinkin' jacket.*

He ushered me inside and released me. Unfortunately.

The lobby soon filled with the officers returning from searching the perimeter. They gathered around the chief and me. I suddenly felt very short surrounded by all the burly cops.

"Why was someone shooting at you?" Seth asked.

"I have no idea."

He stared at me a moment without blinking. "Okay. Write up a report on what happened. We'll keep looking, but it might be a good idea if you kept a low profile for the next little bit."

He retrieved my jacket and walked me to my car. Taking the car keys from me, he unlocked and opened the door. He opened his mouth as if to say something, then closed the door and tapped on the roof.

I could still feel his arm around me on the drive home. Stopping for gas, I pulled out my cell and dialed Blake's number, then hung up before the call went though. What would I say if he asked me to join him right away? My work was still more important? How could I think about a relationship when my head was full of the missing Beatrice, double homicides, serial killers, snipers, my dead parents, stolen cars, and ex-husbands with custody battles?

Beth was jogging up the street with Winston as I arrived. "Getting exercise?"

"Keeping from going stir-crazy and saturnine." She stretched her legs as I got out of the car.

"Saturnine? Word of the day?"

"No. *Amaranthine* is the word of the day. I just can't figure out how to use it yet."

"Never heard of it."

"It means everlasting. Or deep purple-red."

"Sounds like a bruise."

She stared at me. "What's the matter? You look funny."

I walked toward Twin Rivers B and B. "I seem to have picked up an enemy. I think someone tried to break into or damage my — make that *your* car. Then someone shot at me."

Beth spun around, searching for a possible sniper, then charged for the house.

"Last one in is a rotten egg."

Racing after her, I caught the door before it shut, slammed it, then leaned against the wall. I grinned, giggled, then laughed so hard I bent over. I knew intellectually that laughter was a release of tension, but I couldn't stop. "R-r-rotten e-egg?"

Beth's mouth gaped, then she began to laugh. She dropped Winston's leash and the dog took off for our room, I'm sure aiming to get on the bed while we were doubled over with mirth.

We were both sitting on the floor in the hall, still laughing, when Eric came through the door wearing a straw hat and carrying his plastic tub of gardening tools. He stopped at our appearance.

I wiped the tears from my eyes and tried to get control of my aching mouth. "Sss-sorry. Rough day at the office." My comment sent Beth into another fit of mirth.

Eric slipped past us as if concerned that our humor was contagious. Or that we were crazy. The thought reminded me of Holly. Abruptly the laughter was gone. I stood. "Come on, Beth, we have work to do."

After helping her up, I retreated to my room. I'd gotten chilled by the rain, so I changed into sweats. I moved my drawing materials, the envelope with the autopsy report, and the case binder to the game room we shared. Beth emerged, hair up and damp from a quick shower, wearing beige cotton slacks and a cashmere top. "Do you want to go first," she asked, "or should I?"

"I'll go first."

Opening my sketchpad, I told her about the sniper attack in the police parking lot.

"Sounds like someone wants you dead." Beth's face paled. She rubbed her arms, stood, and slid up to the window. After peeking through the blinds, she returned to her seat. "Okay . . . um . . . you're not hurt or anything?"

"Nope."

"Did a SWAT team show up?"

"Not exactly."

"They wear the coolest uniforms, black, with shiny —"

"Beth."

"— helmets. And those special —"

"Beth!"

She glanced at me, mouth still open.

"The Nez Perce Tribal Police in Lapwai, Idaho, does not have a SWAT team."

"Oh." She looked down at her hands folded in her lap.

I gnawed on my lip for a moment. "Um . . . but they did use SWAT sign language."

Beth leaned forward. "Sign language?"

"Like this." I made a circle with my thumb and forefinger, then made a fist over my head. "Sniper. Cover this area."

"I didn't know you knew SWAT signs. Do you know any more?"

"Mm. Just a couple. Freeze. Crouch. Mm . . . pistol . . . I understand. And the super-secret signal." I made a circle with both hands, flashed both hands open and closed, and rubbed my fingers together.

"What's that?" Beth sat up straighter.

"Krispy Kreme hot light is on. Grab a free donut."

"Very funny." She sat back in her chair. "What about your meeting with your former sitter?"

"I did meet with Holly, but she won't be any help. Nor the staff. One thing's for sure, she didn't write those letters to the editor. But I did get some information from a patient." I told her about Amy's revelation. "And there was a J. Pender on staff. Holly called him Jacob, and he was very protective of the woman."

"I'll see what I can find out."

"And I drew this." I pulled out the sketch of four-year-old Jacob and wrote his name on the bottom.

"I tried to locate a Jacob Greene, but

177

that's a relatively common name . . ."

"And he could have changed it."

"There's that as well. Anyway, no luck." Beth took the sketch from me. "You said Holly never married. What about . . ." She held up the drawing.

"I was nine when he was born. I don't remember any men around, never any boyfriends, but there was no doubt Holly'd been pregnant."

"What about when she gave birth?"

Shaking my head, I took the sketch from her and stared at the image. "I don't even have a memory of her going to the hospital to give birth. He'd just . . . appeared."

A sudden memory flashed through my mind. Holly sobbing.

I dropped the art.

"What?" Beth reached over and touched my arm.

Where had that been? And when? Closing my eyes, I focused on Holly's anguished weeping. Pale walls, olive-green carpet, the light coming from windows with white sheer curtains.

"Were you remembering something?" Beth asked.

"Holly. And a room."

Beth leaned forward. "Can you see the room in your mind?"

I nodded.

"Draw it." She handed me a pencil.

"That's a brilliant idea." I opened the pad and began sketching the curtains, then added a sepia-painted door to the right. Beyond that . . . a courtyard, and more apartments. The room had smelled of dry earth and fried onions. I tore off that page and started a new sketch, this time mentally looking to my right. A cheap print hung on the wall, a painted landscape. Beneath the art, a brown sofa squatted with a fake chipped-wood coffee table. Holly was curled up on the sofa, crying. I drew her, then sketched a Christmas tree.

No. I erased the tree. We'd been in Yakima. Yakima, Washington, and were getting ready for Christmas. I closed my eyes. Holly had promised a tree that year, but no tree ever appeared. Or presents. We moved about a month later to Oregon. Jacob was born that August. Opening my eyes, I counted on my fingers. "Nine months."

"What did you remember?"

I put the sketches together and pointed at the drawing of Holly. "This was just before Christmas." Picking up the Jacob drawing, I placed it below the other two. "Nine months later, Jacob was born."

"So —"

"Something happened then. She had a secret boyfriend who broke up with her, maybe a married man. Or maybe she was raped." I took a deep breath. "As a child, I never put it all together. She changed about that time." I nodded at the sketches. "Going from cheerful and singing all the time to crying jags, not getting out of bed, headaches —"

"Clinical signs of depression."

"When Jacob was born, she could barely look at him."

"So you think —"

"She didn't want that baby for whatever reason. I'd put my money on Holly being raped," I finished for her. "I basically took care of Jacob. He was a sweet boy, very quiet, and prone to accidents — No. Wait. That's not right."

Beth raised her eyebrows.

"He seldom had an accident when he was with me. But he was always covered with bruises. Holly was the one who said he'd fallen or run into something."

"Did you ever see Holly hit him?"

"No . . ."

I looked at the sketchbook in my hand. I'd always loved art, filling book after book with my drawings. Without thinking, I drew a cardboard box on the empty sheet of paper. "I was too absorbed with my art," I whispered. And when I'd left, thinking they were both dead, did I leave four-year-old Jacob with his abusive mother?

The old house whispered and sighed around us.

Beth cleared her throat. "Now, as to the plane that crashed with your parents." She cleared her throat again. "Well, I had a long talk with the owner of Meyers' Flying Service here in Lewiston. Turns out it was his brother, Ron Meyers, who was the pilot killed. At first he was very defensive, but I told him . . . well, I lied." She inspected her notes as if they may have changed in the past few seconds. "I told him we were with the top-secret TBIC government agency and were investigating your dad."

I pulled out a chair and sat across from her. "Tibic?"

Beth's face colored. "I had to think fast. He was suspicious that I was investigating pilot error or some kind of lawsuit against his company."

"Yes, but why Tibic?"

"I thought about us and how we're partners, sort of." She quickly glanced at me. "So it stands for Two Broads In Cahoots. TBIC."

My case of giggles threatened to surface.

"I see. What did Ron Meyers tell you?"

Beth's shoulders relaxed and she tapped the papers with a manicured fingernail. "As you can imagine, he remembers that day like it was yesterday. His brother was flying something called a Skymaster." She laid a printout of a plane in front of me. The design was unusual. Instead of the traditional outline, the plane ended just behind the wings, with two pods extending backward, rather like a catamaran design on a boat.

As I studied it, I became aware of the murmuring of guests in the lobby and Winston's snores. The smell of cooking apples and cinnamon drifted up from the kitchen below.

"That smells good," Beth said.

"You're changing the subject."

"I guess there's no other way to say this. Mr. Meyers was present when your parents, with apparently you in tow, came in to book the flight. At first your dad, who said their names were John and Mary Smith, didn't want to tell him where he wanted to go. Mr. Meyers insisted on knowing your dad's destination as he needed to file flight plans. He said your dad wanted to fly over the dam upriver from here to check it out. Meyers thought the whole thing was odd, especially when your dad paid in cash and asked that the flight plans be kept confidential."

"Did he really think a man and woman with a four-year-old child —"

"He said he just had a bad feeling about the whole thing so he made sure the plane's black box would record the cockpit conversation." Beth pulled out a cassette tape and tape player. "He gave me a copy of it."

I couldn't take my eyes off the cassette. My folks' voices. Their last words.

"Do you want to hear it?"

Did I? I licked my dry lips. "Yes."

CHAPTER NINETEEN

Static for a few moments. "There's your target, Mr. . . . ah . . . Smith," the nasal voice of what must be the pilot said. "Put a mess of C-4 inside the drain holes of that dam and boom!" The roar of an engine in the background made it difficult to hear.

"That looks like it would take more than a little C-4 to bring it down," a second male voice responded. My father.

"That's where you're wrong, m'friend. During construction, a whole bunch of cracks formed. Big cracks, some like four hundred feet long. They had to drill drain holes to relieve the pressure. Now they *claim* to have fixed the problem, but don't you believe it." The pilot laughed. "My cousin was an engineer on the repair crew. He said they just applied a Band-Aid to fix the leaks. I figured he should know."

"Useful knowledge."

"If this dam goes, it's a domino effect.

There'd be some delay before the water would hit the downstream dams, so they'd try to push out enough water to hold, but we're talking catastrophic failure. Billions of gallons of water. And at the end of all these waterways? Portland, Oregon."

"There's a road over there. Would that be an escape route?"

"To get away from the flood —"

"No. For law enforcement."

The pilot was silent for a moment. "You're kinda limited on roads out here. That one down there takes you to the highway. From there, go west and you're in the path of the escaping water. Go east toward Montana and it's easy to set up a roadblock. I'd say your best bet is avoid roads entirely. Head north into the Clearwater National Forest. Millions of acres of rugged wilderness."

For a few moments all we could hear was the roar of the engine, then the pilot spoke. "You could take one of those logging roads. Not a lot of traffic." He chuckled.

"It's beautiful," a woman said.

My mom. I swallowed around the lump in my throat.

"Too much clear-cutting for me," the pilot said. "Let me show you some real back country." More engine noise. "Now, down there is God's country. Over four million acres of wilderness."

"You're right," Mom said. "Breathtaking."

"Yeah, but deadly. Grizzlies, cougars, wolves . . . ah." The pilot's voice grew louder as if he'd moved the mic closer to his mouth. "Speaking of deadly, when you booked this flight, you said you were doing a . . . What was the word you used?"

"Scenario. Possible terrorist targets."

"Yeah, that's right. Like something from the Russians or Chinese or Arabs." He pronounced it Ay-rabs.

"Sort of, yes."

"And . . . ah . . I forget. What agency did you say you were with?"

"I didn't say."

The engine sputtered, then grew silent.

"Dear God!" Mom's voice was barely a whisper.

"Look for a place to land," the pilot said. "Mayday! Mayday! Mayday! This is November six-one-one Bravo. Location approximately forty-six miles heading one-sixty-three southeast Homestead. Forty-eight hundred feet."

A snapping, then — *Bang! Bang! Bang!*

"Crack your door," the pilot said.

A crash — *Boom!*

Mom screamed.

An ear-shattering shriek of metal seemed

186

to last forever, then silence.

Beth turned the tape deck off.

I couldn't move. My white-knuckled hands gripped the table.

Beth's hand touched mine with a gentle squeeze. "I'm sorry."

Was my dad a terrorist? Or could he have been doing exactly what he said — checking out scenarios for a terrorist attack? That would make him proactive and probably in law enforcement. I wanted — needed — to believe the second possibility.

"I did some research on what happens when a dam breaks," Beth said. "In China, over 170,000 people died. And the official death toll of the Johnstown Flood, caused when the dam collapsed" — Beth shook her head — "was the third largest loss of civilian life after the Galveston Hurricane and the events of 9/11."

"Those were single dams." I looked out the window. "But if this dam were blown up, it would be catastrophic to every dam downstream. And every town." I looked at my friend. "I need to go to the site of that plane crash."

Someone knocked on the door. "Come in," Beth called.

Lila entered with a tray. "I'm sorry to interrupt. Eric just made a batch of fresh applesauce and thought you might like some."

"That's very kind," Beth said.

Winston stood as she entered, sniffed the air, then slumped to the floor, obviously not interested.

"That is one big dog." She walked to the table and placed the tray down. It held two glasses of what looked like fresh lemonade, homemade bread and butter on stoneware plates, and two steaming bowls of applesauce.

I took a sip of the lemonade. "Thank you," I said. "Does Eric cook all the time?"

Lila nodded. "Two days a week, pretty much all day. Tuesday is shopping, Friday he makes whatever I need for the week, and Wednesday is bread day."

"You have that many guests?" I asked.

"Eric takes food to the homeless shelter and spends time several days a week at the food kitchen." Her eyes were shiny and her cheeks glowed.

"Are you two an item?" Beth asked.

"Well, um, we've been seeing each other, you know, outside of work." Her cheeks were now crimson.

Though I wasn't the least bit hungry, my fingers had relaxed their grip on the table.

Beth glanced at my hands, then winked at

me. "You must have Eric share his recipes with Gwen sometime," she said sweetly.

I scrunched up my face at her.

"Sure."

"Are you disparaging my cooking?" I lifted my head and looked down my nose at Beth. "I'll have you know I recently added canned peas to my tuna noodle casserole. And spices."

"Really? What spices?"

"I don't remember. Something green — maybe oregano — yellow, and a rusty brown. I made leaf patterns on the top instead of using potato chips."

Beth leaped from the table and raced into her room, startling Winston. I could hear her peals of laughter.

"Is she okay?" Lila asked.

"It's been a tense day. She's just . . . letting off steam."

"Oh, well, actually." Lila cleared her throat. "The real reason I came in was something Eric suggested."

Beth returned. Her eyes were red, and the corner of her mouth twitched, as if another fit of laughter was just below the surface.

"You'd asked about the history of the house and guests from before we started the guest book," Lila said. "We have a lost and found. I know that doesn't sound like much, but it goes back to almost the first guests who stayed here, maybe sometime in the sixties. We never threw away anything of possible value."

"It's worth a try, sure, we could go through a box or two —"

Lila laughed. "Oh no. This stuff's not in a box. Lost and found fills an entire room in the attic."

CHAPTER TWENTY

After Kenneling Winston in his mesh pen, we joined Lila in the grand hall. Instead of climbing the main staircase just outside the door to the game room, we crossed the parlor to the hall where we originally entered. "This house was built in 1905 and modeled after a French castle near Vienna," Lila said over her shoulder to Beth and me. "This side of the house was originally the servants' section." We climbed a smaller set of stairs to the second floor, then a narrower and darker set to the third floor. A number of rooms opened off the sparse hallway. She turned to the closest door, took out a set of keys, and opened it.

Steep, dusty steps disappeared into the gloom at the top.

"We've talked about cleaning this all out, but, well . . ." She reached forward, grabbed something, and pulled. A 40-watt bulb dangling from a wire dimly illuminated the stairs. "At the top you'll find a light switch. Let me know when you're done so I can lock it back up."

"You're not coming with us?" I asked.

"No. I . . . I have some work to do in the office." With a final glance up the stairs, she left.

"No time like the present." Beth started up.

"Wait!"

Beth turned. "*You're* not afraid of dark, creepy attics, are you?"

"I'm not scared of the dark."

"Dust? Um . . . toe monsters?" She raised her hands and made claws of her fingers. "Muwhahaha. Are you afraid of ghosties and ghoulies and long-legged beasties and things that go bump in the night —"

"Spiders."

Beth reached over and patted my shoulder. "You keep me safe from serial killers, rapists, snipers, and terrorists, and I'll protect you from spiders. Okay?"

"Deal." I followed her up, pausing at the top as she flicked on the light. The attic stretched the length of the house, with only the middle of the room high enough to walk upright. The sides sloped down following the roofline, and murky dormers appeared every fifteen feet. A line of widely spaced, dim lightbulbs cast pools of light on the floor. The far end of the room held shrouded furniture. Surrounding us were dusty cardboard boxes and brown grocery bags. "We really could use a flashlight."

"How about this?" Beth nodded left. "You sit under that light. I'll inspect each box and bag for arachnids, then bring it to you to check."

"That'll work." I moved to the agreed-upon spot. Night had fallen, and no light pierced the grimy dormers. The overhead illumination flickered every so often, as if to remind me that at any moment the room could be plunged into darkness. Scratching and light tapping — hopefully from nothing larger than mice — came from the wall nearby.

Beth soon placed a folded box in front of me, then a second. Inside was a tie-dyed T-shirt, much faded, a necklace of blue seed beads, two torn and yellowed pocket paperbacks — *In Cold Blood* and *The Andromeda Strain* — and a pair of jeans. I knew without checking they'd be bell-bottoms. A quick peek in the second box yielded similar sixties-era items. The 5th Dimension started singing "Age of Aquarius" in my mind.

A sack and box provided me with several cassette tapes, mismatched socks, single earrings, a belt, reading glasses, and men's underwear. I left the undies alone.

Beth kept bringing more boxes, sacks, bags, and crates of debris from distant travelers. My fingers were soon grimy, my nose burned, and my eyes itched from all the dust. By the time Beth slid an antique wood-and-tweed suitcase over, I was in a canyon of containers.

"This is pretty much the last of the stuff." Beth wiped her face. "There's another section, but someone labeled everything, and the dates are wrong."

The suitcase's latches were broken, and the material had been rubbed from most of the edges. It was definitely the wrong decade, but I couldn't resist.

I expected a treasure trove of forties or even fifties memorabilia. Instead I found women's clothing, all small and well worn. "This looks like a guest left everything." I held up a faded, blue-plaid flannel nightgown. "Though I can't say that I blame her."

Beth sat cross-legged beside me. "You're hardly a good judge of clothing taste. Those look like your pajamas."

"Mine are red." Underneath some underwear was the book *Charlotte's Web*. "I loved this book." On the flyleaf, written in flowery script, were the letters *L. H. G.*

I went cold. The book slid from my numb fingers. "We found it," I whispered.

"What?"

"This is Holly's suitcase."

"Let's take it back to our room. It's creepy up here."

Beth didn't have to ask me twice. I closed the lid, then followed her down the attic stairs. "Um, Beth, let's take this to our room before telling Eric and Lila. I don't want to explain what I'm doing . . ."

"I'll go tell them, you take it to our rooms."

The door at the bottom of the steps was closed. Beth grabbed the knob and twisted it. It didn't budge. "That's strange." She rattled it again. It remained stubbornly immobile.

"Is it locked?"

"I don't know. It's for sure stuck."

Pushing past her, I tried the knob, then shoved against the door. I leaned back and hit the surface with my full weight. I ended up with a sore shoulder and a tightly shut door.

"What should we do?" Beth asked.

"This." I banged on the door and shouted as loud as I could. "Help! Someone! We're locked in!"

"Shhhh, Gwen. You'll wake up the whole house."

I looked at her. "You want to spend the night up here?"

"Heelllllp!" She beat on the door with both hands. "Help us!"

In the distance, Winston started barking. "Well, if that doesn't wake the dead . . . ," Beth said.

The barking stopped for a moment, then resumed, getting louder. Voices joined the rapidly approaching barking dog.

Bang! The door moved as the 165-pound dog slammed into the surface.

"Hang on!" Eric called. "Um . . . I can't get close. Your dog is . . . guarding."

"Winston, sit. Sit," I said.

The knob turned, but the door remained stuck. "Just a minute."

Placing my head against the door, I heard a murmur of voices, someone running on the stairs, a metallic rattle, then — *Bang!* The door swung open. Eric stepped back and dropped a folding shovel into his gardening tub. The door frame was cracked. Lila and various guests in nightclothes stood in a semicircle around the seated Pyrenees.

"I'm so sorry! No one goes up there anymore," Eric said, glancing at Lila. "I never thought the door would stick."

Winston launched himself at me, shoving me backward. I hugged his furry neck. "I'm okay, ol' boy. You did good." Patting the dog one more time, I held up the suitcase. "May we examine this downstairs?"

"Sure." Eric smiled slightly and took Lila's arm. "Once again —"

"We're fine." Beth smiled. "And we're sorry for all the commotion and making you ruin the door molding."

Winston cheerfully led us down to our rooms, where I discovered he'd ripped the nylon crate into shreds. "Aahh, Winston. Did you have to eat the crate?"

"He figured he was rescuing you." Beth stroked his massive head. "Good boy."

Satisfied that we were truly rescued, the dog flopped on the carpet with a *thud.*

I put the suitcase on the table and carefully removed several pieces of clothing. Tucked into the side pocket was a pamphlet titled *Understanding Adoption in Idaho.* I showed it to Beth. "It looks like Holly was looking for a child."

"Apparently babysitting wasn't enough." Beth nodded. "And stealing a child believed to be dead in a plane crash is a whole lot cheaper."

I kept digging. At the bottom was a Lamb Chop puppet.

"Ohhhh." The air raced from my lungs as if I had been punched.

Beth picked it up. "Holly, or your parents, must have bought this for you as a child. That's why you got one for Jacob — you had a vague memory of your own."

"I'll need to show this to Chief Kus. Maybe he'll let me pursue . . ."

"Go ahead and say it. You know Holly isn't behind any of these events. There is, however, a trail leading to Jacob."

I sat at the table holding the puppet. This one was well loved, somewhat grimy, and had a twisted mouth from the threads coming loose.

Beth cleared her throat. "This is intriguing." She held up the directions for a child's cold remedy.

Blinking at it for a moment, I pulled out the sketchpad with one of my lists of knowns and unknowns.

Under *Known* I'd written *recognized Two Rivers house, locations where we moved and when we moved (roughly every year), Jacob, Holly admitted to state mental hospital.* Now I added *plane crash, John and Mary Smith, Holly guest at Two Rivers house, left suitcase, Lamb Chop puppet, giving child cold remedy, later raped? — Jacob result, in mental hospital for at least ten years.*

Beth read over my shoulder. "I didn't think of it before, but the name Jacob means 'supplanter' or 'replacement.' "

"Like he attempted to supplant me?"

She shrugged. "You did say she couldn't look at him and may have abused him."

Under *Unknown* I'd written *Why taken? What happened to Holly and Jacob after I left? Any connection with me and current homicide? When Holly admitted to mental hospital?* I added *Parents' real names? What happened to bodies after recovered? Why in plane in first place? Was I left with sitter because I had a cold? When the plane was reported missing, did Holly see it as a chance to abduct me?*

"That make so much sense." Beth sat at the table. "You wouldn't take a child up in an airplane with a cold."

"I bet my folks made a last-minute decision not to take me on the flight. Maybe Holly offered to look after me that day, or maybe she was my regular sitter."

Winston barked softly in his sleep, his legs twitching as he chased a dream cat. I tapped the sketchpad for a moment, then sketched the puppet and wrote underneath, *Lamb Chop common thread?*

Leaving the cold-remedy directions, book, pamphlet, and puppet on the table, I repacked the suitcase. "At first Holly would have been terrified of getting arrested for kidnapping me, but when I was reported dead, she could relax." I paused. "But she never could know, at least for sure, that her secret would stay safe forever."

"There's another possibility." Beth raised her eyebrows at me. "Someday you might start asking questions, or looking into who supposedly murdered your parents."

"Which I finally did, only I waited over thirty years. The whole time I was with Holly, she told me my parents were murdered and she rescued me. She said the killer was after me, which is why we moved so much and changed our names."

Beth nodded. "Holly's way of keeping your abduction secret. Right."

I rubbed the tiny hairs on my arms down. "But that backfired on her. The day she killed all the rabbits, I saw it as a time to run and never speak of what happened."

Beth's eyes narrowed for a moment, then opened wide. "Holly might have thought you abandoned her."

"Jacob sure would have."

"You were his only protector."

"And for the next" — I did a quick calculation in my head — "twelve years, I left

Jacob with an abusive and progressively more insane mother."

CHAPTER TWENTY-ONE

We both took Winston out for his final walk of the day, with Beth holding the leash and me watching for snipers. When we returned to Two Rivers, I went over the new video tapes for suspects. No one stood out. I paid particular attention to any young man who could possibly look like Jacob — assuming I knew what Jacob looked like. I could possibly age-progress the drawing I did of the four-year-old child, but the drawing was from memory, not a photograph, which is how age progressions are usually done.

Leaning back in my chair, I absently stared at Holly's suitcase. "You know, Beth, something just occurred to me. What we *didn't* find."

"What's that?"

"My parents' suitcases. Or mine. If we were staying here and believed to be killed in a plane crash, our belongings might have ended up in lost and found."

"Good point. Someone must have retrieved their things. I'll double down on trying to find out their real names."

I collected my notes for the morning meeting of the task force. I had a pretty compelling story to tell Chief Kus to convince him Jacob was a valid suspect, or at least someone to be eliminated as a possibility, and that I needed to pursue that angle.

I woke to my cell jangling beside me. "Gwen Marcey."

"It's Seth Kus."

I was instantly awake. The clock by the bed said 5:32. "What is it? Did you find Beatrice?"

"No. We found Kelli LoneBear."

"I didn't know she was missing."

"We didn't either. Yesterday was her day off." He cleared his throat. "She's been murdered."

"Oh no!"

"Her body was found in a field south of Lewiston. Would you meet me there?" He gave me directions.

After I hung up, I sat on the edge of my bed and stared at the phone. *Could it be . . .* I shoved the thought away. I'd know for sure soon enough.

Opening a window, I checked the temperature. Cool, with a residual dampness from all the rain. After dressing in a rush, I woke Beth and updated her on LoneBear. "I'll return —"

Beth shook her head. "No, you're not leaving me here another day. I'm your sidekick. I'm going with you." She shot into the bathroom, emerging shortly wearing jeans and a mixed-media down jacket.

"Ready?" I asked her.

"As soon as you zip up your pants and get Winston."

"It's early. No coffee," I muttered. After zipping my pants, I put a leash on my dog, grabbed my forensic art kit, and headed to Beth's SUV.

Following Seth's directions, Beth, Winston, and I drove south of town to a field that paralleled the road. The early-morning sun cast long, smoky-blue shadows, and few cars slowed our progress. Blue, red, and white strobes flashed from the variety of parked law-enforcement vehicles and lit the faces of the pajama-clad onlookers watching from across the street.

I knew it would be futile to ask Beth to stay in the car with Winston. After opening a few windows partway, I opened the door to a cool wind that cut through the layers of clothing I wore.

The unfenced field sprouted a lawn of green winter wheat stretching for miles. Stakes had been driven into the ground to hold the fluttering, cadmium-yellow crime-scene tape. Seth was standing outside the tape next to several officers. Officer Attao noticed me, nodded, then turned to another officer. Seth spotted me and motioned me over. "Morning, Seth. I'm so sorry."

Seth glanced at the motionless body. "Yeah. Me too. Lewiston PD has the case, but I told them about you and they agreed to let you take a look at her and see if you had any ideas."

Another cool gust of wind swept across the field, rippling the wheat into hookers-green waves. The faint rotten-egg odor of the pulp mill at the edge of town made my nose burn.

I pulled my jacket tighter, ducked under the crime-scene tape, and followed Seth to the body. Kelli LoneBear lay on her back, eyes sightlessly staring at the sky. Several flies had discovered her. Seth shooed them away. Dried blood matted her hair on the right side. She was dressed in the department's rain jacket over a blue T-shirt, jeans, and black Nike running shoes. Purple-red bruising circled her neck.

"The man across the street saw her this morning," Seth said. "He works nights. Said she wasn't here when he left for work. Her car's missing. We're still looking for it."

"Did you want me to sketch or photograph —"

"No. Just observe."

Crouching next to her, I peered closer at her earrings. They were a cluster of brownish stones with glowing golden linear centers. "Tigereye."

"What?" Seth asked.

"You said you couldn't find her car?"

"Not yet."

Standing, I looked him in the eye. "Only two more questions. Was LoneBear familiar with how cars work?"

Frowning, Seth shook his head. "I'm not sure what you mean. Her brother is a mechanic at a garage in Lapwai, but I don't know that *she* was interested in cars."

"How close were you two?"

Seth held my gaze before looking off into the distance. "Is this important?"

"Yes. But maybe the question I really want to ask is just how jealous was LoneBear?"

"We dated some in high school." Seth folded his arms. "I was never serious, but she might have been."

I stared at him.

"Okay, yeah," he finally said. "She married some loser right after high school, moved away, divorced him, then came back and joined the department. She seems to think . . . um . . . thought that we'd pick up where we left off. She was getting quite . . . insistent. Now tell me why you're asking these questions."

"Are you two done?" A plain-clothed female officer approached us. "We need to continue processing the scene."

Seth looked at me and raised his eyebrows.

"Yes," I said. "You'll probably find her car in Orofino, parked somewhere near State Hospital North. That's where she was abducted."

Seth's mouth dropped. "How did you figure that out?"

The officer jotted a few notes and nodded that we could leave. As soon as we passed under the crime-scene tape, he turned to me. "What do you know about LoneBear's murder?"

"I think . . . I suspect LoneBear was trying to do something to my car. She used the long-reach tool to open the door, then popped the hood. She was wearing the same kind of jacket you gave me, undoubtedly with the hood up as it was raining. Her killer would have thought it was me. I noticed the blood in her hair, so someone came up behind her and hit her. She lost a stone from her earring when she fell, a tigereye. I found the stone near the long-reach."

"Why didn't you mention —"

"Um . . . I forgot I stuck it in my pocket." *How many other clues did I miss?*

"Why were you at State Hospital North?" His voice was cool and clipped.

Pulling out a pencil, I twirled it between my fingers. "You remember the connection I wanted to follow up on between an old case and this one?"

"Yes, but I don't see any results. I see one dead officer."

My face grew warm and I stared at the pencil. "I'm sorry."

"You there!" A lanky detective in a navy shirt, tie, and slacks hurried over. I had to tilt my head back to look at his face. He briefly shook Seth's hand, then turned to me. "I understand you might have some information about our homicide." He pulled a small notebook and pen from his pocket.

Tucking the pencil behind my ear, I updated the Lewiston detective. When I was finished, he asked, "Why do you think LoneBear wanted to damage your car?"

Glancing at Seth's face, I cleared my throat. "She . . . ah . . . probably felt I was an outsider . . . and . . ."

"LoneBear was quite possessive of her . . . cases," Seth finished for me.

"You going to be around for a bit?" the detective asked.

"I think so."

"Good. We'll have more questions." He hurried off.

A news van pulled up and the line of curious onlookers across the street grew. Seth took my arm and moved me farther from the gathering of officers, technicians, and now coroner. His hand on my arm felt good. Blake's arm around my shoulders would feel better.

He let go. "You think the killer mistook LoneBear for you. And this same killer was the sniper who shot at you yesterday?"

"Yes."

He tugged at his lower lip. "Okay, I can buy LoneBear getting hot under the collar and trying something on your car."

"Oh, I think she did more than that. I think she also got that mechanic brother of hers to help her drive my car into the Clearwater River. If not for Beth, I probably would have had to return to Montana."

Seth winced. "I'll look into it. Right now what I need to know is who is trying to kill you?"

Taking a deep breath, I told him about all that Beth and I had uncovered about my past. I finished with, "I think your kidnapper and killer is a man named Jacob Greene. That's the angle I want to investigate. All the evidence seems to point in that direction."

Seth listened without interruption, his gaze on LoneBear's body. "Jacob Greene. I'll look into it, see what I can find out." He looked at me. "In the meantime, I need you to do the interviews in Kamiah that you missed yesterday, then you can pursue your line of inquiry.

"Uh-huh."

"One might need a composite sketch. Her name is Lorraine Wolf, and she's an Oglala Lakota." He looked at me pointedly. "From the Pine Ridge Reservation. In South Dakota."

"Right. Okay. Um . . . What are you trying to tell me?" I asked.

"Have you heard of the Pine Ridge Reservation? Or maybe Wounded Knee?"

CHAPTER TWENTY-TWO

"Wounded Knee," I said slowly. "A battle —"

Seth shook his head. "Massacre. Genocide by the US 7th Cavalry. Around three hundred Sioux, mostly women and children, were killed."

"But that was a long time ago."

"December 29, 1890."

"Like I said, a long time ago."

"To some, it's still a festering sore. I'm just warning you that Lorraine is not going to be a cooperative witness." He abruptly strolled away to his patrol car.

I tore my gaze from watching him and headed to Beth. As I approached her car, I could only see Winston's head inside. Glancing around, I couldn't spot her. I opened the passenger-side door.

"Oh!" Beth sat up from the rear of the SUV.

"Were you taking a nap?"

"No." She crawled over the seat, slid down Winston's broad side, and got out of the car, then slipped into the driver's seat. She handed me her phone.

"You were calling someone?" I asked.

"No. Taking surreptitious photos of the crowd." She pushed a button so I could scroll through the images. "I've read the killer sometimes watches the effects of his work or inserts himself into the investigation. I took a few while pretending to be on the phone, then got in the back so no one would see me and took the rest. I kept my hand near Winston's head so it wouldn't be silhouetted, but he kept lying down, so I kept saying, 'Where's the kitty?' and 'Cookie.' You owe him a lot of cookies."

"Beth —"

"I was thinking about going undercover —"

"Beth —"

"— because no one knows who I am and I could listen —"

"Beth!"

"What?"

"You're watching too much television. Again."

Beth squeezed her lips together and started the car. "I was just trying to help."

"You're a wonderful help, Beth." I smiled

at her and started to hand back the phone when I paused at one of the faces. Quickly I checked the assembled crowd still watching from across the street. "When did you take this one?" I held up the phone.

"Um, that was one of the first. Maybe fifteen, twenty minutes ago. Why? Did you recognize someone? Did I photograph the killer?"

"It's just strange, that's all. This is Peter Otskai, the assistant manager of the Clearwater Casino. It was his boss, Sinopa, who was murdered." I handed her the phone. "Could you send that to my computer? Chief Kus might find that interesting."

"Absolutely! Now, where are we going next?"

"Kamiah. Drive down —" My cell phone rang. "Gwen Marcey."

"Hi, Gwen, this is Dan Kus, Seth's dad. Can you drop by the park in Spalding? I have some things to show you and a possible guide."

"On my way." Beth raised her eyebrows at me. "Slight change of plans. We'll be stopping by Spalding on the way to Kamiah. The Nez Perce National Historical Park. Dan Kus may have found me a guide and more information about my folks."

Beth drove toward Highway 95. She didn't

speak until we'd crossed the river and headed east. "Um . . . I don't like to tell you your job, but don't you have an appointment with some witnesses in Kamiah?"

"This stop is on our way. Don't worry."

She glanced at me, then focused on the road. "Gwen, I don't know how to say this without hurting your feelings, but I am worried."

I shifted in my seat to look at her. "Why?"

"You just have a lot on your plate right now."

Making an effort to unclench my jaw, I reached for a pencil out of my purse. "Nonsense. I have a new job that I love —"

"You're still on probation. And you're working a double homicide with a missing child, a fate you thought, until recently, was yours."

"Yes. Well. Work's a bit of a challenge, but my life is going well. My cancer is gone —"

"It's good to know your glass is half full now, but we need to be honest about what's going on and how you're affected."

I took a tighter grip on my pencil. "My daughter —"

"Your ex-husband is seeking to get Aynslee full time. His wife is pregnant." She looked at me. "Aynslee told me when she called."

"Um . . . I found out something about my

parents . . ." My vision blurred and throat closed up. *What's the matter with me? I don't remember them.*

Her gaze returned to the road. "You've forgotten appointments with witnesses, missed clues during interviews, can't even remember to zip your pants and grab your dog. Yeah, I'm worried."

Turning away, I stared out the side window. I focused on nothing, though the day was a postcard-perfect advertisement for North Central Idaho. Beth was wrong. I was fine. I'd found out quite a few earth-shattering things about my life lately. That would make anyone miss a few appointments.

But I needed a friend right now. And Beth was the only one I had. "You're right. Let's get the interviews done, then go to the historical park."

Beth gave me a thumbs-up.

Tugging out the binder with the case information, I read over the autopsy on the body of the young girl. As Seth had mentioned, the cause of death was undetermined with no sign of trauma. She'd been of Asian or Native American background, buried for four to six years, and was wearing a pair of green pants, size 5, and a green-and-white striped shirt.

I tapped my pencil on the binder, then circled the town where the child had lived, Lacey. "Beth, I had you look into murders with a child missing in the Northwest thirty-some years ago."

"Right."

"Would you look again, but this time go back only about ten years?"

"I'm on it, Sherlock. Anything else?"

"Get a couple of maps. One of the Pacific Northwest, one of the Clearwater River drainage."

"Okay, anything else?"

"I'll let you know." We were fast approaching Kamiah and my next interview. I pulled out the information on Lorraine Wolf. She'd been at the Easter egg hunt and mentioned to a neighbor that she'd seen a man watching Beatrice. The neighbor called in the report to police, and Lorraine had reluctantly agreed to an interview. I needed to convince her to give me a composite sketch.

We soon reached Kamiah. I read the directions to Beth. The single-story, white house was just a few turns off Highway 12. A child's bike lay on its side in the front yard and a vegetable garden was on the side. "If you can wait until I make contact, I'd appreciate it. Seth said this might be a reluctant witness."

"Seth?" Beth's eyebrows rose.

"Chief Kus."

"But you called him Seth."

"That's his name." My face felt warm.

Beth could barely hide her grin. "I told you he was a good-looking man. Obviously you did notice."

"It's not like that —"

"Uh-huh. If it's 'not like that' " — she made quotes in the air — "what about you and Blake?"

"Not now, Beth." The warmth turned into a major hot flash. I waited a moment, then cleared my throat. "Did you want to take Winston down to the river and see if he wants to go wading? I bet there's a park or maybe a boat launch. I'll call you when I'm finished."

Beth rolled her lips and muttered, "I wish you hadn't eaten your crate, Winston. You're cramping my style as a sidekick."

Stepping from the car, I approached the house and knocked. Though I'd had the feeling of being watched since we parked, it took a few moments for the door to open. A short woman, barely five feet tall, with long gray hair answered. Sturdily built, she wore oversized glasses, a faded denim shirt, and blue jeans.

"Yes?" she asked, unsmiling.

217

"Hi, Ms. Wolf? I'm Gwen Marcey, here working with the Nez Perce Tribal Police on the missing child. I'm here to talk to you and maybe draw a composite of the person you saw on Sunday."

"I told them when they called and I'm telling you now, I want nothing to do with cops!" She started to slam the door in my face when a meaty hand gripped her shoulder. "What's going on here?" a deep voice asked.

She reluctantly opened the door wider, bringing a large man into view. He was easily well over six feet tall, with broad shoulders and a rounded stomach covered by a faded red T-shirt. A circular logo of a hand making the peace sign and a Native American profile graced the front of the shirt. His gray hair was parted in the middle and tied in the back. "Who are you?"

"My name is —"

"Credentials."

Even though my badge was prominently displayed and hanging from a beaded neck chain, I opened my purse and dug out my leather ID wallet. He took it from my hand and studied it carefully, then stared at my face before handing it back. "What do you want?"

"I'm sure you heard of the double homicide of the Sinopas and the abduction of their four-year-old daughter. Your . . . Ms. Wolf saw someone who could be a person of interest in this case. Chief Kus of the Nez Perce Tribal Police has asked me to follow up and perhaps draw a composite sketch." I held my breath.

"You go back and tell your Chief Kus that *Mrs.* Wolf didn't see anything." He shut the door firmly in my face.

Beth was still parked at the curb waiting for my all-clear sign to drive away. I slowly walked back to the car. "I'm deducing that we need to move on to the second interview," she said.

"So it would seem." I dialed the number for the next witness. After ten rings, I hung up. "Another washout. They're either not home or not answering."

"So what do you want to do?"

"Head to Spalding to talk with Seth's dad. He may be able to help me find out about the death of my parents."

CHAPTER TWENTY-THREE

Beth was silent for the first few miles. She finally cleared her throat. "Um, Gwen, I hate to bring this up again, but you can usually schmooze even the most reluctant witness into giving you a composite."

"There's always a first."

"Don't you think it's another indication that you're —"

"No! I told you I'm fine." I pulled out my sketchbook to keep busy, drawing the logo on the T-shirt Mr. Wolf wore. The wording had long since faded, but the image of a hand making a peace sign with a Native American profile was clear in my mind.

"What are you drawing?" Beth asked.

"A logo on Mr. Wolf's shirt. Seth mentioned that Mrs. Wolf is an Oglala Lakota from the Pine Ridge Reservation and that I might have trouble getting a sketch from her." I gave Beth a meaningful look. "Her husband was, if anything, even more hostile."

"Let me see the drawing."

I turned my sketchpad in her direction. "Look familiar?"

"No. I'm sure they'll know at the park. I do know a bit about Pine Ridge."

"Okay, shoot."

Beth winced. "Bad choice of wording. In the 1970s, Pine Ridge was the location of a shootout between FBI agents and a group of Native Americans camping nearby. Two agents, lying wounded on the ground, were shot in the head, execution style. The killers' trial was contentious."

"That might explain the hostilities toward anything to do with law enforcement."

The Nez Perce National Historical Park overlooked the Clearwater River with a sprawling visitor center and museum. Parking was a distance away with paths leading to the gray-painted building. Beth got out to walk Winston while I went inside. A man in bermuda shorts with a camera around his neck and a woman in sap-green leggings and an orange print top were speaking to the park ranger about a movie that had apparently just ended. A very old, hand-carved canoe was displayed on my right under an impressive mural of a traditional Nez Perce village. Ahead was the gift shop, and to my right a door led to the museum. Entering the museum, I was drawn to a horse made out of wood slats with an exquisite beaded saddle and bridle.

"The Nez Perce were the only tribe to practice selective breeding in their horses," a male voice behind me said. "And they were superb horsemen."

I turned. Somewhere in his midtwenties, the young man was about my height, with black hair pulled into two braids reaching almost to his waist. He was wearing a western-cut shirt and pressed blue jeans. "Oh. It's you."

"Have we met?" I asked.

He shook his head. "Dan said you'd be coming. Let me get him." He left the museum.

I followed, reluctant to leave the displays of Nez Perce arts and crafts.

He headed for a door beside the counter, leaned in, and said, "She's here."

Dan Kus appeared, spotted me, and smiled. "Gwen. Welcome to the Nimi'ipuu Cultural Center."

"Nimi'ipuu?"

"The name we call ourselves. It means 'real people.'"

The young man leaned against the counter. "The name Nez Perce came from the French Canadian fur trappers and means 'pierced nose,' something the tribe never did."

"Impressive center." I waved my hand at the airy lobby area.

"Well then, I'll give you the five-cent history lesson. The Nez Perce National Historical Park is spread out over four states and follows the route of the last great Indian war of 1877." He looked at me. "You, of course, know the story from your school history lessons, right?"

"Well . . ."

"That's what I thought. After years of broken treaties, a young Nez Perce named Wahlitits began a battle with the US Army at White Bird Canyon in Idaho. What followed was a running fight —"

"A fight that had the tribe ambushed at Big Hole," the young man said. "Wahlitits had a dream. He said, 'My brothers, my sisters, I am telling you. In a dream last night, I saw myself killed . . . We are all going to die.' And with the ambush, over ninety Nez Perce were dead, most of them women and children."

"Yes, well." Dan nodded at the man. "About eight hundred Nez Perce, including surviving women and children, fought over two thousand trained American soldiers over four months and twelve hundred miles. Led by Chief Joseph —"

"Real name, In-mut-too-yah-lat-lat," the young man added. "Thunder coming up over the land from the water."

Dan smiled slightly. "Yes, General Howard cornered the remnant of the tribe just forty miles from the Canadian border, where they were seeking their freedom."

The young man gave me a brochure. "Chief Joseph's tactics are still taught at the military academy at West Point." He pointed at a paragraph. "This was reported to be his surrender speech."

I am tired of fighting. Our chiefs are killed. Looking glass is dead. Toohulhulsote is dead. The old men are all dead. It is the young men who say yes or no. He who led the young men is dead.

It is cold and we have no blankets. The little children are freezing to death. My people, some of them, have run away to the hills and have no blankets, no food. No one knows where they are — perhaps freezing to death. I want to have time to look for my children and see how many I can find. Maybe I shall find them among the dead.

Hear me, my chiefs. I am tired. My heart is sick and sad. From where the sun now stands, I will fight no more forever.

I placed the brochure in my pocket, unable to speak around the lump in my throat.

"Anyway, enough history." Dan patted my arm. "I called because I've found an outfitter for you, a good man named Phil Cicero." He handed me a scrap of paper with the name and phone number. "Phil's expecting your call." He led me to a map of central Idaho. "I've also located the coordinates of the plane crash." He touched a spot on the map where he'd stuck a yellow pushpin. "It's in the middle of some pretty rough country."

"It's important that I get there."

Dan nodded. "I understand. This land" — he waved at the map — "is part of *my* history, my connection to my ancestors. You're on a journey to find yourself and your people."

"Yes. I hadn't thought about it that way, but that's exactly what I'm doing."

"The Nimi'ipuu had a practice that when a young person reached a certain age, he was sent out into the mountains alone to find his *Wy ya kin* — his animal or bird spirit. That spirit would speak to him and

225

give him help throughout his lifetime."

"Seth told me about this. He said he went on such a journey."

"I did as well, though I was older. My given name was Shore Crossing."

"With my luck, the critter would be a cougar, I'd be named Mrs. Robinson, and I'd start stalking Generation Z for dates." I grinned at my wit.

Dan stared at me.

"You know, Mrs. Robinson, *The Graduate* . . . the movie . . ." I pivoted and studied the map. "So . . . um . . . how long to reach this spot?"

"I should think you'd easily make it in a day if you went partially by horseback. Why were your parents flying that day?"

Leaning against the wall, I stared out the window as a tour bus arrived and disgorged a number of tourists. "The only thing I've found out so far is . . . maybe . . . my dad was looking at the dam . . . and —"

"Well then, you could start your journey there. I have my boat docked at the Big Eddy Marina."

"I wouldn't want to trouble you —"

"Ha!" Dan grinned. "I was just looking for an excuse to take it out."

"Like you need an excuse." The young man winked at Dan.

"Gwen, this is Thomas Wolf."

"Hi, Thomas. Funny, I just tried to interview a Lorraine Wolf." I stuck out my hand to shake.

Thomas drew his brows together and ignored my hand. "Lorraine is my mom. Why did you try to interview her?"

"I told you earlier, Thomas." Dan patted him on the arm. "Gwen is working with my son on the murder of Alice and Adam Sinopa and the kidnapping of Beatrice."

"I repeat" — Thomas continued to glare at me — "why were you bothering my mom?"

"Thomas!" Dan frowned.

"It's okay," I said to Dan, then turned to Thomas. "Your mom might have seen someone paying too much attention to Beatrice at the Easter egg hunt. I was trying to get a composite drawing."

"I suppose the person you wanted to draw was native? And Seth sent *you* to interview her?"

"Maybe part native. I'm the only forensic artist they have. Seth did warn me your mom might be a bit difficult to interview."

Thomas reached over and straightened a stack of flyers on the counter. "And did Seth say why?"

"He mentioned that your mom was Oglala

Lakota from the Pine Ridge Reservation and asked me if I knew about Wounded Knee."

Thomas's eyes narrowed as he looked back at me. "What about AIM?"

"Now, Thomas," Dan said. "Let's not get into all that."

"Aim?" I glanced back and forth between Dan and Thomas.

"American Indian Movement," Thomas said.

"I'm sorry, but what does this have to do with the murder of the Sinopas and the abduction of their daughter?" I asked.

"Did it ever occur to you that the Sinopas were murdered by whites?" A vein pounded in Thomas's forehead. "That your intrusion is just another example of the ongoing treatment of Native Americans?"

Heat rushed to my face. "I wasn't looking at any particular skin color —"

"You wouldn't understand." Thomas gave me a dismissive gesture. "You're white. You've never known what it's like to be hated because of your race, or belief system, or even your job."

"You don't know me —"

"Okay then." Dan took my elbow and pulled. "Let's go on that boat ride." He ushered me out of the center, up the walk, and to the parking lot.

"How dare he!" My voice shook. "He . . . he . . ." I yanked my arm from Dan's grasp. "How dare he presume I'd act any differently depending on someone's skin color, or background, or —"

"Now, Gwen, you have to consider how he was raised."

Winston spotted me, dropped his head, and launched himself in my direction. Beth had both hands on the leash but was helpless to stop the determined dog. The Pyrenees arrived at my side triumphant at his success with a breathless Beth in tow. "Sorry," Beth said. "He'd managed to water every tree and was getting bored. Hello." She turned to Dan. "I'm Beth Noble, eximious sidekick."

"Word of the day?" I asked.

"From last week. Finally got to use it."

Dan held out his hand. "Dan Kus, purveyor of recondite history." The two of them grinned at each other and shook hands. "Beth, I was just about to take Gwen on a boat ride and share my discoveries with her. I would be most honored if you and your . . . furry horse would join us."

"I'm not sure about furry horses and water, but that sounds great." Beth tugged Winston to her side.

"We can all ride in my SUV. You really don't want Winston in your car." Beth got behind the wheel and I insisted Dan sit next to her so Winston wouldn't hang over his shoulder and demand petting. Not to mention the occasional drool.

"Was Tom's dad at home when you tried to interview Lorraine?" Dan asked.

"If he's a big guy with long braids, yes," I said.

"Nick Wolf." Dan shook his head. "He was caught up in that nasty business on the Pine Ridge Reservation back in 1975."

"I read two federal agents were murdered," Beth said.

"And an Indian, Joseph Stuntz, whose murder was never investigated. Actually, more than forty-five murders from that time were never investigated. The cumulative events from that time formed a perfect storm."

"How so?"

"The Pine Ridge Reservation doesn't have a lot of folks living there. Probably less than twelve thousand residents, but they had more murders than the entire state of South Dakota. It's also one of the poorest parts of the country. Add grinding poverty and injustice to murder . . . It makes for a bitter stew." He opened his window slightly, allowing the wildflower-scented air to circulate.

"Thomas mentioned AIM."

"American Indian Movement. Born out of the civil rights movement in the late 1960s, it was a reaction to the years of mistreatment by the federal government. AIM held protests throughout the country."

We turned upriver on Highway 12 toward the small town of Ahsahka. "I'm sorry," I said quietly. "I can't imagine how hard it was for those folks. But I'm not the government. We shouldn't forget, but that was a different time, a different place, and a different people."

"In the eyes of Lorraine and Nick, you're cut out of the same fabric. The only way they felt they could make themselves heard was to take a stand."

"You sound like you relate to their cause."

"I can understand it." He glanced at me. "But Nick's not someone you want to upset. He can hold a grudge, and when the time comes, he'll get even."

"Is that a warning?"

"Just an observation."

I thought about my stolen and destroyed car, the sniper attack, the murder of Lone-Bear. "Could others besides Nick Wolf have the same . . . resentment against me?"

"Because of the shooter at the police department?"

"And other things."

Dan turned slightly in his seat toward me. "I think the brutal double homicide and missing child has everyone on edge. Having said that, I think you need to be very careful."

CHAPTER TWENTY-FOUR

We drove to Orofino, then backtracked to Ahsahka, which proved to be on the north side of the Clearwater River. A large fish hatchery occupied the mouth of the canyon. As we crossed a bridge identified as the North Fork of the Clearwater, Dan pointed right.

My mouth dropped at the sight. In the distance loomed a giant dam. With water pouring down two spill gates in the front, it looked vaguely like a Mayan temple. We turned toward the structure on a road paralleling the deep, rushing river.

"Impressive, isn't it?" Dan asked. "More than seven hundred feet high, third tallest in the United States."

"There's no way someone could blow that up," I blurted out.

"Blow it up?" Dan turned so he could see me. "So that explains that wounded look in your eyes. You thought your dad was planning some kind of terrorist explosion on the dam? That his plane went down instead?"

I reluctantly nodded.

Dan reached back and patted my arm. "Well, I assure you the dam is quite impervious to attack."

A lump formed in the back of my throat. Why would I think my dad was anything less than a respectable citizen?

Because the name he gave when he chartered the plane sounds like fiction. John and Mary Smith?

"Um . . ." I needed to think about something else. "I don't even know how they build something like this." I motioned at the soaring mass of concrete. We were climbing a road on the left side of the dam that looked like it would take us to the top of the structure.

"They divert the river into a channel or tunnel while they construct the dam, then when they're finished, close up the diversion and allow the lake to fill in. This creates hydroelectric power and recreational access to the lake. And a place for my boat." He grinned at me. We passed a turnoff to the dam's visitor center and crested the hill, and the lake came into view. Pine-covered mountains swept down to the ultramarine-blue water.

"Beautiful," I whispered.

At the bottom of the road was a park with picnic tables, outdoor cooking grills, restrooms, and several buildings hooked together. Soda machines stood in front. "Big Eddy Lodge and Marina," Dan said as we pulled into a paved slot and got out. "A ranger has an apartment in that building, and the park service maintains an office there." He pointed.

In front of us, the ground dropped steeply to a pair of docks extending into the lake, with individual slips for boats. A small shed on the dock sold snacks and gas for the boats. On the right, a sharply pitched boat ramp led to the water with a third small dock nearby. Overhead an osprey called out in its high-pitched whistle and another answered. The warm spring sunshine felt good on my arms. The air was clean and smelled of warm pine needles. Pulling out my purse, I slung it over my shoulder.

Parked in front of the offices were a few cars and forest service vehicles. Two more trucks pulled in and a man got out of one of them. The driver of the second truck remained in his cab.

I swallowed hard and stared at the tinted windows. *Could this be who's been following me? Shooting at me?*

"Gwen, what are you looking at?" Beth asked.

"I . . . uh . . . need something to drink." I jerked my head slightly in the direction of a soda machine in front of the building. Without waiting for a response, I strolled over to the dispenser, grabbed some change from my purse, dumped it into the machine, and punched the first button. A can dropped into the slot. Casually I grabbed it up, leaned against the machine, and opened the can. Pretending to look around the parking lot, I let my gaze drift to the driver of the truck.

A young woman was jabbing away at her cell phone, obviously unable to get a signal.

I took a big gulp of the drink, then almost spit it out. I'd bought peach-flavored sweetened tea. The mass of sugar coated my teeth and tongue. Dropping the can into the garbage next to me, I returned to Beth and Dan.

"What was that all about?" Beth asked.

"I thought someone was following me in that truck. I'm just getting paranoid someone's after me."

"You mean, getting shot at, almost murdered, car stolen —"

"Okay, justifiably paranoid."

"Maybe," Dan said. "Maybe not. I don't

know about the rig you checked out, but that first truck belongs to Thomas Wolf."

"He followed us here?"

Before I could charge over, find and confront Thomas, Dan grabbed my arm and headed to the steps leading to the docks. Beth and Winston followed. We passed by every type of boat from pontoon to rowboat, catamaran to cabin cruiser. A young woman in a light-brown T-shirt with a Parks and Recreation logo waved from the adjoining dock and we returned the wave. Dan's speedboat, almost at the end of one dock, proved to be a Prussian-blue, twenty-foot inboard bowrider. I thought the dog would hesitate to get into the boat, but Winston jumped in and made himself comfortable in the bow. Dan helped Beth and me get in, untied his boat, and walked to the end of the slip before stepping in. "Could you pull in the fenders?" He pointed. "Watch out for submerged logs."

I moved forward next to Winston, pulled in the fender, and sat so I could see into the water ahead of the boat. Once free of the docks, Dan nudged the engine and we cruised to the center of the lake. I drank in the clean mountain air and watched the deep kelly-green water for logs. We rounded a point of land. To our right was the dam, looming several stories above us. I shaded my eyes and stared at the massive structure.

"Now that you see all this from both sides, how do you think your dad could even make a dent in the dam?" Dan shut down the engine and allowed the boat to drift.

"I don't see how, but that was the impression Meyers' Flying Service had, the place where her dad chartered the flight," Beth said.

Dan merely raised his eyebrows.

Wrapping my arms around Winston, I sighed. It was time. Beth nodded encouragement. Slowly I told him of my strange upbringing — Holly, Jacob, the fictional killer, fake names, hiding out, running, and finally being found and raised by Dave's family. I told him about the Lamb Chop puppet and why I thought Jacob was a suspect. He listened quietly.

After I finished, no one said anything. Waves lapped against the boat, the breeze stirred the pines, and a fish jumped somewhere behind me. "And you have no idea who your parents were or why they were here?" Dan finally asked.

"No. I mean, their names really could be John and Mary Smith."

"But not likely," Dan said.

"Not likely." I shrugged. "I'm on to the

next clue — the plane crash itself." We'd drifted down the lake toward where the water was passing through large metal gates to the spillway.

"Um . . . aren't we getting kind of close to that?" Beth pointed at the water rushing through the gates. We were moving faster in that direction.

"That's why there're those buoys and logs over there — to keep boats from going on a wild ride down the spillway." Dan started the engine and moved away from the dam, heading toward the marina. As we passed the docks, a lone figure stood at the end. I recognized Thomas Wolf. He watched us as we sped by.

I glanced at Dan. He seemed focused on steering the boat, but his jaw muscles had tightened.

We rode up the lake for a few miles before Dan again shut off the engine. A herd of elk grazed on the hillside above us. Most of the bulls had shed their antlers, but a few still had impressive racks.

"This is beautiful country." I trailed my hand in the snow-chilled water. "Does the water warm up enough to swim in?"

Dan nodded. "It's about fifty-eight degrees now. It's warm and perfect in July and August. Do you like swimming?"

This wasn't the time to discuss the style of a bathing suit when you had to wear breast prostheses. "Um, I used to."

The sunlight kissed the waves, creating a diamond-sprinkled carpet to shore. A memory surfaced of looking up at an old farmhouse on a hill like the one in front of me. I had no idea where it was but would sketch it as soon as we got back to the car and I could get to my forensic art kit.

"It *is* beautiful country," Beth agreed. "Maybe your folks were just wanting to see it from the air."

"Or looking to buy some land," Dan said.

"Buy land? Isn't this part of the reservation?" Beth asked.

"Yes." Dan leaned back in his seat and rested his elbow on the side of the boat. "But the United States government, back in the eighteen hundreds, gave up to 160 acres of land to individual tribal members. They figured the Nez Perce would assimilate white American life with land ownership. Instead, the tribal members sold the land to the general public."

"So . . ." I opened my hand for him to continue.

"So now more than 90 percent of reservation lands are in white ownership." Dan looked at me. "Chief Joseph, the man we spoke about at the museum, didn't want to move off tribal lands and to a reservation. When he was asked to sign a treaty, he made another famous speech." His eyes grew distant. " 'I do not need your help; we have plenty, and we are contented and happy if the white man will let us alone. The reservation is too small for so many people with all their stock. You can keep your presents; we can go to your towns and pay for all we need; we have plenty of horses and cattle to sell, and we won't have any help from you; we are free now; we can go where we please. Our fathers were born here. Here they lived, here they died, here are their graves. We will never leave them.' "

In the silence that followed, an osprey whistled across the water to be answered by his mate.

"Powerful words," I said slowly.

"Powerful feelings." Dan nodded. "And I believe the events of the past impact all that happens in the present."

Chapter Twenty-Five

We were all silent on the way back to Big Eddy Marina, each lost in our own thoughts. I was relieved to see Thomas Wolf and his truck gone when we returned. As we climbed the steps from the dock, a radio somewhere played Kenny G's haunting "Going Home." I paused and listened.

Before getting into the back seat, I opened the back end of the SUV and pulled a sketchpad from my forensic art kit. Beth got behind the wheel and Dan took the passenger seat. As Beth drove, I sketched the farmhouse from my past. The roof had been red metal, the house painted white with a wraparound porch.

My phone rang. I reached into my purse and pulled it out. "Gwen Marcey."

"Yeah. This is Jay Pender."

My brain went blank for a moment. "Um."

"Lucinda Greene's physical therapist."

"Oh. You mean Holly."

"Yeah, whatever. After you left, Lucinda started talking about books. Then she said your name. You wanted to know if anything changed with her . . ."

"Thank you! I'm just outside Orofino, coming from the dam. We'll swing by." I disconnected. "Dan, would you mind a slight detour? Holly — that's my sitter I told you about — is talking. Well, sort of."

"Not at all. Another clue on your quest?"

"Hopefully."

Dan gave Beth directions and we soon reached the state mental hospital. Both Beth and Dan chose to wander across the grounds rather than go in and meet Holly. I hurried across the parking lot to the building. Jay Pender was waiting for me behind the reception desk. He nodded toward the large multipurpose room where I'd seen Holly before. Amy, the woman who'd pretended to be a nurse during my last visit, was sprawled on a sofa. She waved at me, then went back to using a highlighter pen as a cigarette and reading a magazine.

Holly was seated in the same place as before, facing the window.

My breath quickened. I started walking faster, but Pender grabbed my arm. "After I called you, I asked one of the older staff members about Holly's books. She said we should check the storage area to see if Holly has anything stowed there. We can check that out after you talk to her."

Approaching my former sitter, I bit back the thousands of questions I wanted to pepper her with. I reached her side and saw her blank face. "Holly?"

Holly blinked but continued to stare.

I pulled up a chair and sat beside her. "Holly, it's me. Gwen. You remember me?"

This time not even a blink.

I took a deep breath, turned, and stared out the same window. My vision blurred. I'd come so close to unraveling the threads of my past, only to have that door slammed shut with Holly's mind. *God, this isn't fair.*

I caught Pender's attention and shook my head. If Holly had been talking earlier, she wasn't now. He motioned me over. I stood and looked at the old woman. "Holly, try. Try to remember. Please? What were my parents' names? Who were they?"

Not even a flicker of change. Her gaze covered a thousand miles.

My feet seemed encased in concrete. I shoved them forward toward Pender. If only I wouldn't get my hopes up that Holly would reveal my past.

We traveled down several corridors and through several locked doors until we reached a laundry area. A room lit by buzzing fluorescent lighting, with built-in shelves around the sides, opened off the laundry. Suitcases and plastic tubs of various sizes and colors lined the shelves, each with a neatly printed name on a piece of masking tape. Thinking about Holly's suitcase I'd found in the attic of the Two Rivers Bed-and-Breakfast, I checked the luggage first. None had the name Greene. The plastic tubs were next. Pender stood in the middle of the room, watching me as I shifted and checked each item. Moving faster and faster, I completed a circuit of the room. Nothing had Holly's name.

A brick formed in my throat. *Not again!*

"Looks like Holly was just rambling." Pender turned and moved toward the exit.

"No." I spun around, checking the names again. *Griesinger, Garlock, Harris, Ingram, Jacob* — "Jacob!" I snatched the small blue container from the shelf.

"No!" Pender grabbed my arm and yanked me away. The bin hit the floor and the lid flew off. Five cheap sketchbooks tumbled across the floor.

I recognized them immediately. My drawing books, the ones I'd spent so much time working on during the years I was with Holly. I yanked my arm from Pender and reached for the books.

Pender caught my wrist. "I let you in here looking for Holly's books. Those belong to someone else. You have to leave."

"They're mine!" I tried to tug my arm away, but Pender squeezed harder.

"Prove it."

I stopped struggling and stared at the drawing books. I'd filled many times that number in my years with Holly. "I . . . I liked to draw horses."

"Too general. Lots of people draw horses."

A hot flash shot up my neck and into my cheeks. My brain became muddled. *Think!* Pender dragged me toward the door and reached for the doorknob.

"Wait!" I planted my feet. "There would be . . . um . . . a drawing of a . . ." Looking at the top sketchbook, bright yellow and green with a bear on the cover, I tried to think of where I was, what I was doing. "A dog, a collie, but just his head. And a year, 1991, and location . . . um . . . Missoula." *Please, Lord, let this be the right book.*

Pender let go of my wrist, stepped to the pile of books, and lofted the top one. Swiftly he flipped through the pages. "Nope. Nice try." He picked up the plastic tub to place the sketchpad inside.

I remembered. "Look in the back. There's

a portrait of a young boy. Not very good. And you'll see my name, Gwen, on the bottom."

He sighed but flipped to the back. "It's the same as the others."

"What do you mean?"

He turned the drawing so I could see it. Black marker scrawled across the page, obliterating the sketch.

Taking the pad from him, I flipped through all the pages. Someone had scribbled over every drawing, in places tearing the paper. I checked the other sketchbooks. The results were the same. In the bottom book, not only were the drawings scrawled across, but the paper was crumpled and ripped. "I need to have these processed for fingerprints."

"Then come back with a court order." Pender took the destroyed drawing books from my numb fingers and placed them in the bin with the others. "If these sketchbooks were yours, someone sure hated your art. Or you."

CHAPTER TWENTY-SIX

Beth, Winston, and Dan were strolling under the pine trees at the edge of the parking lot. I angled in that direction. Just as I caught up with them, my phone rang. I fumbled the phone from my purse. I didn't recognize the number, but it had an Idaho 208 prefix. "Gwen Marcey."

"Hi. This is Phil Cicero, Wilderness Outfitters. Dan Kus gave me your name and said you needed a guide into the Clearwater National Forest."

"Hi, Phil. Yes. I need to go to a small-plane crash site. Can we meet somewhere and go over the details?" We arranged to get together at the bed-and-breakfast later that afternoon.

After I hung up, Beth asked, "What happened with Holly?"

"Mixed results. Holly's still not talking to me, but she kept some of my sketchbooks. But either she or someone else destroyed the drawings. If that someone was Jacob, we might get a lead on him through finger-prints, but Seth will need a court order to process them."

Dan glanced at his watch.

"We should be going." Beth headed for her car with Winston. Dan and I followed.

Once we loaded up, I reached in my purse and pulled out my sketchpad. I'd written the list of knowns and unknowns on my background. Under *Known* I read *recognized Two Rivers house, locations where we moved and when (roughly every year), Jacob, Holly admitted to state mental hospital, plane crash, John and Mary Smith, Holly guest at Two Rivers house, left suitcase, Lamb Chop puppet, giving child cold remedy, later raped? — Jacob result, in mental hospital for at least ten years.*

I updated it with *my drawing books damaged, need court order to process.*

Under *Unknown* I read *Why taken? What happened to Holly and Jacob after I left? Any connection with me and current homicide? When Holly admitted to mental hospital? Parents' real names? What happened to bodies after recovered? Why in plane in first place? Was I left with sitter because I had a cold? When the plane was reported missing, did Holly see it as a chance to abduct me?* I added *Why fly over dam?* I handed the notes to Dan. "This is what I've been working on."

Dan read through my writing. "You think the accidental plane crash that killed your parents launched the events, culminating with the murder of the Sinopas and the abduction of their daughter?"

"I believe that might be a possibility."

He handed the materials back. "I believe you're right."

My eyes burned with unshed tears and I quickly looked out the window. *Someone besides Beth believes me.*

We dropped Dan back at the Nez Perce visitor center. "Now where, Kemosabe?" Beth asked.

"Kemosabe? What does that even mean, Beth?"

"There are many theories, but one says the name dates back to one of the founders of the Boy Scouts —"

"Never mind. Why do I even ask you these questions? Let's head over to the police station. I need to update Seth."

Beth drove the short distance and parked near the front door. "It's cool enough outside. I'll just wait in the car with Winston."

Seth was standing in the lobby when I entered. My pulse rate ratcheted up a notch and I smiled.

He didn't return it. "There you are. Come into my office."

The smile died on my lips. "Did something happen?" I said to his retreating back. "Did you find out something about Lone-Bear? Or . . . Beatrice?"

He sat across his desk from me and motioned for me to sit. "Nothing on Beatrice. We talked to LoneBear's brother. He was pretty torn up about Kelli's murder. He said Kelli called him and asked him to move your car. She hoped you'd go back to Montana. He'd parked it on a boat ramp but didn't set the parking brake. When Kelli told him the car ended up in the river, he was furious."

"And the long-reach tool?"

"He said Kelli had one. Lewiston police found her car parked at the Orofino High School, which is next to the mental hospital. No leads yet on her murder. That's not why I wanted to talk to you in private."

I swallowed hard.

"I got a call from Thomas Wolf. He said his parents were very upset by your visit."

"I didn't —"

"He also said you were boating on the lake instead of working on this case."

"Your father —"

"Right after I hung up talking to Thomas, I got a call from your boss, Gary James, asking how you were doing."

"Wait a minute —"

"I had to tell him you missed appointments and seemed to be distracted. I didn't tell him about the boat ride."

"Did you tell him about the progress I made?"

"Commander James said you were on probation. He mentioned someone named Kirt was to have worked this case."

"Kirt's a whiner. And he's probably pushing the commander because he wanted this case. And Commander James is a micromanaging, overbearing, nasty, grumpy . . ." Words failed me.

"I stood up for you —"

"I bet you did —"

"But he wouldn't listen. He said you wouldn't be offered the job when you returned. He wanted me to collect your badge and gun."

"He's a coward to boot," I whispered around the lump in my throat. My stomach contracted in pain, my vision blurred. Fumbling, I removed the badge from the holder around my neck, then slowly took the Glock from my purse and placed both on Seth's desk. I dropped the leather holder and beaded neck chain into my purse.

Seth left the items where I'd set them. "If there's any good news, it's that you can now go back to Montana where hopefully you'll be safer."

Standing, I shook my head. "No. I'll get Beth to bring you the three-ring binder with the notes and Beatrice's teddy bear." I turned, then twisted back. "And I'll find the Sinopas' killer. And Beatrice . . ." My voice broke. I spun and raced from the room, not wanting him to see my tears.

I kept my head down until I'd slipped into the car. Beth took one look at my face, opened her purse, and handed me a lavender handkerchief. As I dabbed my eyes, she started the car and tore out of the parking lot. "You lost your job," she finally said.

"How did you guess?"

"You're not wearing your badge."

I grunted and blew my nose. Winston leaned over the seat and stuck his head on my shoulder. "I'm okay, big guy." I patted him.

"You'll find another job," Beth said softly.

"Yeah. I know. It's just . . ."

Beth glanced at me. "You liked him."

"Silly me."

"Gwen, it's okay to let your guard down and like someone."

I dry rubbed my face with my hands. "I don't know how to do that anymore, Beth. Maybe Robert is right. Maybe I'm toxic to men. Look at what happened with Blake."

"Ha! Robert is never right. He's toxic to you."

Without asking, Beth turned toward Lewiston. "There's a time and season for everything, Gwen." She drove for a few minutes, then finally asked, "What now?"

"Keep going forward. And we don't have much time. Beatrice has been gone for four days. Generally speaking, every hour a child is missing from an abduction, the outlook grows worse, and after seventy-two hours, well . . ."

"Do you think there's a chance she's still alive?"

"A chance. There was no sign of trauma on the body they found. I cling to that. But in the meantime . . . we need to focus on finding Jacob."

On the way to the Two Rivers B and B, we decided to keep my employment status, or lack thereof, private. Beth parked as close as she could to the door of the old house. "You run inside," she said. "I'll bring the dog in. Your sniper is still on the loose."

I bolted inside and nearly tripped over a body sprawled across the hall.

Chapter Twenty-Seven

Beth was right behind me with the dog. "Oh no! Who is it?"

Half the body was in the office, lying facedown with blood matting the brown hair. I picked up his hand and checked for a pulse, relaxing slightly at the strong *thump-thump-thump*.

"It's Eric. Someone conked him on the head." His gardening tools were scattered across the hall. I could see blood on the handle of a shovel. "Call 911."

"Winston, sit." Beth looped the leash around her arm and reached for the office phone.

"Ohhhh." Eric moaned and put his hand to his head.

"Eric, what happened?" I asked.

The man rolled over and sat. "I don't know. I just came in when — *wham*, the world went dark."

Beth had finished talking to the police.

She found a wet towel from someplace and handed it to me. I gingerly applied it to the vertical gash on Eric's head. He winced but took the towel.

Lila entered carrying a bag of groceries. She dropped the bag and raced to Eric, almost knocking me aside. "Oh, darling, what happened?"

Beth and I moved back and picked up the spilled produce, returning it to the grocery bag. "It looks like someone attacked Eric. Beth called the police. Can you tell if anything was stolen? Cash or . . . ?"

"There's never much money here." Lila stood and peeked over the counter into the office. "People usually pay for their rooms by credit cards. The cash drawer is closed."

"Do you have other guests?" Beth asked.

"Not until later tonight."

"Well then." I looked at Beth. "Um, Lila, the police will be here shortly. We're going to check our rooms." Beth gave me an understanding nod.

The door to the game room stood partially open. I nudged it open the rest of the way with my foot. Our papers were strewn across the floor. The blank foam board was tossed aside and the Sinopas' crime-scene photos were missing.

"Well, we know who was here," I said.

"Someone wanted to find out what we knew."

"What did they find out?" Beth asked.

Crossing to my room, I checked to see if the door was still locked. It was. "Not much. The three-ring binder and Beatrice's teddy bear are locked in here. I had the sketchpad with all my notes with me. All that we left in this room was the Sinopa investigation notes and photos. What about your room?"

Beth checked. "Door still locked. My computer and notes are in there." She glanced around again. "But I don't see my cell phone. I left it plugged in over there."

"Leave everything in here as is. The police will want to check for fingerprints." Rubbing down the small hairs that were standing up on my arms, I looked at Beth. "He's getting bold, so maybe we're making headway. Let's go in my room and work on this case before anyone else gets hurt."

Beth moved her computer and books as well as a paper bag of supplies to the antique sofa in the alcove. I retrieved the unused foam board and propped it against a dresser.

Beth sat and opened up her computer. "Give me a minute. The Internet is spotty in this old house. You're sure —"

"Jacob. It can only be Jacob."

"Um . . . you're pretty focused on the man who attacked Eric and the killer being Jacob. What do they call that?"

"Tunnel vision. Focusing on a limited range of possibilities for suspects. That could be true." My gaze drifted to the one-eyed teddy bear. "But only Jacob would be driven enough by our progress to break in here and attack Eric."

Several sirens howled, getting louder. "The police are here. Don't mention we're working on the identity of the perpetrator, or that I no longer work with the Inter-agency Major Crimes Unit. Also that the crime-scene photos are missing. Let's keep it simple."

"My lips are sealed."

It wasn't long before a Lewiston patrol officer knocked on my door. Winston pushed me aside before I could answer. I grabbed his collar and opened the door. The officer took a step backward when he saw the dog. "Does he bite?"

"Mostly dog cookies. Come in." I opened the door wider.

The officer remained standing as he asked questions, carefully writing down our answers in a small spiral notebook. We left out any mention of snipers, mistaken-identity murders, or serial killers.

"What do you think happened?" I asked him.

"Well, I'm not a detective, but it looks like teenagers got into the house and were making a mess. When they heard Mr. Winchester, they panicked and ran, whacking him on the head so he wouldn't call it in right away. We've had a number of these break-ins recently, though this is the first anyone's gotten hurt."

"How is Eric?" Beth asked.

"They were transporting him to the hospital for stitches, last I checked. Someone will be by shortly to take your fingerprints to eliminate them from the crime scene. Please don't touch anything in the next room until they're done dusting for prints." He nodded and left.

My cell rang, and I answered without looking at the screen. "Yes?"

"I just found out you got fired," Robert said. "You shouldn't even bother going to court for Aynslee."

"How did you learn about my job?"

"Your boss. I called to get the address where you're staying. We'll be moving her things out of your house."

"I'll have my lawyer —"

"What lawyer? You can't afford one. And no judge will let a child live with someone who was fired for gross negligence and incompetence." *Click.*

I threw the cell at the bed.

"Robert?" Beth asked.

"Just when I think he's out of my life, in the past, forgiven, and I'm moving on, he does something horrible."

"Would it help to talk about it?"

"No."

"In that case, what next, Miss Marple?" Beth asked.

"Did you get those pushpins I asked you to buy?"

"Yes. In that sack." She pointed.

"Excellent. Do you have a map of the Pacific Northwest in your car?"

"Of course. I'll go get it."

She opened the door just as a technician was about to knock. "Oh, hi, I just need to get your fingerprints," the woman said. "Big dog." She patted Winston.

"You can start with me while Beth gets something from the car."

I shifted the foam board off the dresser so we could use that surface. Winston sauntered over and rested his head on the dresser to observe our moves. Beth returned just as we finished up, and I washed my hands while she was printed. Still drying my hands, I entered my

Beth was talking to the technician. "No, I'm sure it was the episode involving the Gig Harbor killer where he uses his —"

I stopped dead. "You are not talking about some crime show —"

"Of course." The technician finished Beth's last finger. "But it was the one with the superhero victim, Beth. Don't you remember?" She picked up her kit, waved, and left.

Beth had placed several maps on the bed, and I mounted the one I wanted while she washed up. "Here's what we're going to do. Phil Cicero, the outfitter I hired, will be here in a few hours."

"Why doesn't it surprise me that you're still planning on going to the plane crash?"

"Employed or not, I'm going to see this through to the end."

"You're sure you don't have tunnel vision on this?" Beth asked.

"This is about *my life.*" I picked up the sketchpad and turned to the drawing I'd done of Jacob as a child. "But if I'm wrong, the worst that could happen is I find Jacob."

"And if you're right, we might find Beatrice."

"If I'm right" — I turned the drawing toward her — "then this is a portrait of vengeance."

Chapter Twenty-Eight

Settling in an antique wingback chair, I opened my sketchpad. "Here's a thought I had. Lapwai is near Lewiston. And Kamiah, of course. And Lacey is near Olympia."

"Right," Beth said. "Profound. What on earth are you talking about?"

"I'm going to write down all the places I can remember living while with Holly. Once I've given you those locations, could you look up similar events, murders, child abductions?"

"Of course."

"Then we'll visualize it by posting it on the foam board."

"That sounds great. But how would Jacob know all the places you lived? Why would he care?"

"The sketchbooks I had growing up. Holly kept them, but someone destroyed the drawings."

"Either Holly or Jacob." Beth sat on the sofa.

"Right. But I remembered I always dated the drawings and put where we lived. Jacob would have seen the sketchbooks. As to why he would care — I'm working on that."

It didn't take me long. After handing the list of towns and cities to Beth, I returned to my sketchbook notes on the knowns and unknowns. What was I missing? We worked in silence for a while, with only the clicking of Beth's fingers on the keyboard and the muted conversation of the police dusting the game room.

"There!"

I jerked at Beth's voice in the quiet room. "There what?"

The answer came from her portable printer clacking through several pages. "I think I have the information you need to profile Jacob as the serial killer we're looking for."

"But you're not a criminal profiler."

Beth sniffed. "Neither are you, but you do it all the time." Beth opened a textbook she'd brought from my place. "Did you know the term *serial killer* was first used by Robert Ressler, a profiler in the Behavioral Science Unit of the FBI?"

"Yes. I met him once."

"Noooo!" Her eyes grew round. "I'm such a votarist."

"Someone who plays a votar? Like a guitarist plays a guitar? Get it? Huh?"

"I see your warped sense of humor is intact. A votarist is someone who is devoted to something. Word of the day from last week." She stood, picked up the printouts, then handed me a stack. "The top page is a summary. What I could find on the individual cases are underneath in chronological order." She then crossed to the foam board and held up the first sheet. A photo of a child.

I closed my eyes. "No. No photos. No names."

"Why?"

"Names and photographs of the children are meant to personalize the cases." I looked at her. "They're designed not only to give clues to victimology but to remind those working on the crimes what's at stake. And what's been lost. But those names and faces become seared into your mind. They will change you. Haunt your dreams. Disturb your days. Prey upon your soul."

"You sound like you're speaking from experience."

I grunted. "We know what's been lost and

what's at stake. Leave the names and photos off."

"Okay, I won't put the photographs up." She placed the printed-out photo on the dresser, then paged through and found a second image. She glanced at me, then pulled more photos from her stack, spreading them out on the surface. "Gwen, you need to see something."

I stood and walked over. My mouth dropped. Seven children were lined up. They could have all been brothers and sisters. And they all looked like my sketch of Jacob. "We know how he chose his victims. Holly would have said 'save the child,' meaning she believed she 'saved me,' but Jacob would have believed *he* was the child who needed saving. So he chose children who resembled himself." I gathered the images together and turned them face-down.

"You're right about not looking at them." Beth turned to the foam board. "Staring at their little faces would make me want to cry."

I gave her a hug.

She took a deep breath. "Anyway, I started with the body found Wednesday outside of Lapwai. The child was abducted in Lacey, which is next to Olympia, Washington, one

265

of the towns you lived in. The problem here is the parents are still alive."

"Maybe Jacob had a learning curve with the murders." I sat at the table. "Attach the information to the board and put a pushpin in the location. Put a different color pin into the town where I lived. Do you have Post-it notes?"

"Of course."

"Write the date of the abduction on that."

She did as I asked, placing a green and a red pin on the map, then adding a round, light-green Post-it note.

I grinned. "No purple, lavender, lilac, or violet pushpins?"

"I asked. They didn't have plum, am-ethyst, heliotrope, or violaceous either. I'd have to special order. And it would take a week —"

I tried not to smile. "You actually asked about special ordering —"

"Never mind." She sniffed. "The red stands for possible cases. The green for where you lived. Get it? Green for Greene?"

"Right. Um . . . the round Post-it notes?"

"I kept with the red-and-green Christmas theme. Round is like a Christmas bulb. I had lavender notes, but the colors clashed."

"Of course they did."

She pinned the case information on the

board, then stepped back to admire it. "Wait, I saw this on television." She raced from the room, returning quickly with a ball of purple yarn. "Don't say a word. I can switch colors later. This is the best I can do." Wrapping one end of yarn around the pin holding the sheet of paper, she connected it to the red pin in the small town in Washington. "We wouldn't have even known about this first murder if the body hadn't shown up."

I did some mental calculations. "Holly would have been institutionalized three years before that event. Jacob would have been twenty when this part started."

"What do you mean, 'this part'?"

"Serial killers don't just wake up one morning and start their killing spree. I'm sure if we looked carefully enough, we'd find Jacob starting fires, then abusing animals, then on to being a peeping Tom before carrying out his fantasy of abduction and murder."

"According to your textbook," Beth said, "Jacob's been able to go on so long not just because the crimes were committed in different states, but also because of something called nomothetic. That's a false theory where the crimes are too narrowly investigated."

"Right. A homicide, rape, arson all may have the same motive, which is separate from the behavior. A rape may lead to homicide to protect the identity of the perpetrator. A homicide may have sexual aspects."

"Why did you have me research it if you already knew that?"

"I needed a reminder."

Beth sighed. "The next place you lived was Boise, Idaho. No abductions, no murders fitting the template. The nearest I could come was a fire in Caldwell that killed a family."

"Caldwell is less than thirty miles from Boise. Was there a child involved?"

"Yes," Beth said reluctantly. "Interestingly enough, same age, Native American, and body not recovered from the fire."

"So a second case."

"I marked it as inconclusive."

"Record it anyway. That's too many points of similarity."

Beth attached the paper under the state of Idaho and looped the yarn to connect the pin and paper.

Someone tapped on the door. I answered.

"We're done processing the room." A crime-scene technician smiled. "Watch the fingerprint powder. Gets on everything."

"Thank you." I left the door open but made no effort to shift to the game room. "For now let's stay in here. We'll listen for Eric and Lila to return."

Beth nodded and looked at her notes. "So, the next place you lived is Ellensburg." She applied a red and a green pin, then ran the yarn to the case notes on the side of the map. "I found a single mom, a student at Central Washington University, murdered and her daughter taken."

I put a check next to the case on the summary she'd given me. "The case matches."

"Age and race, yes, but once again, not exactly. A single parent, shot, not hacked with an ax —"

"Splitting hairs, if you pardon the expression. I see The Dalles is next. That's the one Andi Tubbs mentioned. Jacob was born there."

A door opened and closed somewhere in the house. Winston stood, but I caught his collar before he could investigate. Shortly Lila and a bandaged Eric appeared in the game room.

"What a mess." Lila glanced around at the tossed papers, fingerprint smudges, and rearranged furniture.

"How's the head, Eric?" Beth asked.

"Five stitches and a headache." Eric

touched a bandage on the side of his head. "The doctor said I was lucky. No concussion. What did the police say?"

"We just spoke to a patrol officer," I said. "He thought it might be teenagers."

Eric nodded. "We'll get this cleaned up later."

"We'll do it," Beth said. "You should just go lie down."

"I might just do that." Eric smiled slightly. "I was planning on making baklava tomorrow, and we'd hoped you both could join us for dinner."

"Are you sure you're up to it?" I asked.

He waved his hand. "I'm not letting a gang of vandalizing teenagers interrupt my life."

"We'd love to, I mean . . ." Beth glanced at me and I nodded. "Well then, yes, we'd love to dine with you both. I tried making baklava once. It takes forever."

"It does, but it's worth it." He took Lila's arm and the two of them left.

I released Winston's collar and shut the door.

Beth cocked her head at me. "I noticed you didn't tell him it wasn't teens who attacked him but rather a serial killer bent on murdering you."

"Mmm." I leaned against the door. "He

has enough to deal with. What is it you say?"

"Sufficient for the day is its own trouble."

CHAPTER TWENTY-NINE

Beth turned her attention to the map. "The Dalles, Oregon, is on the Columbia River. This was the nearest match to the present murders of the Sinopas. Both parents killed and a child taken. Same age, part Native American. But once again the weapon was a gun, not an ax."

"Jacob is twenty-seven by now." I sat in the wingback chair. "You do remember the difference between modus operandi and signature?"

"Of course. Modus operandi are actions taken during a crime and can change. Signature is why — the underlying motive or, in many cases, the fantasy that he is carrying out."

"Right. The signature is staying the same — a 'rescue' of a child." I made quote marks in the air. "The child being him, and the murder of one or both parents — substitute Holly. We have four possible abductions at this point, all the same age and race. The next place I lived was Coeur d'Alene, Idaho. I see you found a case in Post Falls, just a few miles away."

Beth put a green pin in the North Idaho town and a red pin next to it. More yarn led to the case notes. "A single father stabbed, badly hurt but not killed. He was from the Coeur d'Alene tribe. Child taken. The last one, not counting Beatrice, was from Frenchtown, Montana. It was ruled a murder-suicide, but the child is missing. You lived in Missoula, within a few miles." She placed the last of the pushpins and case notes on the foam board.

"Counting Beatrice, seven children over as many years."

"Don't you think law enforcement would see the pattern?"

"Every murder crosses state lines, so local agencies might not see a pattern. But federal law requires missing children to be reported to the National Center for Missing and Exploited Children. Most of the children are runaways. About ten percent are family abductions, and about one percent are stranger abductions."

"Four-year-olds don't usually run away." Beth finished writing the dates on the Post-it notes, then took a seat on the sofa.

"No, but the police might think a family member has the child. There are more than four hundred thousand reports of missing children every year."

"How do you know all this?"

"I've done reconstructions and age progressions for some of them."

We silently contemplated the need for reconstructions and age progressions on children. Beth typed on her computer a bit more, then printed out a sheet, which she posted on the board. She stood back and stared at it. I joined her. The only sound came from the sleeping Winston, who pursued dream cats with muffled barking and twitching feet.

Once more I scanned the dates on the list. "We can definitely consider the Caldwell fire as one of his. The cooling-off period is about the same."

Beth reddened. "Cooling off?"

"Not just the time to plan, act out, and relive the experience. Some serial killers can have a normal life where they completely mask their homicidal instincts. Or they can be giving clues that no one understands."

"That's frightening."

"Yes."

Another knock broke the silence. This time Winston moved to the door and stood

Lacey, WA	2009	Child taken Body found in Lapwai Jacob 20
Caldwell, ID	2011	Fire, parents killed child?
Ellensburg CWU, WA	2012	Mom murdered, child missing
The Dalles, OR	2014	Parents shot, child taken
Post Falls, ID	2015	Father stabbed, child missing
Frenchtown, MT	2015	Couple murdered (murder suicide), child missing
Lapwai	2016	Sinopas

at alert. I checked my watch, got up, grabbed the dog, and opened the door.

A tall, broad-shouldered, dark-haired man with a mustache and goatee took a step back when he saw Winston. "Whoa, a polar bear?"

"This is Winston." I kept my grip on his collar to keep him from launching at the man's crotch. "And you must be Phil Cicero."

Phil offered his hand, then glanced behind him at the chaos of the game room. "A bit of excitement?"

"You could say that. Let's move into the parlor where we have more room."

Phil led the way through the game room and across the hall, then politely waited for us to sit before sitting down. Even seated he was a big man, easily six foot four or taller. He wore pressed khaki slacks, a matching safari-style shirt, brown hiking boots, and carried a leather messenger bag. Reaching into his bag, he pulled out a detailed map.

"I'm Beth, by the way."

Winston followed us and flopped onto the floor next to my chair.

"Ma'am." He looked at me. "Dan Kus gave me the coordinates of the plane crash." He'd marked a spot on the map with a yellow highlighter. "You know, a helicopter would get you there a lot easier."

"How much would that cost?" I asked.

He told me, then gave me his fee. Both were steep, but the helicopter was impossibly high. "Um, I'm good with you as the guide."

"Okay then, two questions. Can you ride a horse?"

I grinned as I thought of my last horseback ride. "Yeah, but I prefer daylight with a saddle and at a relatively calm speed."

Phil frowned. "You'll have a saddle. You'll also do a lot of walking. What condition are you in?" He reached over and grabbed my thigh.

I leaped to my feet. "What are you doing?" Winston lunged for Phil's hand. I caught the dog before he could chomp the man.

Phil had the decency to turn red. "I'm sorry. Just checking your muscle tone. I'm used to taking men out hunting."

"I'm fine."

"This will be one long day, unless you want to spend the night in the wilderness."

Still feeling his hand on my leg, I said, "A long day is good."

"I'll meet you at oh-four hundred. Take Highway 12 to Lowell. It's about two hours from Lewiston. Park here." He handed me a card for a hotel and rafting company. "I'll pick you up and trailer the horses up the Selway Road to about here." He pointed. "We can take an old logging road for a few miles on horseback, some back-country riding, then walk in. It's only a couple of miles, but the terrain is steep."

"I'll be there." Opening my purse, I took out my checkbook and wrote the requested amount. I tried not to think about my income now that I didn't have a job. I'd just have to jump off that bridge when I came to it.

After Phil left, Beth crossed her arms and glared at me. "So, you're still planning on going to the crash site even though someone has tried to kill you at least twice."

277

"I'll be fine. I'll be leaving here before two tomorrow morning. And I'm heading to a place you can't even get to except on foot or by helicopter." I slumped in my chair. "Beth, try to understand. I don't remember my parents. I don't know anything about them. With Holly's mind gone, this is the only link I have to them."

Beth uncrossed her arms. "Okay. I guess. You'll be driving my car, so I'm stuck here. What did you want me to do?"

"If Jacob is the killer, and if he's the one trying to kill me —"

"Two insurmountable 'ifs' in my book."

I ignored her interruption. "I left when Jacob was only four. I want you to figure out how he recognized me in order to make me his target."

CHAPTER THIRTY

Sleeping only sporadically, I spent the few hours in bed flipping the pillow to the cool side and checking the clock. I got up before the alarm sounded at one thirty. Beth had packed virtually my entire wardrobe, minus my rain jacket. I layered a sweater over a long-sleeved shirt, then a T-shirt with *Don't Drink and Draw* on the front. I grabbed my purse and police raincoat, then quietly slipped out.

Winston was in Beth's room for the night, but I could hear him panting on the other side of her door as I tiptoed across the game room.

Even though the probability of a sniper waiting for me at two in the morning was slim, I still raced to the car. I didn't relax until I'd reached the edge of Lewiston, where I stopped for coffee at a twenty-four-hour convenience store.

I didn't need the coffee to stay awake. My

brain bounced around like a ping-pong ball. *Is Beatrice still alive? Why didn't Seth defend me against my boss? What will I do for a job? How can I convince a judge not to take away custody of my daughter? What do I hope to learn from visiting the crash site? Should I try calling Blake? Where is Jacob?*

Traffic was almost nonexistent. I made it to Lowell on time and pulled up next to a pickup hauling a two-horse trailer. Grabbing my wallet and cell phone, I locked Beth's car. Phil started the truck as I got in, and I barely snapped my seat belt before he started moving. The road paralleled the Selway River, which I'd looked up the night before. During the season, rafters considered the river to be one of the toughest whitewater challenges in the West. Designated a National Wild and Scenic River, the forest service only allowed one permit a day for rafters. In the predawn blackness, I could only catch brief glimpses of the rapids. After a few miles, we crossed a bridge and headed into the mountains on a gravel road.

"You believe your parents died in this plane crash?" Phil asked.

"How did you know that?"

"Dan Kus told me."

"I wonder who else he told."

Phil glanced at me. "Is this some kind of secret? I left a copy of our itinerary with my company as well as the forest service. They post hikers, hunters, and campers on a big map in the office. Anyone who asks or drops by can find out where I am."

"Um, can you call and tell them not to reveal your location?"

"No cell service. Why the hush-hush?"

Go ahead and tell him. Oh, by the way, someone is trying to kill me. He's already killed one person and put stitches in another. "Um . . . I was just wondering, that's all."

Phil once again concentrated on driving, his expression clearly showing he didn't believe me. The darkness around us gradually lightened to where I could see the steep mountains parading off into the distance. We finally turned onto a small, overgrown road on the right and parked. "This is as far as we can drive." He opened the door, letting in cool air, the smell of pine needles, and a faint whiff of skunk. I climbed out my side and helped him unload the mounts. Two rangy horses, one a bay with a white rump and spots, the other a red roan, were already saddled and both had well-stocked day packs in the saddlebags. They wore halters, their bridles attached to the saddle.

"An Appaloosa?" I patted the bay.

"Nez Perce horse. Both of them are. The tribe used some of Chief Joseph's original stock and bred with a rare breed from Turkmenistan called Akhal-Teke. Are you interested in horses?"

"Right about now I don't think I can afford one."

"I hear ya. You can ride the roan." He tightened the cinches on both horses as I bridled them, then he tugged a day bag and rifle out of his truck. A scabbard was already secured on the saddle and he slid the rifle into place, tied on the day bag, and mounted.

I dropped my cell and wallet into the saddlebag and got up on my horse, then turned to follow him up the logging road. The first downed pine blocking the trail confirmed why we were on horseback and not driving.

The terrain grew steeper, trees and underbrush denser, and the temperature warmer as the sun climbed in the sky, although patches of snow still appeared on the shady side of some hills. I slipped off the rain jacket and sweater and tied them to the saddle. My thighs and rear informed me I was in for major saddle-soreness as soon as I dismounted.

"Do you bring people up here to hunt?" I

asked over the squeaking of leather and clopping of hooves.

"Yep. Bear, deer, elk, moose, bighorns, mountain goats, you name it, somebody wants to shoot it."

Following a game trail, we startled a small herd of deer that huffed their displeasure. Overhead, a massive golden eagle rode an updraft in lazy circles, looking for a meal. A soft breeze fluffed my hair. Spring rains blessed the scenery with every shade of green. "What kind of wildflower is that English red ochre one?"

"English what?"

"English red ochre. Sort of a garnet with maybe ultramarine . . ."

He stared at me.

"Never mind."

Phil finally pulled up his mount and checked a compass. "We're almost at the spot where we'll be leaving the horses. See that big ponderosa at the top of the hill across there?" He pointed. "We'll climb up to that. The crash site is about five miles due west at the end of an open slope."

We dropped down a steep slope, the horses scrambling to keep their footing, and ended in a narrow draw with a small stream running through it. He dismounted and let his horse drink from the stream.

Sliding off, I handed him the reins and moved slightly upstream to cool and wash my dusty face. I bent down.

Something burned across my shoulder.

Before I could move, Phil landed on top of me, knocking me to the ground. Inches from my nose, an arrow stuck in the earth.

Adrenaline surged through my body.

The horses snorted, whinnied in pain, then bolted, their metal shoes clattering on the rocks as they tore down the stream bed.

"Phil?" I whispered.

The man didn't answer. Or breathe.

In the silence broken only by the gurgling stream came a *thurrrrrp,* then a *thump.* An arrow skidded through my shirt, scraped my ribs, and embedded into the ground. It had to have gone completely through Phil.

Whoever was shooting at us had the total advantage. *Whoever? Don't kid yourself.* Jacob may have thought he had killed me with one or both arrows. He was probably watching me through field glasses, waiting for movement.

The second I tried to shift Phil off my back, Jacob would launch a storm of arrows. And that wasn't the only problem. The last arrow pinned me to the ground. I had no cover other than Phil's body, no place to hide. And having a large, dead body on top of me sent my creep-meter off the charts.

Play dead.

What if he keeps shooting? Or walks over and cuts my throat? He'd murdered two people with an ax. He'd want to get up close and personal.

Don't move.

What choice did I have? The arrows were upright. He was above me, shooting down.

A rock dug into my hip. My left hand, still showing scars from my last encounter with a rock slide in Kentucky, trailed in the icy stream. Mosquitoes found my other hand and invited the neighborhood in for a meal. Phil's blood grew cold on my back. His weight made breathing difficult.

How long before Jacob left? Or moved closer?

My nose itched. Flies discovered Phil's body. Their buzzing grew louder as more flies joined them. They'd be laying eggs. Maggots. Bugs.

I clenched my jaw to keep from screaming.

Concentrate on something besides your misery. How did he find us?

That was easy. Dan pointed out the location of the plane in front of Thomas. He'd marked it on the map in the visitor center. And the forest service probably had a Post-it note with my name on it. He could have come out here last evening and simply waited for us to show up. I listened for approaching footsteps.

My shoulder and side burned where the arrows had scraped a furrow of skin.

Make a plan. I can't just lie here until someone finds me.

The day pack with supplies along with Phil's rifle were long gone with the horses. I hadn't paid enough attention to our route to find my way to Phil's truck. What had Seth told me? The Nez Perce–Clearwater National Forest was over four million acres with almost half of that wilderness. That's a lot of land to get lost in.

Sweat added more wetness down my back, mixing with Phil's blood. I did know the direction of the plane-crash site. If Phil still had his compass on him, I could go there. That would be where search and rescue would look first.

Just one minor problem with that plan. No one would even start searching until I was overdue to return. Meaning tomorrow. At the earliest.

One thing was for sure, I couldn't remain under a dead body. I had to move. And pray the shooter had already gone. Slowly, ever so slowly, I pulled my frozen hand from the stream.

No sounds of running feet or thump of an arrow.

Opening and closing my numb fingers hurt like the dickens, but it helped warm them. Once I had enough feeling, I reached down my side until I encountered the shaft of the arrow, sticky with drying blood. I tried to pull it out of the ground.

The arrow didn't budge.

I shifted sideways as far as I could, disturbing a cloud of flies, then pulled, hoping my shirt would rip.

No such luck. *I really wish I had a solution that didn't require me to undress.*

Unbuttoning my shirt, I scooted over farther, then tugged at my T-shirt. The material was thin and old and tore relatively easily. I left my long-sleeved shirt under Phil's body. I kept low, crawling to a small patch of snowberry bushes. With only a torn T-shirt, I felt naked and exposed.

No one moved on the hillside above the draw.

Taking a deep breath, I crept over to Phil's body. His eyes were open, staring at nothing. Swiftly I checked his pockets. The compass and truck keys were in one, a pack of cigarettes and paper matches in another.

Thank you, Lord.

A T-shirt was scant protection for a wilderness overnight. I wiped my hands on my pants, took a grip on the arrow holding my shirt, and gave a tug. It didn't move. I rocked it back and forth, trying not to look at Phil's body as I did so. The arrow came out of the ground enough that I could retrieve my shirt, now soaked in blood.

I couldn't put it on. Not yet. Not fresh.

Overhead, a hawk screamed. Branches in the distance snapped, then I heard a moan and a clacking sound. Squinting, I made out a mama black bear clicking her teeth at two cubs up a tree. They seemed to be ignoring me.

Before I could relax and take a breath, something moved above me to the right. I ducked behind a bush, then peeked through the branches.

Halfway up the hillside, a cougar stared down at me.

CHAPTER THIRTY-ONE

My heart hammered in my chest. My mouth dried. Run? Freeze?

The big cat twitched its tail.

Would the cat target live food? Obviously the bloodbath lured him here. I dropped my soaked shirt, stood up from behind the bush, then stepped away from the body.

The cougar watched intently.

Another step, then another. *My dandy pink camo rifle would be nice right now.* My foot caught a rock, almost tripping me. *Don't go down. He'll think you're injured.* I didn't want to turn my back to the cougar, but I'd reached the hillside. I couldn't climb it backward.

Half turning, I climbed out of the gully sideways, checking each step before committing to it, then shooting my gaze to the cat. Sweat soaked my T-shirt and dripped off the end of my nose. The cougar moved just as I'd reached the halfway point toward the tree Phil had pointed to.

I kept climbing. No longer seeing the cougar, I stopped my crab-like crawl and charged up the hill. Was he staying with Phil's body or coming after me? Stopping to catch my breath, I listened for his approach. The only sounds were the *shhhhhh* of wind through the trees, birds chirping, and my gasping for breath.

Reaching the top of the hill, I looked around for the big ponderosa. All the trees looked big. Phil had pointed one out as the start for the trek to the crash site. What if I started too far one way or the other?

I spun in a dizzying circle, looking for the big tree. Nothing, nothing, nothing.

Stop it. The world kept twirling. I sat. *If you panic, you'll be lost.* I stopped looking up and just looked around. A tall tree would need a big trunk. *Find the biggest trunk.* Standing, I walked twenty paces north, turned, twenty paces east, twenty paces south. I spotted the tree. I wanted to hug it, but that could lead to becoming a vegan. Using the compass, I put my back to the trunk and faced due west. Straight ahead was a rocky cliff with a streak of cobalt green. I headed toward it.

The cliffs were on the other side of a steep, narrow valley. I slid part of the way down on my bottom, grabbing branches to slow my progress. My unprotected arms soon were covered with welts and mosquito bites, and a persistent horsefly buzzed around my head. I finally broke off a branch from a pine tree and swatted at it until I whacked it into fly purgatory.

From the bottom of the ravine, a game trail offered a route up the cliff. I followed it, praying the game that used the trail were just amazingly surefooted mountain goats or bighorn sheep.

I finished the last part of the trail on hands and knees, grabbing shrubs to pull myself up. I paused at the top to check my progress. A tawny gold movement on the opposite hillside caught my attention.

The cougar.

My stomach contracted and blood rushed from my face.

The big cat passed in and out of sight, stalking my trail.

Checking my compass, I set off at a trot. I had to make it to the crash site before the cougar caught up with me. I could build a fire and wait for rescue.

I reached a ridge, trees pressing in on all sides. Not able to see beyond a few feet, I kept the compass in front of me. The sun dappled the pine needle ground from directly overhead. If it was noon, I had about seven and a half hours before sunset. But I would need to gather firewood and get a fire going to keep that cougar at bay. Assuming he didn't catch up with me first.

Pushing on, I increased my speed, chipmunks chattering their displeasure as I passed.

The ridge ended, trees thinned, and I could see the mountains cascading in the distance. Ahead, across a rugged valley, was the small clearing Phil had mentioned, with a spot of burnt sienna at the far side.

A lump rose unexpectedly in my throat. This was the last place my mom and dad had been alive.

I swallowed hard a few times, then took a reading with the compass. The sun was getting lower in the sky, and I had a lot of ground to cover. I headed downhill at a trot.

Bad idea.

The trot became a headlong run, my arms windmilling to keep me upright. My feet caught on a downed tree limb. I pitched forward, smashed against the ground, and tumbled like a rag doll in a dryer. A pine tree stopped my forward momentum.

I lay on my back and stared at the sky, sure I'd broken some bones. A small avalanche of rocks and dirt pelted me. "That's gonna leave a mark."

My voice worked. I wiggled my toes, then raised my hands so I could see them and moved my fingers. So far, all systems checked out.

Maybe I could just lie here and wait for help.

Cougar.

Maybe not. I slowly got to my feet, holding on to the tree. The world spun a bit, everything hurt, and I was going to have some dandy bruises, but thank the Lord, nothing was broken.

Pushing on, I tried not to think of that cool stream where I'd last had a chance to drink some water. *Don't forget, lying beside that stream is Phil's body.*

As usual, Gwen, you made a bad decision to head into the wilderness to pursue some crazy idea.

Ugh. Robert.

"Finding out my history isn't crazy."

What difference does it make?

"Maybe no difference to you, but —" I slid a few steps and caught a branch to slow my progress. "But it does to me. For ten years I lived with Holly's lies. I left a child with his abusive mother."

You're going to have to forgive yourself for leaving Jacob, Beth whispered in my mind.

You were little more than a child yourself. And who you are, what you are, what you believe about life, death, love, loss is all genuine and real. You became the person you are for a reason. That reason hasn't changed.

"You're siding with Robert."

No. I am throwing a bucket of cold ice over your pity party. Find out what you need to and move on. Like seasons of the year, you're having your winter, but spring follows.

"Yeah. Well," I muttered. "Spring brings allergies. And mud."

Beth didn't answer, but I could almost feel the bucket of ice on my head.

A tiny stream burbled through the rocks at the bottom of the mountain.

I charged over and flung myself down on the bank and drank. Nothing tasted so delicious. I plunged my face into the icy water, instantly cooling it. *Thank you, Lord.*

With the cold water, I rinsed my scratches and the gouged areas where the arrows scraped my skin. Bruises checkered my body. Standing, I looked for movement behind me. I didn't see the cougar, but the terrain was heavily timbered.

Shadows started to stretch across the small valley. Night would not be my friend if I had no flashlight or lantern. Moving as swiftly as I could through the underbrush, I crossed the valley and started up the mountain.

The climb was steep, with loose rocks that carried me backward one step for every two I made. Dust clogged my nose, branches snagged my clothing, and my toes felt like they were one big blister. Partway up, I paused to catch my breath. Sweat again soaked my torn T-shirt and mixed with Phil's blood, creating a reeking stench. I turned and watched for the cougar. The trees and shrubs framed a small section of creek far below.

The cougar stalked to the creek, sniffed, then looked up.

His eyes stared directly into mine.

CHAPTER THIRTY-TWO

Turning, I sprinted up the slope, plowing through the underbrush, shoving pine limbs aside. A grouse burst from the bushes near me. More crashing came from my left as something very large and dark moved away. I caught a glimpse of lighter fur on the rear. Elk.

The noise could be covering up the sound of the approaching mountain lion.

Running faster, I gasped for breath, my legs made of cement, my muscles burning. The dense woods around me darkened. Indigo clouds blocked the sun.

I tripped, fell forward, and landed on a patch of pine needles. The ground leveled.

A long clearing dotted with small pines and patches of wild daisies narrowed toward a massive pine in the distance. The remains of a small plane wrapped around the base of the tree.

The sight blurred for a moment and I

blinked hard. My hands made fists, my nails digging into my palms.

A brisk wind stirred and bent the tops of the forest surrounding the field, and more clouds moved in, blotting out the sun.

If it rains, I'll never get a fire started. And without a fire, that cougar . . .

I ran as fast as my tired legs would propel me. The nearer I came to the wreck, the smaller the plane looked.

The burnt sienna color I'd seen wasn't the paint on the plane, it was the rust. The landing gear was gone, the fuselage resting on the ground with the front facing me. A pine had crushed the pilot's side. A large, horizontal branch the size of a small tree had destroyed the windshield, slicing off the top of the cabin to where the wing attached to the roof. Evidence of that long-ago recovery showed with the passenger door cut and pried open. It now swung gently in the breeze. Rescuers had removed the seat — reduced to wire and rotted leather — and placed it on the ground next to the cabin.

I walked around the wreckage. The plane was now a part of the giant ponderosa. The scars from the crash were gone, but it appeared the plane tried to land, sliced into the tree, wrapped around the trunk, and finally was stopped by the tree limb.

Beth had called the plane a Skymaster. Without the traditional tail, only the fuselage remained. The right-side wing rested partly on the branch. A support structure still kept the wing horizontal, though the tip had rusted through. The left wing was a crumpled mass of metal some distance away. Over the thirty-plus years, pines had sprouted around the plane.

My parents were sitting there when the plane spun around the tree. No time to duck.

A drop of rain pulled me out of my sooty-black thoughts. I'd need a dry spot for the night. The right wing afforded some protection. Quickly I gathered fallen tree branches, dried pine needles, and pinecones, placing them in a pile under the wing.

Dusk took on a jaundiced hue with the approaching storm. The breeze turned cool and smelled of rain.

Pausing, I glanced down the field. A flash of tawny fur at the far end told me I was out of time. The cougar still stalked me. Gathering the dried needles, a bit of old bark, and a few small twigs, I opened the matchbook. I had six matches. Six chances to start a fire.

The cat approached.

I lit a match with shaking hands, then dropped it. It went out. A second match was no better.

The cougar moved steadily through the brush and grass, tail low and twitching.

The third match went out with a puff of wind.

Please, Lord. I tore the top off the matchbook, adding the bit of paper to my small pile. The next match caught some needles on fire, burned for a moment, then went out.

The cougar grew larger. He was at least three feet tall at the shoulder and over two hundred pounds.

If I couldn't get the fire going, I'd have to stand and try to appear larger than the cat. I had two rocks I found to throw. After that . . . well, I needed to get the fire going.

The fifth match I placed under the paper, then cupped my hands around it. The paper caught fire, which spread to the needles. Gently I blew on the small flames as I fed the fire more needles, then a pinecone.

The mountain lion stopped twenty feet away and hissed.

"Get out of here!" I stood and threw a rock. Missed.

The cougar hissed again and crouched.

My lips were numb. Even though the air was chilly, sweat broke out over my body. I added more pinecones and sticks to the fire.

The cones flared and popped.

The cougar flattened his ears, hissed again, and moved a few steps away. I could barely see him in the dark. Behind the mountains to my right, lightning flickered like a strobe light and distant thunder rumbled. A *shhhhhhhh* grew louder as the rain splashed through the trees before pinging on the airplane wing above me. I piled more wood onto the fire, then checked my supply of fuel.

I didn't have enough wood to last until morning. Not even close.

A streak of lightning lit up the field. The cougar crouched thirty feet from me.

Help wouldn't come before morning, especially with the storm.

Boom! Thunder rattled the metal wing above me.

Lifting a small burning branch, I inspected the fuselage next to me. The tree limb had peeled the roof of the cabin as far back as the rear seats. I could crawl inside that area to be safe, but a four-foot gap remained where the front passenger seat had rested. If I could put the removed seat back in place, the cougar couldn't reach me. Maybe. Assuming I could keep the door shut. And attach the seat.

And there could be spiders.

I stuck the burning branch inside the space and moved it around, hoping any creepy-crawly bug would die or leave.

You're worried about a spider when a cougar is just waiting to make you his dinner?

The two rear bucket seats of the plane were still somewhat intact, protected by the remnants of the wing and large tree limb.

The lightning flashed every few seconds, with thunder rolling across the sky. The cat lay a short distance away in the rain, ignoring the storm, watching me.

Saving one good-sized branch, I added the last of the wood to the fire. It blazed with a welcome warmth. After throwing the branch into the rear of the plane, I stepped into the rain and grabbed the rotting seat. I was instantly drenched. I manhandled the seat into the front of the plane.

Closing and fastening the door would help keep the seat in place, but the latch was broken. A piece of rope, shoelace, or belt would hold it shut. I had none of these.

Slipping my arms inside my clammy T-shirt, I reached back and unfastened my bra. I removed the breast prostheses, Ginger and Mary Ann. Pulling my arms back out, I chucked them into the rear of the plane. I tied the bra firmly to the door, crawled under the tree limb into the fuselage, and pulled the door shut. The undamaged portion of the cabin smelled of moss and mildew. Weaving the bra between the metal frame of the rotted seat, I fastened the door closed.

The icy rain pounded overhead. My hands shook so hard I could barely jam the chunk of wood through the wires, connecting the two front seats.

The storm continued, with the lightning and thunder getting less frequent, but the rain increased. Large droplets of cold water dripped down my back and neck. I brought my knees up to my chest, wrapped my arms around my legs, and shivered. The fire I'd left burning looked warm and inviting as it flickered on the undersurface of the wing. The cougar would come as soon as the fire died down.

I was wrong.

Thump! The fuselage rocked as the giant cat leaped to the wing overhead. Two glowing eyes appeared between the rotted seats.

CHAPTER THIRTY-THREE

The cougar jumped forward into the remains of the cockpit. He spun and faced
me, just beyond the pitiful wire seat barrier.
He hissed.

I could barely breathe. I shrank away as
far as I could, pressing against the back of
the cabin. "Go away." The words came out
as a whisper.

The cat wrapped his claws around the
metal framework separating us and pulled.
The rusting plane rocked and squealed. The
wire bent.

"Get out of here!" My voice was louder,
but high-pitched.

The cougar leaned in and grabbed the
wire seat with his teeth. His hot breath
smelled of rancid meat and coppery blood.

My stomach clenched. *I will not go through
cancer, divorce, and losing my job only to be
dinner for an overgrown cat.*

I grabbed the only things I had to throw

— my prosthetic breasts, Ginger and Mary Ann. Ginger whacked the wire by the cat's mouth. The cougar let go of the wire and reared back. Mary Ann followed, thwacking the wire with a satisfying *thump.*

In the dying light from the fire, the cat blinked at me.

"Go on, get! Go away!" I kicked the wire.

The cougar stuck his foot through the narrow opening between the seats, claws extended. I found Mary Ann and threw the breast form at the paw. The cat snagged the prosthetic and pulled it through the opening.

"Take that, you miserable creature." I kicked the wire again.

The cougar jumped from the front of the plane.

I couldn't stop shaking. The small amount of light from the dying campfire was fading. The clouds would keep out any moonlight. I didn't want to fight a mountain lion in the pitch dark.

The cat returned, attacking the wire seats with teeth and claws.

I screamed, kicked at his face, then threw the remaining prosthetic at the small opening. He grabbed it, narrowly missing my wrist with a sharp claw, and jumped away.

Rustling, growling, thrashing came from

beside the plane.

Clutching my legs tighter, I prayed for mercy.

The soft flickering changed to a glow, the glow faded to nothing.

Darkness enveloped me.

The rain continued to steadily thunder on the cabin roof as I grew even colder. Oversized drops gathered and dribbled through the rusted holes above me. The sound drowned out any noise the cougar might make. Had he gone?

I was afraid to close my eyes. If I fell asleep and leaned against the wire front seats, the cat could reach me.

What if no one came in the morning?

Someone will come. I'll make sure of it. Beth's calm voice spoke in my mind.

My throat closed up and eyes brimmed with unshed tears. When was the last time I'd told Beth how grateful I was for her friendship? *She thinks she hangs around me for excitement. The truth is, I hang around her for her wisdom and friendship.*

I tried again to hear the cougar. The rain responded by pounding harder on the metal roof.

Dan Kus's words echoed in my head. *The Nimi'ipuu had a practice that when a young person reached a certain age, he was sent*

305

out into the mountains alone to find his Wy ya
kin — *his animal or bird spirit. That spirit
would speak to him and give him help throughout his lifetime.*

"Cougar, don't you know the legend?" I
spoke out loud. "You're supposed to help
me, not attack me as an hors d'oeuvre. I'm
freezing, wet, smelly, and squashed into the
rotting end of a crashed airplane."

I listened again. "I will say you have
patience, waiting for your prey —"

Waiting. Prey. I'd asked Beth how Jacob
would recognize me after all these years. He
wouldn't. He couldn't even be sure I'd have
kept my name.

"It would be nearly impossible for him to
find *me.*" I tried to keep my teeth from
chattering. "But not impossible for me to
find *him.* What if he re-created the crime
that Holly said occurred — the murder of
my parents and my disappearance? Maybe
in the same towns or cities where I lived."

A trap, Beth murmured in my brain. *Like
a South American margay, a jungle cat that
lures monkeys down from the trees by making a sound like a hurt baby monkey.*

"One problem, though." A particularly
large dollop of rain hit my neck and ran
down my spine. I curled up tighter to retain
my body's heat. "He'd have to be assuming

I would notice the murders."

Not so much bait for the trap, but more like a line of breadcrumbs.

"Or even several different kinds of bait. The murders would be one, and the letters to the editor would be another. That's how I located Holly in the first place. Subtle, using the name I knew her by, and giving the location by using the letters of the state mental hospital. He must have figured I'd wonder if she was really dead after all."

Brilliant, Beth muttered.

A scream like a woman getting murdered made every hair on my head stand on end. The fuselage rocked, metal clanged. The cougar had returned.

I screamed back and grabbed for the seat, unable to see anything in the inky night. The wire twisted and pulled under my fingers. A sharp *crack* told me the wood holding the seats together had splintered. Still holding the wire, I groped around me, grasping for something, *anything,* to throw. My hand encountered rotting leather seat material with attached springs.

A sharp, searing pain ripped through my upper arm. The cat's claws were making headway.

My fingers were burning with the pain of holding the seat. I reached behind me with my other hand, wrenching my shoulder, and fumbled between the bucket seats. Feeling only soft, squishy moss, I grabbed a handful and threw it.

The cougar didn't slow.

I stuffed my hand behind the seat and found something metal. Flinging it, I heard it clang against the wire.

The tugging stopped for a moment.

Frantically clutching in the same area, I grasped more objects and thrust them forward.

The cat hissed.

I bit my tongue.

Reaching behind me now, my fingers caught a round stick. With a jerk, I freed it and stabbed at the cougar.

A yelp told me I'd hit my mark. I jabbed again. The stick broke, leaving a small piece in my hand. The cat snarled and spit. The cabin squealed and flexed as the feline jumped off the fuselage. The rain beat on the metal roof, making it impossible to hear any other noise. *Please let him be gone.* The rain slowed slightly, and I tried to quiet the sound of my ragged breathing. I waited.

The cougar was gone.

My fingers ached from clutching the stick. With an effort, I relaxed my hand. Rain turned to sleet, then a late spring snow. I was going to die of hypothermia. My hands and feet burned. I shook uncontrollably. Reaching between the seats where I'd found the stick and things to throw, I carefully felt around. *Please, Lord, don't let this be a spider's hangout.* This time I found a scrap of material and pulled it out. A clasp and metal edges showed it had once been a purse. Mom's purse. The material was a cotton duck, like the fabric found in beach bags. Most of it had rotted away. Opening the purse, I felt papers and a chain.

Paper. That was important. My shivering slowed. Yes. Paper. I had . . . one match. If I burned the paper, I could be warm.

Fumbling, I pulled the matchbook from my pocket. I was so sleepy. Crumpling one sheet of paper, I set it by my feet. I struck the match on the striking surface. Missed. Tried again. And again. It flared to life. I dropped it.

I moaned. *Please, God . . .*

A tiny light flickered at my feet. I crumpled another scrap of paper and added it to the small flame. Then another.

The remains of a lace hankie from the purse joined the paper, then the purse itself. The fire warmed the small area around me. The tree branch was dry on the underside and I gouged some bark, adding the pieces slowly.

The snow stopped, leaving a white frosting on the fuselage.

Two remaining pieces of paper and I'd be out of fuel for the fire.

I fed one scrap of paper to the dimming fire. The flames wrapped around the edges and burned inward until one word remained. *Water.*

Water. I was thirsty. And hungry. The fire gobbled up the last piece of paper.

I held up the broken stick I'd used to drive away the cougar and paused. It was blue. A blue stick. My mind was filled with cotton and it took time to work out what it was — part of a fiberglass fishing rod. I wasn't going fishing. Or was I?

Using the fishing rod, I stabbed at the tree limb, harvesting more bark. The effort exhausted me.

I must have dozed off. I thought I'd just closed my eyes, but when I opened them, I could see the tiny cabin in the faint light of dawn.

A spider dangled inches from my face.

I shot backward the tiny distance I had, screaming. The movement sent the spider swaying at the end of its web. Kicking clumsily, I managed to squish it against the

310

rusted wall.

My frantic movements warmed me slightly. I slapped around my head, just in case a spider had landed on me overnight.

On the floor, next to the ashes of my tiny fire, rested some items. After a few moments I worked out what I was looking at — a tube of lipstick, a chain, and a broken compact. I picked them up with numb fingers. They weren't mine. They had to belong to . . . my mom. Pulling the cap off, I twisted up the light peach lipstick. It was flattened, dried out, and covered with dirt. *This means something.* I forced myself to concentrate. The cap had been on the tube . . . Raising my head, I stared at the large branch resting across the front of the plane, now scratched and gouged on the underside. Anyone sitting in those two seats would have died instantly. But someone in the back?

Beth said . . . I rubbed my head to remember. Beth said the rescuers didn't get to the crash right away. Everyone was dead when they arrived.

Had my mom survived the crash, albeit briefly? If she had . . . did she write something with the lipstick? I examined the compartment. If she'd written on the seats, the leather had rotted away. The inside of the cabin was probably covered with fabric, also gone.

A shape in the corner of the floor looked odd. I knew that shape. I nudged it with my shoe. Metal. Plastic. I kicked it. The barrel rotated from under the seat. A pistol. I even knew what kind. A . . . a . . . *Why can't I remember?*

Why was my mom or dad carrying a gun? Or did it belong to the pilot? Or me? I shook my head.

Whap-whap-whap.
The air is vibrating.
Whap-whap-whap.
I know that sound.
Whap-whap-whap-whap-whap.
A helicopter.

Thankyouthankyouthankyou! I shoved against the seat. It didn't move.

I shoved harder. The wires had tangled from . . . the cougar. That's right, I'd fought a cougar.

Whap-whap-whap. The copter grew louder, though I still couldn't see it.

Grunting with effort, I rocked the seat to loosen it. What if they decided I wasn't here? What if they just flew off? Leaning away, I kicked at the seat. It jammed against the side. Grabbing the wire seat with both hands, I rocked it as hard as I could. It barely moved an inch.

My hands and feet burned. Blood pounded in my head.

The copter came into view, hovered above the clearing, then landed. Dirt, leaves, grass, and other debris flew in all directions. I ducked and covered my ears.

Something touched my arm.

I screamed and slapped at it.

Other sounds replaced the helicopter's steady drone. Words, but they didn't make sense. I blinked and stared at the face peering at me. Seth Kus. His mouth moved again. This time I understood him. "Gwen? Gwen, you're okay now. We're here —"

I burst into tears.

CHAPTER THIRTY-FOUR

Heat rushed up my neck to my cheeks, but the tears didn't stop. I covered my face with my hands. *Stupid, stupid, stupid. Get it together. Be cool.* Swallowing a few times, I wiped my runny nose on my arm. *Oh, that was cool.*

"Are you hurt, Gwen?"

The concern in his voice almost set me off again. I shook my head, clamped my jaw, and looked up. "It was a long night." My words still sounded slurred.

Seth touched the metal cabin. "I imagine you didn't get much sleep. Let's get you out of here." He looked behind him and jerked his head. A man appeared and yanked the door open.

My bra, holding the door shut, ripped in two.

The two men froze and stared at the tattered remains for a moment. The man turned bright crimson and didn't seem to know where to look. Seth grinned at me.

I shrugged.

The men recovered from the bra encounter and made short work of removing the rotted seat. Seth held out his hand to help me out.

I stared at it. *When he pulls you out, there will be no hiding your flat chest.*

Sucking in a deep breath, I took his hand. *So be it.*

My legs gave way as soon as they touched the ground. Seth wrapped his arm around my waist and held me up while the other man draped a blanket around my shoulders. The warmth was a slice of heaven.

A young, wiry man in a baseball cap with some kind of medical patch on it placed a bag on the ground next to a coffin-shaped wire stretcher. He wore a navy zip-up jacket, a blue uniform shirt, and black pants with pockets everywhere. "Can you tell me your name?" he asked me.

"Yes."

He tried again. "What is your name?"

"My first name is Gwen. Right now that's all I'm sure of."

He exchanged glances with Seth. "What's the date?"

"I don't know. Is it important?"

"How do you feel?" he asked.

"Like I spent the night in a crashed plane fighting off a cougar."

He picked up my wrist and took my pulse. "You say you saw a cougar?"

"No. I fought a cougar with a fishing rod."

"I see." He lifted the blanket and peered at my shredded T-shirt. "Are you cut anywhere? You seem to have a lot of blood on you."

"Phil's blood."

"Did you say you had your fill of blood?" He paused in his probing of the scratch on my arm.

"That too. But Phil is dead."

"I see." He tucked the blanket back around me and studied my hand. "Can you feel your fingers?"

"Yes."

"Your toes?"

"Yes."

He pulled out a thermometer and popped it in my mouth, then looked at Seth. "She seems to have a lot of confusion, probably dehydrated —"

"Excuse me, but I'm standing right here." It came out, "Loose me, ba I'n nandy lite he," around the thermometer.

The EMT — his name tag said *Redwood* — removed the thermometer and studied the results. "Let's help you get onto the

316

stretcher —"

"I can walk." I straightened.

"No, you can't." Redwood picked up his bag. A pile of flesh-colored goo was on the bottom. "What's this?" He nudged the remains of my breast prosthesis with his boot.

Poor Mary Ann. Ginger, still somewhat intact, lay nearby. The cougar had taken out a lot of frustration on those pieces of silicone. I tried to smile. "I'd say it's the definitive answer to 'Which one did you like better, Ginger or Mary Ann?' "

Redwood glanced at Seth. "She needs medical help right away."

"Wait." I turned to the fuselage. "I need to get something."

"I'll get it for you," Redwood said.

"There's a small pile of items on the seat. And a pistol."

The man raised his eyebrows but retrieved the pitiful reminders of my parents — the lipstick tube, compact, purse frame, chain, and pistol. He held them out for me to check.

"Okay." I reached for them, but Seth shook his head. "I'll take them for now." He grabbed the pistol and checked to see if it was loaded, then placed all the items in his pockets.

A blast of cold wind had the men eyeing the sky. Redwood took my arm. "Let's get going." Another gust of wind shook the trees. The sun dropped behind slate-gray clouds.

I wanted to protest, but before I could get the words out, I was placed unceremoniously on the wire stretcher and surrounded with blankets. The stretcher was hard, but this was the warmest I'd been in over sixteen hours.

Redwood and Seth strapped me in and lifted. At least they didn't grunt at the weight. As we crossed to the helicopter, Seth asked about Phil. I gave him the *Reader's Digest* condensed version. He raised his eyebrows when I told him it was murder, but only asked, "Can you direct us to the outfitter's body?"

"I think so." The rotors were still turning on the helicopter, so I raised my voice to be heard over the din. "Head straight east. You should pass over a ravine, then a ridge, then a second gulch with a small stream. He's beside the stream."

Seth nodded understanding. We reached the helicopter and my stretcher was strapped into place.

"I am capable of sitting in a seat," I tried pointing out.

"This is your seat." Redwood tugged a final strap in place. Seth sat in the copilot's seat while the technician sat next to me. I hoped they'd reverse their seating.

The pilot gave a thumbs-up to Seth, then spoke into the radio. "Dispatch, this is fifty Romeo, we are airborne, en route to St. Joseph's ER in Lewiston with the patient plus two onboard, ETA thirty-five minutes. Please advise St. Joseph's of our ETA status." We took off with a stomach-plummeting swoop.

The noise made conversation impossible. We rose, dropped, and swerved across the sky. I closed my eyes after one particularly big bump. When I opened them again, we weren't moving. The door opened next to me and several orderlies unstrapped my stretcher from the helicopter and placed me, still in the stretcher, on a gurney. When we arrived at the hospital, the nurses moved me off the stretcher to an ER room containing a slightly less uncomfortable bed.

Immediately I was questioned, stripped of my bloody T-shirt, and given an ugly blue paper gown. Then for the next few hours I was prodded, scrubbed, stitched, bandaged, drained of my blood, started on an IV, given chicken soup, and left alone in a cubicle for extended time periods. I dozed at first, waking up every time a nurse or doctor remembered I was there. After the last temperature check, sleep no longer seemed so attractive. I thought of my mom's tube of lipstick. While Mom was severely injured, waiting for help, what had she written? What desperate message had she left? But the rescue had come too late, the message never received.

"Mom," I said out loud, my voice a shaking croak, "why can't I remember your face? Why couldn't I have looked for you before now? Maybe what you wrote would have still been in the plane."

Maybe not, Beth whispered. *You can't change the past, merely learn from it. Finish your season of searching and move on to mending.*

Finally a nurse unhooked me from the IV saline, removed the needle, and went over my treatment plan before leaving a small pile of discharge paperwork. Shortly, Dan Kus appeared, followed by Seth. Seth's black hair tumbled across his forehead, his face looked drawn, and his eyes were red. "The doctor said they were about to release you. LoneBear's funeral is today, so I brought Dad to be sure you got back to your place safely."

"Thank you." Aware that I still wore the

ugly paper shirt with no bra or breast forms, I kept the blanket wrapped around me.

"We've been unable to locate Phil Cicero's body." Seth finger-combed his hair back, but a chunk flopped forward again.

I wanted to brush it from his forehead. Instead I asked, "What about Phil's horses?"

"They know the area better than most outfitters," Dan said. "And Phil had tough horses."

"They're safe," Seth said. "They headed for the trailer. Officer Attao found them early this morning when we were searching for both of you. Your wallet and cell were in one of the saddlebags. I'll get them to you as soon as I see Attao. We didn't have the keys to Phil's pickup, so we sent a couple of rigs to tow his truck and haul the horse trailer."

"Good." My voice caught. I'd neatly place Phil's death in a box and tie a ribbon around it. But Phil was dead because someone wanted to kill me. I looked around for a tissue.

Dan pulled one out of the tissue box on the counter and handed it to me. Both men tactfully ignored my loud honking as I blew my nose. When I finished, Seth held up an unmarked evidence bag. "I brought you these." Inside were the few items I'd found at the crash — the compact, lipstick, purse frame, chain, and rusty revolver.

I took the bag. "Thank you."

"Someone really wanted to keep you from getting there. Any ideas?" Seth asked.

"I'm leaning toward Jacob. Counting the sniper event outside of the department and the death of LoneBear, who was mistaken for me, that makes three attempts on my life."

"I had my deputy do a follow-up on that pistol," Seth said. "Smith and Wesson model 36. Serial number places it from the early 1970s. You'll need to clean it up before it will fire. Any reason someone would be carrying it? Especially on a plane?"

"A Chief's Special." I turned the clear bag over, examining the weapon. "I thought I recognized the revolver back at the crash, but my brain was pretty scrambled." I looked at Seth. "Wasn't this the gun of choice for law enforcement at that time?"

"Some." He leaned against the wall. "Or a backup weapon because of its small size."

Reaching into the bag, I removed the chain. "Seth, this is a beaded chain. It's what I had my leather badge holder attached to. Maybe more proof that Dad was with law enforcement?"

"That would be a reasonable conclusion."

I dropped the chain into the bag, then hugged it. "I thought my parents could be . . . well, maybe terrorists or something. They gave fake names, or at least I think they did, and were checking out the dam."

"I'd say they were more likely *looking* for terrorists."

I gaped at him.

Seth's mouth twitched. "Maybe working undercover."

My dad was a cop? Or with the FBI? I wanted to pump my arms in the air. "So why would anyone think there was a terrorist ready to blow up a dam in North Central Idaho in 1984?"

"That's a question for Dad here."

We both turned to the man. He looked down and pursed his lips. "Eighty-four? I can do some research . . ."

"Wouldn't it help," Seth said, "if we had an idea of which agency your dad might have been with? I mean, FBI looks into terrorist activity. Federal marshals might have a fugitive. Other agencies could be after drug traffickers."

"So if I put it all together, I'd want to see if some law-enforcement agency was doing an undercover operation, possibly on a terrorist attack on the dam thirty-plus years ago. And that officer was killed in an accident."

"A lot of speculation," Dan said.

"Yes, but specific. Beth and I have a lot of research ahead of us."

"Well then, let's get you back to the B and B." Seth helped me to my feet.

"I'll get the car warmed up and meet you by the front door." Dan winked at Seth before leaving.

Seth wrapped his arm around me. He smelled of cedar, rain, and a hint of Old Spice.

I wanted to fold the blanket around both of us, but only if I could turn Seth into Blake. And take a shower. And wash my hair. And put on makeup. A little perfume. Maybe change into . . .

I clutched the blanket over my paper clothing and enjoyed the feeling of a warm arm around my waist. We slowly made our way to the lobby.

Why am I snuggling up with Seth? The words rose unbidden to my brain. *He betrayed me to my boss.* I stiffened. "I can walk from here."

"What's the matter?"

"Let's just say I miss my badge. And my job. Thanks to you."

Seth's arm stiffened but he didn't let go.

"I told you I argued with him. He wouldn't listen. I had no choice."

"There's always a choice." A brick formed in my stomach.

Seth turned so I was facing him, holding on to my arms. "Your boss, Commander James, asked about your performance. He wanted to know only about the tasks I'd assigned you. I was honest. He didn't ask about your working a different angle, or your skills as an investigator, or your devotion to your craft." His brows were drawn together, his eyes searching my face.

My chest tightened and stomach churned.

"Come on, Gwen, give me a chance. You were going to connect the death of your parents to the present case. You haven't finished that yet. I didn't mean to get you fired."

I wanted to believe him. *Everyone lies to me.*

Not everyone, Beth murmured. *I've never lied to you. Or Dave. Nor has Aynslee.*

Not now, Beth! Dropping my head, I studied my tightly clenched fists. *Time.* I needed time to process all this.

Seth let go of my arms.

All I had to do was turn and walk away, head high, in solitary pride, but my legs had a mind of their own. I stumbled, tripped, and fell against the wall.

Pride went before that fall, Beth muttered.

Without saying a word, Seth found a wheelchair and placed me in the seat, then propelled me outside to where Dan had a large, silver Sequoia SUV waiting. After helping me in, he paused, his face inches from mine. "Connect the dots, Gwen."

CHAPTER THIRTY-FIVE

"Gwen!" Beth's hair was mussed and her face flushed as she rushed from her bedroom and hugged me. Winston flew from my room and crashed into me. If Dan hadn't been beside me, I would have gone flying. He caught my arm and kept me on my feet.

"Steady, Winston. Good boy." The dog continued to dance around me, mouth wide open in a massive doggy grin. The game room had been returned to a respectable level of tidiness, all traces of fingerprint powder and tossed papers gone. Beth had moved the foam board with the map and trail of Jacob's destruction from my room to the easel.

"I was so worried when you didn't return!" Beth took a chair next to me. "Last night Eric, Lila, and I waited for you at dinner, then when you didn't show up or phone, I had Eric call Chief Kus. I think, if anything, he was more worried than I was."

Dan helped me to a seat, then took one himself. "Because of LoneBear's funeral today, the department will be pretty short-handed. Here's my number." He took out a card and wrote on it. "Call me if you need anything." He slid the card over, then patted me on the shoulder. "Try to stay out of trouble. I'll check in on you later." He left.

I could see Beth was gearing up for another barrage of questions. I held up my hand. "Let me get a shower and into clean clothes. Then I'll answer all your questions."

Forty-five minutes and two aspirins later, I felt human. I'd put on my remaining prosthetics — Laverne and Shirley — beige sweats, and a cotton paprika-red sweater. Beth was sipping tea when I entered the game room.

"Lila brought us tea and Eric's baklava." She indicated a tray loaded with sweets and a teapot.

Both sounded outstanding and I wasted no time in helping myself. "I can't believe he felt well enough to cook after the bang on the head."

"I heard him going downstairs to cook at the crack of dawn."

I grunted.

"I meant to mention it before," Beth said,

"but Chief Kus forwarded me the crime-scene photos while you were still working on the Sinopa case. I printed them out again." She tapped a file. "I also did some work on trying to find your parents. About all I managed to do was collect some wanted flyers from that year, but the printouts are in this file."

"Thanks, Beth." I told her about Phil, the cougar, and my rescue. Placing the clear bag with all that remained of my parents' possessions on the table, I pulled out the pistol. The lipstick followed. "I think my mom survived the crash. At least for a little bit of time. The lipstick is broken off and dirty, as if she wrote with it. I believe she left a message."

My mouth tasted sour. I got up and paced. "It was long gone before I got there." I looked at my friend. "That's it, isn't it? I've kept my head in the sand my whole life. I left Jacob, an innocent four-year-old, with an abusive mother, not seeing the abuse. I didn't even bother to check out what happened to Holly that day, why all the blood. I just ran —"

"You were only fourteen!"

"If I'd stayed and found out she wasn't hurt, I could have asked her about my folks before her mind was gone." My stomach twisted.

"But if Holly lied to you for all those years about your parents' fate, why would she ever tell you the truth?"

I picked up a pencil from the table and twirled it in my hand. "That's *my* MO. Take the easy way out. Don't get to the bottom of the problem. That's why my husband divorced me. That's why my teenage daughter is alienated from me. If any man shows interest in me, like Blake, I don't have time —"

"Are you quite done?"

I gaped at my friend. "Um . . ."

"Shoulda-woulda-coulda. You're one big pity party today." Beth's face was flushed. "Yeah, you got handed a raw deal when your folks died, but you lived. You weren't a perfect teenager, surprise surprise, because you didn't notice child abuse. Guess what, Sherlock, professionals sometimes miss abuse. You ran when you saw evidence of murder because you'd been told your whole life to run. You put your past into a box and didn't open it for over thirty years." She stood and glared at me. "But you're looking now. We have work to do and no time to indulge in your meltdown!" She pointed at the foam board and map.

Slowly I sank to my chair. "Where did that come from? You sounded like —"

"You." If possible, Beth's face got even more crimson. "I just imagined what you would say to me if I were talking like that. You're rubbing off on me."

"But is that a good thing?"

"It worked, didn't it? I've told you this before. Sufficient for the day is its own trouble."

Silence stretched between us as I let her words sink in. "The last thing Seth said before heading to LoneBear's funeral was for me to connect the dots." I looked at my friend.

"We can't change the past, but we can learn from it. Jacob isn't going to stop until you're dead."

"Which I don't intend on becoming." I picked up another pencil. "Okay, so we'll connect those dots." I pulled out my sketchpad with all my notes and opened it to the first page. Under *Known* I read *recognized Two Rivers house, locations where we moved and when (roughly every year), Jacob, Holly admitted to state mental hospital, plane crash, John and Mary Smith, Holly guest at Two Rivers house, left suitcase, Lamb Chop puppet, giving child cold remedy, later raped? — Jacob result, in mental hospital for at least ten years, my drawing books damaged, need court order to process.*

Under *Unknown* I read *Why taken? What happened to Holly and Jacob after I left? Any connection with me and current homicide? When Holly admitted to mental hospital? Parents' real names? What happened to bodies after recovered? Why in plane in first place? Was I left with sitter because I had a cold? When the plane was reported missing, did Holly see it as a chance to abduct me? Why fly over dam?*

I opened a new page of the sketchpad and listed what I needed to learn about my parents.

1. Was my dad with a law-enforcement agency?
2. If so, which one?
3. Undercover for that agency?
4. Who or what were they investigating?
5. Death should be noted on that agency's honor roll/memorial.

"I think I've found some connections." Suddenly hungry, I took a bite of baklava. Heavenly. "For now, we'll ignore who my folks were and what they were doing prior

to the crash." I circled *What happened to
Jacob?*

CHAPTER THIRTY-SIX

I stepped over to the foam board. "Now we need to build the case. If we can prove that my research into my past wasn't some kind of dereliction of duty . . ."

"You'll get your job back!"

"Well, maybe." I shrugged, then touched the pin in Lapwai with the current date. "I had time to think about how Jacob could recognize me after all these years."

Beth nodded. "So did I."

"You go first." I sat beside her at the table.

Beth had sorted all her notes, placed pale-lavender Post-it notes on some, and somehow found purple floral file folders. She pulled one out. "Jacob would have no way of knowing if you changed your name or what you'd look like. He'd have to wait until you went looking for some piece of your history."

"That's what I thought too."

She held up a list. "We identified and I

marked on that map seven children he potentially took and presumably murdered over the past eight years."

"Right." I tapped my pencil on the table. "He wanted to draw my attention, but not the attention of law enforcement. He abducted kids from places where we'd lived, just in case I'd moved to one of them." I stared at the map. "But I didn't bite."

"He must have moved on to phase two, the letters to the editor in Holly's name." Beth opened a file. "If the similarity between the child abductions and murders didn't get your attention, he thought eventually you'd look into your history and search for Holly."

"Wait." I stopped tapping and grabbed the file. "Look. The last letter was over a year ago."

"Right. I told you that."

I stood and taped the last letter to the editor to the board.

"Then what did you just figure out?"

"What if he assumed his traps weren't working — the letters and the murders staged to resemble the story Holly told me about my parents. He decided that I *wasn't* going to return. He gives up writing the letters, but the murders fulfill his needs — his fantasy."

"Okaaaay. I'm not sure where you're going with this."

"Stay with me, Beth. Just as he concluded he'd never identify me, I showed up and somehow gave myself away as the Gwen who'd betrayed him so much earlier. His trap has sprung. I'm here. Instead of hiding, he provides the body of an earlier victim."

"Why not just murder Beatrice and lead you to her?"

"Then we wouldn't have looked at the past, looked for the pattern of murder and abduction."

She nodded. "He goes back to plan A. He now wants to let you know it's him. He tries to abduct you —"

"But he gets Kelli LoneBear instead." I tried not to think of her body lying in that field. "He's frustrated. Angry. No more subtlety. He tries to shoot me in the police parking lot, gets into our room here, and later attacks Eric, then, out in the wilderness, kills Phil Cicero."

"And almost kills you with that cougar."

I grinned at her. "According to Dan Kus, the cougar was to be my spirit guide. Apparently if I wear a symbol of that spirit throughout my life, nothing will harm me."

"Seems to me you're already doing that."

She pointed to the cross I wore around my neck.

"So I am." I touched the cross.

"So." Beth tugged the drawing I'd done of the four-year-old Jacob. "Why don't you age-progress this drawing to what Jacob might look like today?"

"I could, but the drawing is from memory, not a photograph like we usually use, so it will be a guess at best."

"You've told me often enough that a drawing may do more than eliminate those faces that aren't similar."

"I *am* rubbing off on you. And I still don't know if that's a good thing." Beth had brought my old light box with the rest of the supplies. I found it in my room and brought it to the table in the game room. Taping the sketch to the light box, I then placed a clean sheet of bristol paper over the top. I sketched the top of the head down through the eyes, then slid the paper down to lengthen the bottom part of the face. I removed the top drawing and set it on my drawing board. A child's eyes are wide set with large irises. I increased the white around the eyes as well as enlarged the medial canthus — the inside corner of the eye. Thicker eyebrows and more depth to the eyes came next. After broadening the nose to bring it to adult size, I added more shading to enlarge the sides. The lip shape remained the same but would widen as the lips stretched over adult teeth. I increased the size of the mandible, keeping the shape similar to the child's jaw. Leaving the hair shaggy over the forehead meant I didn't have to figure out his forehead shape.

"Done." I showed her the drawing.

"Your sketches look more like portraits." She took the drawing from me. "As you said before, a portrait of vengeance."

Someone softly knocked at the door.

Winston sauntered over and sat in front of it. Beth stood and opened the door.

Eric smiled. "I'm sorry to interrupt you."

"No problem," I said. "How's the head?"

"Healing." He wasn't wearing the bandage now. His blond hair was shaved on one side, and a three-inch purple line rose horizontally from his temple with a neat row of black stitches.

I winced.

"Lila and I are glad you made it back safely. Beth here was quite distraught when you missed dinner."

"I'm so sorry about that."

Lila joined him in the doorway. "Did you ask them yet?"

"Since you missed dinner with us last

night," he said, "we'd like to try it again tonight."

"Are you sure?"

They both nodded. "Everyone's checked out so we have the place to ourselves. We'd like the company."

"In that case, that sounds great," I said.

Lila glanced at the table strewn with papers and drawing supplies. "Oh! Is that one of your sketches? Is that the man who took the little girl?"

"It's an age progression, and yes, I think he's the one responsible." I held up the drawing so they could see.

"He looks familiar," Eric said slowly.

Beth's eyes widened. "Was he the person who assaulted you?"

"I didn't see who hit me. He was behind me."

"Can you think of where you might have seen him?" Beth said. "Were you at the Easter egg hunt?"

I frowned at her leading question, but no one seemed to notice.

"No." Eric scratched his chin. "Maybe . . . maybe it was someone who came to the door selling something?"

I thought about the composite I'd done of the man standing at the Sinopas' door the night before their deaths. Both drawings had dark hair and were about the same age.

"Let me think about it," Eric said. "Dinner at seven in the parlor." The couple left, closing the door behind them.

I looked at my sketch of the adult Jacob. "Beth, Eric's right. He does look familiar. We need to compare this to everyone I've met since coming to the Clearwater valley. There's no doubt I've already met him."

CHAPTER THIRTY-SEVEN

While I made a list of every place I'd visited and people I'd seen, Winston stood, stretched, then headed to the door.

"I'll take him out." Beth picked up his leash.

"Before you go, do we have a different color pin? And maybe an enlarged map of the Clearwater drainage?"

"Sure." She went to her room, returning with black pins and a folded map, then handed them to me. "Be right back."

After she left with the dog, I opened the smaller map and mounted it on part of the foam board. I jabbed a black pin in Kamiah and one in Orofino. Another set of pins went into the casino and Lapwai. On the top of the board I taped the age-progressed drawing. Picking up a final pin, I looked at the map, then picked up the business card Dan Kus left and called him. He answered immediately.

"Hi, Dan, Gwen here. I have a question for you. Thomas Wolf, the young man you work with at the center . . . What do you know about him?"

"Why do you ask?"

"Well . . . ah, you seem to know a lot about his background, his parents . . ."

"And if you remember" — Dan's voice was serious — "I also told you to steer clear of his dad, Nick Wolf."

"I plan on it. But —"

Dan's sigh came clearly over the receiver. "Nick, Lorraine, and I go way back. Nick's been in a lot of trouble with the law, though he's doing well now. He was very active with the American Indian Movement and paid dearly for his activism. I took Thomas under my wing when he was in his teens. Troubled kid, but coming around. I didn't think he would make it."

"Oh? Was he sick or . . . ?"

"Foster child. The Wolfs were foster parents."

I chatted further before disconnecting. Taking the black pin I still held in my hand, I jabbed it into the tiny town of Spalding.

Beth and Winston returned. "Beautiful afternoon. You should smell all the flowers."

"I'm sure all of Eric and Lila's flowers now smell of Winston pee."

"Winston only watered the trees," Beth said righteously. "And one tire on my car." She took off his leash and finished placing and looping yarn on the cases. "What are the black pins for?"

"Each pin represents someone I met who fits Jacob's profile. We know what made him start, what he's done, where he's been. Now we need to figure out who he is."

"Do me a favor. Draw each suspect." Beth handed me a sketchpad. "We may not want to look at the faces of the missing children, but don't we want to look for him? Plus, how many detectives can draw like you?"

"More than you think," I muttered, taking a seat. "And all of them will be lining up for my job if I can't make this work."

"You'll convince everyone."

"Okay then, I'll do a quick sketch, then we'll go through the likelihood of him being Jacob. Of course, we could be totally off base and it could be someone not on our radar."

"Naaah." Beth took a piece of baklava. I was pretty sure it was her third or fourth slice. How she kept her minus-zero clothing size was beyond me.

"By any chance do you have a tapeworm?" I asked.

"What?"

"Never mind. We want to look at males in their midtwenties, dark hair and eyes, overhanging eyelids, slightly fuller mouth, medium skin tone. Maybe rounder face or with pronounced cheekbones."

"Got it."

I sketched a face. "The first person I met when I reached the Clearwater valley that fits the description was Officer Attao with the Nez Perce Tribal Police. He was at the Sinopas' murder scene, LoneBear's dump site, supposedly found Phil's horses, and was at the site where they found the child's body. He was the first officer on the scene when the sniper attacked in the parking lot of the police station. Come to think of it, the shooting stopped before he arrived and didn't resume."

"He looks like your sketch. Who better than a police officer to keep a watch for you and know how to get away with murder?"

I wrote *Attao* under the sketch. "He's definitely on the short list. Next is Peter Otskai, assistant manager of the hotel and casino." I drew his face with a few deft lines. "He could easily have planted the notes trying to throw off the investigation. He knew I was staying at the B and B, and you took a photo of him at LoneBear's murder site. He lied to me during an interview. He also claimed to keep close watch over people coming and going at the hotel." Otskai's name went under his drawing.

"He has a rounder face, but otherwise looks like your drawing. So two possibles." Concentrating hard, I developed a rough sketch of Randy Wait. "Randy here" — I stood and attached his sketch to the board — "was the witness who lied to me in Kamiah. It's not unusual for some killers to want to insert themselves into the investigation. In a sense, he called me, so I can't exclude him, but . . ."

Beth nodded. "He looks a bit young, and we haven't seen him at any other place."

I sketched another face. "What about this?" I held up the finished drawing.

"I've never seen him."

"Jay Pender. Holly's nurse. Holly called him Jacob, and he was at the hospital when LoneBear was taken."

Beth took the drawing from me and studied it. "If someone was waiting for you to show up, what better place than near Holly?" She attached the sketch to the board. "Is that the lineup?"

"One more. Thomas Wolf, the guy who works with Dan Kus at the museum. Dan said he talked to Thomas about Phil Cicero as an outfitter for me. He knew exactly where I was going, and, through Dan, would have known of my arrival here in Lewiston long before I met him." I swiftly drew in his features.

"Didn't I hear about parents —"

"He's a foster child." I finished the thumbnail and handed it to Beth. She taped it to the board, now quite crowded with images.

I stood and looked at each image, comparing it to the age-progressed drawing of Jacob.

A clatter of dishes, the clinking of silverware, and the smell of baking cheese and bread foreshadowed the call to dinner. Winston stood and moved expectantly to the door leading to the parlor. "Let's get you some kibble so we can eat in peace." I filled his food dish and added fresh water to his bowl.

"I'm starving. Let's not wait." Beth opened the game room door. "Oh! You startled me."

Lila stood in the hall with arm raised about to knock. "And *you* startled *me*. Dinner's ready." She blinked at the foam board covered with maps, drawings, and case information.

"Looks like you're making progress." She turned and strolled to the parlor. After closing the door to the game room behind us,

Beth and I followed.

Tapered candles in silver holders rested on either side of a bowl of pink tea roses. The round oak table sitting in front of the carved fireplace was covered with a white linen tablecloth. The tossed green salads were already on the table. A small fire crackled in the fireplace.

"This is exquisite." Beth lifted a white bread plate painted with pink roses.

"The bone china was Eric's grandmother's." Lila touched a dinner plate. "Spode Billingsley Rose. As you can imagine, he doesn't use them for the regular guests. Please, have a seat."

We sat at the indicated places. Night had fallen and the Victorian parlor was transformed by candlelight. *I should have changed clothes.* I felt totally underdressed in my beige cotton sweats and sweater.

Eric entered with a plate of sliced bread, placed it on the table, and joined us. "Please enjoy." He passed the bread. "What have you two been working on all day?"

I took a slice. "Well —"

"I think we're closing in on the killer." Beth took a bite of salad. "Yum, this is delicious."

I tried to get her attention to let her know

not to talk about the case, but she was on a roll.

"Gwen's narrowed the field to five suspects. Now we just have to figure out the right one and get him to tell us where he has Beatrice." She glanced at me, then ducked her head and concentrated on her salad.

"That's easy," Eric said. "We'll set an irresistible trap for him."

CHAPTER THIRTY-EIGHT

"It's not quite that easy." I didn't want to tell Eric and Lila that I was no longer connected to any law-enforcement agency. "I don't have . . . the power to arrest someone."

"Oh." Lila speared a tomato. "I thought you were an investigator."

"Umm . . ." I gave Beth a *let's change the subject* look.

"This salad is awesome," Beth said. "What is it?"

"Warm roasted eggplant salad with bell peppers and tomatoes," Lila said. "We can help you set a trap and get the bad guy."

"Well . . . I'm not sure that's such a good idea." I smiled. "What's the main course?"

Eric nodded at a warming tray on the sideboard. "Roast duck with orange and ginger. Wild rice. Glazed onions. Why can't we help you?"

"For one thing, it's dangerous." I put

down my fork. "He's dangerous."

Eric straightened, then touched the side of his head. "I'm aware of that. I didn't buy the idea of teenagers breaking in here. The only things they touched were in the game room — your things. When he hit me, it became personal. He could have just as easily gone ahead and chopped me up with a hatchet. Lila and I have sat on the sidelines of this whole investigation unable to do anything to help."

"Please, we have to do something," Lila said. "Even if it's just narrowing down who it might be."

In the silence that followed, a clock *tick-tick-ticked* in the hall. The candlelight and fireplace created dancing shadows on the walls. The old house rustled and moaned. Beth looked at me, raised her eyebrows, and gave a small shrug. "I think we should flush out the killer." Both Lila and Eric nodded.

"We can't arrest him. It's a police matter." I gave them a sharp look. "We're not even going to get near him. He's a killer, and you were lucky, Eric. The last guy he whacked on the head he also killed."

Lila laid a hand on Eric's arm.

"All we need to do is get him to show himself," Beth said. "The police can do the rest. They will need him to tell them where

Beatrice is."

"You think she's still alive?" Lila asked.

"I do," I said. "At least I pray she is."

"Then let's go public," Lila said. "Print something in the paper, or give a television interview."

"Difficult to set up." Eric picked up the salad plates, put them on the sideboard, and served dinner. "And that would take too long. What about the Internet? Social media? YouTube?"

I kept shaking my head.

"How would we know he would see it?" Beth tasted the duck. "This is outstanding, Eric."

"Not just see it, but in a timely manner." Lila pointed with her fork.

"What if . . ." Beth bit her lip. "What if we sent a letter to the editor? Like he used to do?"

"Letter to the editor?" Eric looked from Beth to me. "I don't understand."

"It was a trap he set for me," I said slowly. Eric, Lila, and Beth gave me encouraging smiles. They were going ahead with this harebrained scheme, with or without me.

All I can do is keep them from getting hurt. Or killed. "A letter in the newspaper won't work."

"That would take too long," Beth said.

"If we could somehow e-mail our suspects . . ." Eric leaned forward.

"Do you have their e-mail addresses?" Lila asked.

"No, but . . ." Beth took a bite of dinner and slowly chewed it. We watched her. I could tell she was enjoying the attention. If I had a pencil, I would have chucked it at her head.

"What, Beth?" I asked through clenched teeth.

"I'll find their e-mails." She grinned.

"She was a researcher at Microsoft," I said to Lila and Eric. To Beth I said, "We'll use the wording from one of his letters to the editor, sign it Gwen, and add a time and place to meet."

"Where would you meet?" Beth asked.

"I have no intention of meeting him —"

"Why not?" Eric dabbed his lips with his napkin. "Wouldn't you want to say something to someone who's tried to kill you a couple of times? He tried to kill me." He touched his stitches. "I'd want to ask why."

Dinner lost its appeal. I laid down my fork. "I know why he is trying to kill me. I don't know that facing him, talking to him, will change how he sees me."

"You *know* him?" Lila's eyebrows rose.

"Knew him. It's a long story, but let's just

352

say I don't think he'll ever forgive me for what he thinks I did. Someday I'll forgive myself."

Lila opened her mouth to ask more questions, but Eric touched her arm. "Just have him come here. We'll lock the doors — and believe me, our doors are thick."

"What if someone shows up inquiring about a room?" Lila asked.

Eric shook his head. "After the attack on me, I listed us as having no vacancies. No one is booked into here until next week."

"That's true," Lila said slowly. "We do have the place to ourselves. And we can have someone waiting with a phone to call the police. Actually, we can call the police the minute he pulls into the driveway. They'll be here in three minutes or less."

I sat back in my seat. "In three minutes he could hack through several of us. Or he could bring a gun and shoot us all in less than a minute."

Beth's eyes were wide open. "He's used a number of different weapons in the past."

"You mean he's killed people other than the Sinopas?" Lila put a hand over her mouth.

I counted on my fingers. "At least eleven, not counting the children."

"I don't know, Eric." Lila looked at him.

"He knows you're here." Eric stood. "Unless you leave, he could come back at any time and finish the job he started." He touched his stitches again. "Unless you leave," he repeated, "none of us are safe."

"So give up and run, wait for him to return, or bring him here on our terms where we call all the shots." Eric's logic made a strange kind of sense. "Okay, but we're calling the police first. We're not going to wait until he shows up."

"What if he doesn't appear?" Eric asked.

"He will," I said grimly.

We cleared the dinner dishes and worked out the details of our plan. Beth would find the e-mail addresses of the five men. I would work on the wording of the message. Lila would call the Lewiston police. Once the message was sent, Lila would wait upstairs on the third floor in the middle bedroom, which had the best view of the parking lot. She'd have a phone to keep the police informed. Beth would be in the corner bedroom with binoculars to watch for his arrival and see if there was anyone, meaning Beatrice, in the car. Eric would park our car out of sight so when the suspect arrived looking for me, Eric could simply call through the door and say they were closed and we'd checked out. I would stay out of sight and hang out with Winston.

After giving Eric the keys to her car, Beth and I headed to the game room to work. Winston greeted me, then collapsed on the floor with a sigh.

Shortly after Beth announced she'd succeeded in finding the e-mail addresses, Eric tapped on the door. "Your car's out of sight behind the house. I'm checking with Lila."

Constructing the e-mail message, I copied one of Holly's letters to the editor word for word. At the end I wrote, "8:00 PM Two Rivers B and B. A life for a life. Save the child. Trade her for me. Gwen."

Another knock on the door. "Lila got hold of the police. It took her a few minutes to explain the situation, but they said they'd send a patrol over to keep an eye out. He'll park out of sight. I don't think they believed her, but she reminded them of the attack on me."

"Thank you." Beth clicked on her computer for a few more seconds, then looked up. "Done."

Did I just do the dumbest thing in the world?

CHAPTER THIRTY-NINE

"Beth, I'm having second thoughts."

Beth paused in unpacking her binoculars. "I thought you liked the plan. You agreed to it."

"Something's not right."

"Nothing's right. You counted eleven people dead plus the kids. He has to be stopped."

"Let me use your phone and at least call Seth. And double check with the Lewiston police."

She put her hands on her hips. "Where's your cell?"

I snorted. "Possibly with one of the suspects, Officer Attao. I put it in the saddlebag when I went out with Phil to the crash site."

"My phone is missing, remember? It's been missing since the break-in."

My neck muscles tightened. "What about the house phone?"

"Do you have a phone in your room? I

don't. And I've not seen a phone anywhere in the place."

Now the tiny hairs on my arms stood on end. "Check your computer and see if you're online."

She peered at the screen. "Nope, but remember, the Internet is spotty here."

My mouth dried. Slowly I looked at the age-progression drawing mounted on the foam board. Picking up a kneaded eraser, I approached the sketch, then tapped the iris, lifting out graphite. The eyes were now lighter in color. I stepped away and put my hand up, blocking the dark hair over the forehead.

My hand trembled. Turning to the table, I opened the file on the Sinopa murders. The autopsy photos Beth had reprinted were on the bottom. I pulled out the one with the head wound on Adam Sinopa. The exact wound was on Eric's head, but going in a different direction, as if struck from a different angle. I thought about Eric's comment at dinner: *When he hit me, it became personal. He could have just as easily gone ahead and chopped me up with a hatchet.* The police hadn't revealed that a hatchet had been used on the Sinopas.

"Do me a huge favor, Beth. Stay here for a few minutes." I worked to control my voice. "And lock this behind me."

Beth's face drained of blood. "Why? Where are you going?"

"I need to find Lila. She has a phone." Listening carefully at the door, I could hear no sound of movement. I opened the door a crack and checked for any sign of Eric. *Or should I just call him Jacob?*

The house was eerily still, as if holding its breath, with not even the usual creaks and moans. Slipping off my shoes, I crept through the hall, then up the stairs, wincing every time the floor squeaked.

The second-floor hall had a jag in it, so I couldn't see from one end to the other. It smelled slightly of old carpeting and furniture polish. Wall sconces dimly lit the hunter-green and cranberry wallpaper. I tried the door nearest me. Locked. Moving carefully, I tried each door. All were locked. I reached the end of the hall where the back stairs were located — originally the stairs used by servants. Below was Eric's office. Taking even more care, I tiptoed up to the third floor. This hallway was far narrower, the odor of age stronger, doorways smaller, and light dimmer. One window opened to the front of the house and provided a little extra light. The doors were all locked on this level as well. Counting over, I found

the room where Lila should be. "Lila," I whispered, then tapped softly. "Lila?"

Pressing my ear against the wood, I heard no sounds. I tried one last time. "Lila?"

Downstairs, Winston started barking furiously.

Adrenaline shot through my body. I raced to the window.

A car had pulled into the lot. A man stepped out and looked around. He raised his face slightly to the front of the B and B.

Jay Pender, Holly's physical therapist.

Did I just make a mistake? No. I couldn't have.

Running to the end of the hall nearest our rooms, I stopped at the top of the stairs.

The doorbell rang.

Sliding my foot down gently to prevent the old wood from creaking, I moved down the steps.

On the first floor, someone strolled into the hall and to the door.

My knuckles turned white. My nails dug into the bannister.

"Can I help you?" Eric's voice carried clearly.

"Hi, I'm Jay Pender. I'm looking for Gwen Marcey. I believe she's a guest here."

"Come in."

The air shifted, and the light scents of

fresh flowers and old house drifted upward. *Oh no!*

The door closed, then I heard a scuffle, ending with a *thud.*

Someone rapped on wood, followed by a murmur of voices.

Creeping down a few more steps, I almost reached the landing above the great hall. My only advantage at this point was that Eric didn't know my location.

A door opened and closed. More quiet talking.

A scream.

I froze and clutched the bannister with white knuckles. *Look? Hide? Return to another floor?*

"You can come on down, Gwen." Eric's voice was calm.

I turned the corner and came into view of the great hall.

The doors to the game room were closed. Winston, on the other side, resumed barking and began digging at the carved surface. Beth was leaning against the entrance to the parlor, clutching the wall as if it were the only thing keeping her upright. Her head was turned toward the front door. Jay Pender lay unconscious on the floor, blood seeping from a wound on his head.

"Move into the parlor." Eric's voice came

from the shadows. Beth didn't move. "Move or she's dead." Eric stepped into the light, a large carving knife at Lila's throat. The woman's eyes were closed, her lips moving as if in prayer. Tears trickled down her cheeks. "That goes for you, too, Gwen." He looked directly at me, his eyes onyx-black. The hate radiating from his gaze was almost physical.

I clutched the railing, afraid I'd fall if I let go. I could run down the stairs, get to the door to let Winston out . . . I measured the distance. *I'd never make it in time. He'd slice Lila's throat and stab my dog before I could run for help.*

"Don't even think about it, Gwen." He jerked his head toward the parlor, then moved to block the door to the game room. Winston, as if sensing Eric so near, redoubled his barking, then threw his weight against the door, making the paintings rattle on the wall.

One step at a time I descended the stairs, crossing to the side farthest from the man. "You were very clever, Eric. You colored your hair. Green contacts. I didn't recognize you, not at first."

"But you did."

When I reached the bottom, I backed into the parlor until I was level with Beth. "What happened?" I whispered.

"He tapped on the door and asked for you. You didn't tell me he was the one, so when I saw Pender, I thought everything was okay. He told me to leave Winston in the game room."

Beth wrapped her arms around her shoulders. "It wasn't until I closed the door behind me that I saw he had Lila."

I looked at Lila. "You didn't have a chance to call the police, did you?"

She shook her head. "Eric said he'd call."

"And I did," Eric said. "I told them you'd checked out and would contact them in a few days."

I squeezed my hands into fists. *Will they believe him? Why not?*

Eric forced Lila ahead of him into the parlor.

Beth and I backed away.

Lila's eyes were pleading.

"Jacob," I said.

The man flinched. A thin line of red appeared on Lila's neck.

The woman turned as white as a sheet. More tears streamed down her face.

"Let her go, Jacob," I said. "Let Lila and Beth go."

"I can't do that."

"But I'm the one you want. I'm the one

who left you."

Jacob's tongue darted out and licked his lips. "Yes."

I could barely hear him over the racket from Winston's assault on the door. "Please, Jacob. Let them go."

"Please." Lila's voice shook. "Please, Eric. I love you. I've always loved you."

"See, Eric," I said. "Lila loves you." *I have to make him see her as a person.* "Neither Beth nor Lila ever hurt you."

"Shut up, Gwen. I've waited a long time for you to return. I knew you were out there."

"W-what do you mean?" Lila asked.

"You silly sow," Jacob whispered in her ear. "You never asked me why I traveled so much for my 'charities.' I was baiting a trap for Gwen here."

"What about your mom, Holly?" I asked.

He winced. "I'll take care of her when I'm done with you. She was more bait."

"Jacob, please, it's me you want."

"You're right." Jacob's eyes glittered. "I didn't want to lose my cover. I wanted to get you alone so we could spend time together, but you kept leaving. But now, well, I never would have imagined this would work out so well. No one will bother us here until next week. I have all the time in the world. I can't wait to have you experience all the things my insane mother did to me." A vein pounded in his forehead. "Then I'll just disappear."

Lila tried to jerk away. I grabbed Beth and dashed to the door. With a quick slash, he drew the knife across Lila's throat, then leaped in front of us. Lila crumpled.

Beth screamed. Winston redoubled his barking.

I didn't dare look at Beth or Lila. I watched Jacob.

The man dropped the bloody knife and reached for the sideboard. I grabbed Beth and shoved her behind me.

Jacob held up the small shovel he'd used to open the attic door. "Military-issue folding shovel. Nice, isn't it? Folds to nine inches and comes with a carrying case. One side is designed to be used like a hatchet. Or an ax." His smile didn't reach his eyes. "You have no idea how much pleasure I get from letting you see it. And how much joy I'll get from using it on you."

Oh, please, God. His voice made the hair on my arms stand on end. "What happened to Beatrice?" My voice was shrill. I swallowed hard.

"Don't worry about her. You'll never find her body. You'll never find any of their

364

bodies. Beatrice, Amanda, Ethyn, Olivia, Jess, or Noah. Not for a long, long time."

"Wait —"

He swung the shovel with both hands.

I dodged, but not quite enough. The razor-sharp blade sliced through my sweater. I backed away, keeping Beth behind me.

He moved forward. I quickly glanced around. Two doors opened to the room — one to the hall, the other to the office area. To reach either exit, I'd have to get past Jacob. The massive, carved fireplace was to my left. I was running out of time. And room to maneuver.

He swung again. The blade sliced across my stomach. Not deep, but enough to hurt like the dickens.

He glanced down. "Ah. I drew blood."

Beth gasped.

Risking a glance at her, I made a hand motion. She froze.

Sweat ran down my back. My heart felt like it would explode in my chest. I took a shaky step closer to the fireplace. No handy pokers.

Jacob's lip lifted off his teeth. His eyes narrowed.

I gave the hand signal for *crouch*, praying Beth remembered.

He took a quick leap forward and swung the shovel at my head. He couldn't miss.

CHAPTER FORTY

I dived to the floor. Beth dropped next to me.

The shovel passed over us, embedding in the wood fireplace mantel. Jacob cursed and tried to pull it out.

Beth and I leaped to our feet. Beth ran for the door to our rooms. I followed, but I couldn't seem to get any traction. The floor was slick with Lila's blood.

Jacob tackled me from behind.

I crashed to the floor, and my breath left me. Jacob lost his grip on my legs. Gasping for breath, I kicked at him, then got on my hands and knees, scrambling to escape.

Jacob punched me in the side.

I rolled away from him, trying desperately to breathe. Another blow landed on my ear. Sparklers erupted in my eyes. I flipped onto my back and kicked him again.

The blow pushed him away. He scooted backward, then leaped to his feet. His eyes were slits of hatred, his face a white mask. Lila's blood soaked his clothing and smeared his cheek. He looked around, his head jerking from side to side.

The knife.

We both spotted it at the same time. I crawled toward it, still trying to suck in some air.

A door banged open. A snarling bellow sounded, then a flash of white fur charged into the room.

Winston. Every hair on his back and neck stood on end. His mouth was open, lips pulled back, exposing gleaming teeth. His roar of fury filled the room.

Jacob crouched, backpedaling away from the dog, arms extended.

The full rage of Winston's 165-pound body smashed into the man. Jacob howled as Winston bit into his upper thigh. Man and dog crashed to the ground. Jacob's head snapped backward, slamming onto the floor, momentarily stunning him. Winston lost his grip on Jacob's leg. The giant dog grabbed Jacob's forearm, pulling him to a seated position.

I got to my feet and searched for the knife. It lay near Jacob. I leaped for it, missed, dodged Jacob's swinging fist.

Jacob punched Winston in the nose. The

dog let go, but just for a moment. He dived for the man's crotch.

Jacob screamed.

Spinning, I looked for something, anything to use as a weapon.

Jacob seized the knife, raising it over his head to plunge into Winston.

Vase, dishes, books, tray . . . I lifted the warming tray from the sideboard and smashed it on Jacob's head.

CHAPTER FORTY-ONE

Jacob went limp.

Winston grimly held on to the man.

It took a few moments before I finally had enough breath to speak. "It's okay, Winston." My voice was weak and shaky. "Let go. He's not going anywhere."

The dog released Jacob and came over to me.

Beth appeared in the doorway, ghost-white. "I didn't know what else to do."

"You did just right. You saved my life, or rather, Winston did. Again."

"Lila. Is she . . ."

For the first time, I looked at the motionless form. "I'm afraid so. Um . . . could you do me a favor? I'm not so steady on my feet yet. In my purse you'll find those flex-cuffs, the disposable restraints. Could you bring them to me?"

"You mean he's not dead?"

I staggered over and stared at Jacob,

unwilling to touch him to check for a pulse. "He's breathing. But I think he's going to sing soprano in the prison choir for a while."

"Good." Beth left, returning shortly with the restraints.

We quickly bound his hands and feet. I next moved to Pender, still in the hall. He was sitting cross-legged and holding his head.

"Are you okay?" I asked.

"What happened?"

"Long story." I helped him to his feet and over to the stairs. "Please stay here for a few minutes. I need to find a phone —"

The doorbell rang.

Winston raced toward the front door, growling.

"Beth, get his leash." I moved to the game room, located my dad's rusty revolver, and met Beth at the front door. "Who is it?" I called out.

"Police! Chief Kus and Officer Attao." After snapping the lead on my dog, I pulled him away and nodded for Beth to open the door.

Attao and Seth froze, staring at me. Seth finally spoke. "Gwen, please put down the gun."

I dropped it.

The men stepped in but abruptly stopped

at Winston's rumbling growl.

"He's really protective right now." I handed the leash to Beth, who wrapped it around her hand several times. "Could you take him to my room?" She nodded and led him away.

"You're hurt," Seth said.

I looked at the gash on my stomach. "Just a slight cut. Most of the blood's not mine. I have your serial killer." I pointed to the parlor.

Seth spotted Pender still sitting on the steps. "Who are you?"

"Jay Pender. Some crazy guy whacked me on the head."

Attao glanced into the parlor. "Chief. We have a homicide." Seth joined him at the doorway. "I'll call Lewiston PD," Attao said.

I wandered into the game room and sat on the sofa before my legs gave way. Beth joined me, still shaking. I covered her with the throw from the back of the sofa, then patted her shoulder.

"I can't get it out of my head," Beth whispered.

"It was an awful way to die —"

"Oh. Yes, but I don't mean that. I mean he knew their names. The children he killed. He knew their names." She covered her face with her hands. "I know now why you didn't let me say the names or put up their photos."

I rubbed her back, unable to think of anything to say.

In the hall, Officer Attao was on the radio calling in the homicide and asking for an ambulance for Jacob and Pender.

Still holding his head, Pender came in and sat at the table. "What is going on around here?"

"You had the misfortune to meet up with a serial killer." I sat up straighter. "Why did you come here?"

"You sent me an e-mail that made no sense, but I was reminded that you seemed to have an interest in Lucinda Greene, Holly."

"She was my . . . caretaker for about ten years."

"Well then, I'm sorry to have to tell you she died."

My hand flew to my mouth. "Dead? How? Why?"

"Pick a reason. She had a bad heart. Her mind was gone. She had stage-four lung cancer. It was only a matter of time."

Bringing my knees up to my chest, I wrapped my arms around them. *Holly is gone, and whatever secrets she had locked away in her ravaged mind are gone as well.*

"You came here to tell *me*, not . . . her son?" I nodded toward the parlor.

"Her son is the serial killer? Wow. Looks like mental disorders run in the family. I didn't know she had a son. No next of kin are noted in her records."

"No one came to visit her?" I asked.

"Not that I know of."

A heavy weight settled in my stomach. Whatever she'd done to Jacob, whatever bad decisions she'd made, she'd been good to me.

Sirens approached. Lots of sirens. Winston howled from the bedroom.

Attao stepped into the room. "Sir," he addressed Pender. "There's an ambulance here for you."

Pender started to shake his head, then winced. "Yeah, maybe I'd better get the ol' noggin checked out." He got to his feet and slowly followed Attao from the room.

The sound of slamming car doors was followed by the front door banging open and a barrage of voices. In my room, Winston barked and dug at the door.

Seth came into the room with us, pulled up a chair, and sat down. "What happened?"

I told him, working backward from my cold-cocking Jacob, Winston's rescue, Lila's

374

murder, then to our investigation. Seth listened, eyes growing wider as my story unfolded. "The foam board in my bedroom connects the dots, but right now Winston's in there, and . . ."

"Okay. There's a lot to sort out." He stood, reached out and stroked my cheek with the back of his hand.

I stiffened, then warmth flooded my face. *You're toxic to men, Gwen,* Robert's voice whispered into my brain.

No, Robert. Not toxic. Afraid.

Afraid of men? That's a laugh.

No. Afraid that love is like tissue, easily torn, irreparable when damaged. Like ours was, Robert. Like Blake.

Blake's not Robert, Beth murmured in my head. *Seth's not Robert. Give them a chance.*

I leaned slightly against Seth's hand.

Attao entered, carrying something. "That Pender guy asked me to bring you this." He handed me a bag. "Said it was one of Holly's few possessions. He thought you might want to have it."

It was a small jewelry box with a gold velvet cover and interior. I recognized it as one she'd carried from place to place as we moved. Inside were several pairs of button-shaped clip-on earrings, a rhinestone necklace with a broken clasp, and a copper pin

375

in the shape of a leaf. I remembered her wearing each of them. "Thank you."

Seth glanced at the hall. "You can't stay here. Lewiston police will be sealing this all off. I'll find you a motel room —"

Beth sat up. "I'm driving home. With Winston. Tonight."

"Oh, Beth, are you sure?" I looked at my friend's pale face. "You've had a really big shock —"

"I'll be fine, but Winston's a basket case. While he's around, no one can get near you. He's in the process of tearing through that door, and you can't crate him. He ate it. When you're ready to question me, I'll come back."

Seth studied Beth's face for a moment, glanced at the bedroom door currently under assault by the frenzied dog, then stood. "Let me talk to Lewiston PD." He left the room.

I patted Beth's arm, got up, and slipped into my room. Winston greeted me as if I'd been away for years. *Beth is right. Winston will end up with doggy PTSD if I don't get him out of this house to someplace he knows is safe.*

I sat on the floor, hugged Winston, and promised him a large steak dinner when this was over. He finally lay down and put his head in my lap. We stayed like that for a long time.

I knew before I heard the tap on the door that someone was there. Winston walked stiff-legged and sniffed, then growled. "Yes?"

"It's me, Seth. I explained the situation to the lead detective with Lewiston PD. He's letting Beth go home with your dog. She's already packed up her things and is waiting in her car."

"What about me?"

"You have a long night of questioning, then they'll get you a room somewhere else."

"Okay. Tell everyone to clear out of the game room, hall, porch, and parking lot until I get Winston loaded."

"Is that necessary?"

"My dog's on red alert. If they don't think that means anything, point out what he did to Jacob. I think they'll see the wisdom in getting out of range."

"Got it." A short time later Seth said, "All clear. Count slowly to five, then bring him out."

I wrapped Winston's leash around my hand several times, then cautiously opened the door. As promised, no one was in sight. Beth stood beside the open rear door, her car idling outside. The dog was promptly loaded and she shut the hatch behind him.

"Are you sure you're okay to drive all the way to Copper Creek?" I asked.

"I have so much adrenaline in me I could drive to Denver." She gave me a hug. "I'll return and pick you up when you're done with all the paperwork and formalities. Call me when you get a chance. And be careful." Another hug and she drove off. Winston watched me out the back of the car until he passed out of sight.

The parking lot was suddenly full of people. Someone draped a blanket around my shoulders.

Seth came over. "They want to take you to the hospital and get you checked over, photograph your injuries, and get your statement. Okay?"

I nodded.

"I did want to ask you one thing before you go. Did Jacob say anything about the location of Beatrice?" He took out a small notebook.

"He said we'll never find her body. Any of their bodies. Then he said their names — the names of the children he's killed over the years." I closed my eyes and thought of their faces lined up in the photographs Beth had spread out. I opened my eyes. "Now can you answer *me* one thing before I leave?

What made you come here, like . . . like the cavalry?"

"Officer Attao received a strange e-mail from you. He was going to return your cell phone anyway, but he thought something was wrong. He called me and I agreed."

A slender woman in slacks and a blazer walked up. "Gwen Marcey? I'm Detective Perez. Are you ready to go to the hospital?" She didn't wait for an answer but pointed to a gray sedan.

Shortly we arrived at the emergency room, and once again I found myself on a hard bed wearing a paper shirt and blanket. After Detective Perez photographed the various bruises and cuts Jacob had inflicted, she placed my sliced sweater into evidence. The same doctor and nurses tut-tutted at my injuries and patched my cuts.

"I'd like for you to come down to the station and give us a statement of the events of the evening," Detective Perez said.

"Can we go by way of the bed-and-breakfast?" I asked. "I need to grab something to wear."

"I have a clean sweatshirt at the station."

I agreed to the compromise. Detective Perez drove me to the Lewiston Police Department, where she handed me an Orofino Maniacs sweatshirt. At my raised eyebrows, she shrugged. "The name of the high school team. The school overlooks the state mental hospital. Political correctness isn't a virtue in this part of Idaho."

After pulling on the sweatshirt, she led me to an interview room. With another detective present, I told her the events of the evening, backtracking through our investigation, the deaths of Phil Cicero and Lone-Bear, and my car still in the river. I finished up the interview somewhere on the far side of four in the morning with the story of my search for Holly and my parents.

The two detectives looked as exhausted as I felt. They stepped out of the small interview room, and I fell asleep with my head on the table.

"Gwen?"

A slight shaking of my shoulder pulled me out of my stupor. I was pretty sure I'd drooled on the table. "Huh?"

"We're taking you to a motel for the night." Detective Perez yawned.

I glanced at my watch. "It's six a.m."

"Yeah, well . . ."

Trailing behind her, I came out of the station into the early-morning light. "McDonald's?" she asked.

"Bed."

The motel was part of a generic budget

chain, the room clean and bland. I hung a Do Not Disturb sign on the door and turned to the bed. The detective said something just before she left, but my head had already hit the pillow.

Opening my eyes, I stared at an unfamiliar ceiling. It took a few moments to try to work out where I was. *Jacob. Blood. Beth left. Winston's attack.*

I sat bolt upright, wide awake.

The bedside alarm said four o'clock. Light peeking through the drapes told me it was afternoon. I was still wearing a crumpled Orofino Maniacs sweatshirt and beige cotton sweats spattered with Lila's blood. Standing, I found the lilliputian coffee machine and fake white stuff calling itself creamer. If Detective Perez had a contact number, she hadn't left it. No cell, purse, or transportation.

A call to the front desk got me a comb, a small container of deodorant, a toothbrush, and toothpaste. They regretted to inform me that clean underwear wasn't part of guest services.

After a shower and cup of coffee, my stomach admitted I was starving. I called the front desk again and they said I could order food from the restaurant and it would go on the room bill.

The restaurant menu, in the top drawer of the desk, featured comfort food. I ordered the biggest comfort plate on the menu — chicken-fried steak, mashed potatoes, a mess of gravy, and grits — a dish I'd grown fond of while in Kentucky. I couldn't decide between a slice of lemon meringue pie or a brownie. I ordered both.

The meal was delivered by a waitress who winked at me for the two desserts. I signed for an extra-large tip. *Expense accounts are lovely.*

Beth mentally scolded me. *Gwen, you'll clog your arteries and gain weight because you never exercise.*

"How can you say that, Beth?" I took a bite of steak slathered with mashed potatoes and gravy. "Grits are corn, and corn is a vegetable."

You told me grits were an excuse for butter, salt, and pepper.

"Well, that's true . . ."

And two desserts?

"Excuse me? *Lemon* meringue pie? Plus, everyone knows chocolate is good for you. And fighting bad guys constitutes exercise." My impeccable logic silenced my friend.

Partway into the meal, my scratches hurt, my eyes drooped, and the fork became exceptionally heavy. The unmade bed beckoned for a quick nap. This time I undressed before crawling between the sheets.

When I opened my eyes, it was still daylight. I glanced at the alarm to see how long I had dozed. The digital clock read eleven thirty.

Checking my watch, it said the same. I stood and peeked out the blinds. *Did I really just sleep for . . .* I worked out the time in my brain. *Seventeen hours straight.*

No wonder I felt stiff, sore, and starving. And smelled like a barnyard.

A light flashed on the phone. Had I actually slept through a ringing phone? In tiny type I found an explanation for how to retrieve messages. Seth's voice came on the line. "Hi, Gwen, things are crazy here. I'm sending Dad over to take care of you. I just got a call from some folks in Lenore. They think there's a possibility of . . . Well, let's just say we'll be doing some digging. I'll probably be there until really late. Law enforcement's spread pretty thin right now, so I won't see you for a bit. I'll . . . um . . . call you. Bye."

"Bye, Seth." I pictured his deep sepia eyes, smooth skin, full lips . . . I reached up to fluff my hair. The smell reminded me of my original goal. A shower.

A shower took care of the stench, but I still had to wear clothes I would rather have burned. Last night's leftovers were disgusting, and the brownie had turned to stone. I was considering trying to reconstitute it with coffee when someone knocked on the door. I peeked, then opened it to Dan Kus. "Greetings." He held up a Starbucks cup.

"I think I love you." I opened the door wider and took the steaming cup.

"Have you turned on the news?" He entered.

"No. I can't believe I've been out of it for almost two days."

"I suspect you needed time to rest and recover."

"So it would seem." I eyeballed the brownie again.

"To catch you up, let's just say your capture of Jacob Greene has stirred up a beehive of activity in the law-enforcement community. Everyone wants to talk to you, but Seth said to keep you hidden for now. I'm charged with making sure you've eaten a real meal." He glanced at the tray of congealed food, then stepped back and gave me a head-to-toe evaluation. "I see we need to get you some proper clothing."

"Seth left word you were coming over. Food first? I'm starving."

384

"Barbecue?"

"Perfect."

Dan drove me to the tiny town of Culde-sac, just south of Lapwai. The day was warm, the air clean, and traffic nonexistent. We pulled up to a log building where the fragrance of smoky barbecue had my mouth watering. Opening the door set off a loud cowbell.

I winced, but none of the diners even raised their heads from conversation. The waitress didn't blink at my Orofino Maniacs sweatshirt and bloody pants.

Over a massive meal, Dan caught me up on what had happened since I'd left Two Rivers B and B two nights before. "I suppose there's no way of breaking this to you easily. Jacob Greene is dead."

CHAPTER FORTY-TWO

"Oh no!" I put down my fork. "How?"

"He was unconscious in the emergency room, or so they thought. Somehow he got hold of a sharp instrument and . . ." Dan shrugged.

"But that means . . . that means they won't know where to look for the children's bodies."

"According to Seth, they're already doing soil samples off the one body to see if they can at least pinpoint the region. They're still following up on active leads." The cell phone Dan had placed on the table vibrated. He picked it up.

"Yes." He listened for a few minutes. "Okay. We're almost done." After hanging up, he looked at me. "Lewiston PD said you can retrieve your things at the bed-and-breakfast. They want you to stay at the motel until they've had a chance to think of more questions."

"Okay. I'm done eating."

"Why don't you take the rest of that with you." Dan pointed at my still-loaded plate.

Though the idea of food wasn't all that appealing at the moment, I agreed. Something tickled the back of my brain, but when I focused on it, all I could think about was the duck Eric had fed us.

I'd never eat duck again.

We drove to the Two Rivers B and B. The parking lot was full of police vehicles, and an officer was near the front recording who entered and exited. Television trucks with mounted satellite-dish antennas lined the street. The coppery stench of old blood permeated the hall and game room.

An officer spotted Dan and waved. *"Ta'c halaxp."*

"Ta'c halaxp." Dan waved back. "Greetings to you too."

"Dan, it will take me a few minutes to pack up. Go ahead and talk with your friend."

Dan smiled and wandered over to chat.

The foam board showing Jacob's killing rampage was missing, but all my notes and drawing supplies were still on the table in the game room. I closed the door to my bedroom and showered again, then changed into cream slacks, a collarless matching blouse, and a peach-colored merino-wool sweater. Adding a matching cream-and-peach scarf, I felt ready to take on the world — or at least appear in public without finding my picture on the "People of Walmart" page. I found a plastic bag and folded Detective Perez's sweatshirt into it.

Beatrice's teddy bear, the Lamb Chop puppets, and the three-ring binder of the Sinopas' case were sitting on the dresser where I'd left them. I added the bag with the sweatshirt, opened the door, and placed the items on the sofa in the game room. Returning to my room, I packed the rest of my clothes and Holly's jewelry box into my mismatched luggage.

I did a final room check, then moved toward the game room.

Dan stood at the table. "Gwen, what do you want me to do with all this stuff?"

He'd set a box on a chair and placed my light box inside along with some of my drawing supplies. He waved at the sketchpads, files, drawings, and notes still on the table.

"The teddy bear, puppets, and binder go to your son." I pointed. "The sweatshirt in the bag goes to Detective Perez. I can finish up the rest of this stuff. My suitcases are packed in there." Dan headed to the bedroom to load my luggage into his SUV.

I sat down to sort through the jumble of papers. Opening a file, I found the summary of the missing children stapled to one side and the flyers from the year of my parents' deaths on the other. I put my hand over the file and said a quick prayer for the remaining families, then stared, my eyes unfocused, at the stack. A weight settled on my shoulders. *How could I have gotten so far in the investigation and then failed at the most important part — finding the children?*

Someone softly coughed.

I jumped.

"I'm sorry." Dan stood in the doorway. "I was trying not to startle you."

"Don't worry. I was a million miles away." I glanced at the cases. "I was just thinking about the carnage Jacob left behind."

Dan moved closer. "The children?"

I nodded.

Dan pulled out a chair and sat. "Our people never reveal the identity of our *Wy ya kin,* our animal spirit guide."

Blinking, I looked at him. "Excuse me, but —"

He held up his hand. "Humor me here. I have to ask you, what animal did you first see when you went into the wilderness?"

"A cougar."

"Are you sure?"

"Of course. I . . . No, wait. A bear. A mama bear with two cubs. Why?"

"Yes." Dan nodded. "That's what I thought. A bear often means you'll have a tough time in life, such as the loss of your parents."

I bit my lip but remained silent.

"It also means you value protection of life."

"I'm afraid I didn't do much to protect the lives of the kids." I lifted the file. Underneath, Beth had clipped the autopsy report on the body found in the tarp to the case information she'd downloaded. In the box describing the description of the deceased's clothing was written: *long green pants, size 5, green-and-white striped shirt and white sweater, also size 5.*

Frowning, I turned to the missing-person's flyer. *She is described as being 38 inches tall and weighing 35 pounds. She was last seen wearing a pink top and white shorts.* "She was wearing different clothing."

"Gwen, are you okay?"

"Look." I unclipped the two reports and placed them side-by-side. "Her height, her weight. She was wearing summer clothing." I pointed.

"Yeeess?"

"But here." I pointed again, this time at the autopsy report. "She's wearing a sweater and was a size 5."

"Right, right." He picked up both reports, then put them down. "Um . . . he bought her some clothing?"

"No. I mean, yes, he did, but look here." I underlined a sentence with my finger. "She'd been buried for between four and six years."

"Uh-huh." He stood and pulled out his cell. "Excuse me. I need to make a phone call."

I put my hand over the phone. "I'm not going nuts. I'm pointing out the significance of what she was wearing. He didn't *just* buy her new clothing, he bought her a bigger size. She grew. He kept this little girl alive for some time after he abducted her."

In the silence that followed, the murmur of voices came from the other room. I hadn't peeked in when I passed, not wanting to remember that horrible scene.

Dan put away his phone. "You think that Beatrice is still alive?"

"Maybe, yes. I wanted to believe it, because the body we found showed no sign of trauma, but something tickled my brain at the restaurant where we just ate. I couldn't figure out what it was. When you told me to take home the food, I think it triggered a memory. Lila told me Jacob took food to the homeless." I stood and paced. "I bet if we checked with the different homeless shelters, no one would know who Jacob was, or that he provided food."

"She would have to be nearby." Dan slowly nodded.

"A reasonable distance, say, within an hour or so." I stopped and picked up a pencil. "And he brought Beth and me applesauce. In the Sinopas' cupboard was applesauce. Maybe Beatrice's favorite food?" I put the pencil behind my ear, opened the sack I'd set out to go to the police, and picked up the teddy bear. "But where would he keep her?" I asked softly.

Dan once again took out his cell and dialed. When someone answered, he handed the phone to me. "Hello?"

"Hi, Gwen." Seth's voice was brisk.

I updated him.

Seth listened, asked a few questions, then had me put Dan back on. Dan said, "Okay, yeah, not a problem," and hung up. "Seth said if she's still alive, she'll soon be out of food if she isn't already, and water. He's going to set this up as a joint investigation with Lewiston. Everyone will search the B and B again, along with phone records, the com-

puter, credit-card purchases, gas receipts,
you name it."

"Weren't they going to do that anyway?"

"Yes, but there wasn't any reason to hurry.
Now we have a ticking clock."

CHAPTER FORTY-THREE

I hugged Beatrice's teddy. "What does he want me to do?"

"Go over all of your notes and see if you can find something else, some other clue."

I looked at the pile of papers, sketchpads, files, and printouts still covering the table.

"I'll help you." He patted my arm, then started gathering the scattered pencils and placing them in a pencil box. I snagged another one and twirled it in my fingers as I paged through a sketchpad.

Dan picked up a pad and opened it. The sketch was of the logo on the T-shirt Mr. Wolf had been wearing. "Where did you see this?"

I took the pad from him. "Mr. Wolf was wearing that on a shirt when I tried to interview his wife. Why?"

"It's the logo of the American Indian Movement. AIM."

"That's right. You talked about it. Pine

Ridge." I flipped the page. The next drawing was the farmhouse I'd remembered while on the boat. I stared at the image for several moments. Red roof. Mr. Wolf. Red. Blood. Wolf in Kamiah. "Dan, do you think you could drive me to Kamiah?"

"Did you remember something?"

"I don't know. I just . . ." I shrugged.

"Sure. Let's load all this into my Sequoia. If nothing pans out, I can at least get you and your things to the motel."

The sun was setting as we loaded the SUV. "It will be dark by the time we reach Kamiah," Dan said.

"I know. But I don't want that little girl to spend one more night alone." I kept the teddy bear in my lap.

We drove in silence for half an hour before Dan said, "Do you have any children, Gwen?"

"A daughter, Aynslee. She just turned sixteen."

"Husband?"

"Ex. Aynslee . . . stays with him when I travel. How about you? Other children besides Seth?"

Dan was silent for a few moments. His jaw muscles tightened, then loosened. "I did. A daughter. She and her mother, my wife, were murdered."

"Oh. I'm so very sorry."

"It was a long time ago. Seth was just a baby."

I looked down at my fingers, trying to figure out how to get my foot out of my mouth. "Did you raise Seth by yourself?"

"Yes."

"You did a great job. You must be very proud of your son."

"I am. I am."

I glanced at his profile, barely visible now in the gathering darkness. A slight smile played around his mouth. "Seth's the first one in my family to graduate from college. And the youngest chief of police in Idaho."

We finished the drive to Kamiah in comfortable silence. We stopped for gas at a convenience store at the edge of town. Taking my farmhouse sketch, I went inside the station and showed it to the clerk. "Do you know where this house is?"

"No. But I'm new." The woman turned to an older man thumbing through the paperback-book rack. "Hey, Tony, would you look at something?"

The man shuffled over to the counter.

"Have you lived around here long?" I asked.

"My whole life. Seventy-three years come this July."

I showed him the farmhouse drawing. "Does this place look familiar?"

He shook his head.

"It may be run-down . . ."

He continued to shake his head.

I sighed and turned to leave, then stopped. *The house in Kamiah . . . the one I fled from so many years before . . . on that day I went to a store . . .* Returning to the old man, I asked, "Is there a grocery store around here that was open twenty-some years ago? Actually, it may still be in business, but it was at the bottom of a hill."

The old man pursed his lips and closed his eyes. "Let's see. Thirty or more years . . . hill." Slowly he nodded. "Pat's. Pat's Market. Outside of town. Became a thrift store, then a car-repair business. Closed down completely ten, twelve years ago." He gave us directions.

Dan and I returned to the SUV and got in. "Should I give Seth a call?" Dan asked.

"Not yet. I have no idea if this place still exists and, if it does, if it's where Jacob was keeping Beatrice. This could be a total wild-goose chase."

If the old man hadn't told us to watch for a broken-down Studebaker on the right, we never would have found the building in the dark. Our headlights picked out a parking area overgrown with weeds. The building was boarded up and decorated with graffiti, and a tree was growing into the side.

"Now where?" Dan stopped his SUV.

"I'm not sure." I stepped outside. The cool night air enveloped me, bringing the scent of freshly turned soil. A coyote wailed in the distance, answered by several dogs. A few stars glinted between the clouds. The road we'd taken to get here was void of traffic.

Nothing looked familiar.

I stuck my head back into the SUV. "Do you have a light?"

He reached under the seat and pulled out a small LED flashlight. I took it and wandered around the parking lot, flashing the light. *If I walked from here, there should be a road.* Circling the lot, I found only discarded beer cans, a rotting shoe, and broken glass. The weeds didn't look crushed as if a car had driven over them. Returning to the Sequoia, I got in and shut the door, then slumped in my seat. "I'm sorry. This was a waste of time."

Dan used the parking lot to turn around. The headlights swept across the building, making it look even more run-down, then over a line of pines that edged the lot. Behind the pines stood a large cottonwood. "Wait!" I said.

Dan obligingly stopped his SUV again.

Jumping from the SUV with the flashlight, I approached the pines, then pushed through them to the cottonwood. A dirt track angled upward and away from the main road. I followed the track back. When I'd cleared the trees and could see Dan, I waved him over. As soon as he pulled next to me, I jumped in. "There. Straight ahead."

Haltingly we climbed the rutted lane, quickly passing out of sight from the road below. "Well, I'd never have found this route." Dan slowed even more. Grasses stroked the underside of the SUV. Craggy ponderosas hemmed us in. We climbed for what seemed like forever but was probably less than ten minutes. "You're sure there's a house up here?" Dan finally asked.

"I think so. Someone's been driving up here enough that they've kept the grasses from growing." I pointed to the two worn trails we followed.

We finally leveled out. Ahead something glinted in our headlights. An old metal mailbox with part of a reflector still attached. Beyond that, the farmhouse from my drawing.

CHAPTER FORTY-FOUR

The muscles across my shoulders tightened. I wiped my hands on my slacks. "We found it," I whispered.

The farmhouse was completely boarded over, paint long peeled off, and the porch had collapsed in the middle. Dan turned off the engine, then the headlights. No light escaped the rotting building.

A shiver crossed my neck. *Is poor little Beatrice somewhere in this crumbling house?* Dan found a second flashlight, I grabbed my light and the teddy bear, and we stepped from the SUV. A portion of a picket fence lay in the knee-high weeds that formed a lawn. The grasses appeared undisturbed leading to the front door.

"Gwen, I don't think anyone's been here in quite a while. That front door is inaccessible."

"Let's try the back." With Dan leading, we pushed through the overgrown landscape to the rear of the building. A pack of coyotes yipped and howled, much closer than before. Though I knew coyotes almost never attacked humans, their cries slid up and down my spine.

We stumbled on a worn path. Dan bent down and inspected the dirt for a moment, then stood and waved me forward. The rear of the house was also overgrown, but here the weeds and grasses were trampled. A rusty swing set swayed gently in the breeze, letting out a slight squeak as the chain rubbed against the metal. A faint foul odor made me blink.

The back door was off a small porch. I aimed my flashlight on the door. A shiny new padlock held it shut.

"Wait here." Dan left me and headed back to his SUV.

Squeak, squeak, squeak. The metallic screeching got on my nerves. *Please, Lord, let us not be too late.* I hugged the teddy bear tighter.

Soft footsteps approached and Dan reappeared carrying the handle of a car jack. Wordlessly he handed me his flashlight, then used the hunk of metal to rip the latch from the doorjamb. The sound was like a shotgun in the quiet evening. We entered a kitchen with a dirty brown linoleum floor and white painted cupboards. Dan put his hand out to stop me from moving farther into the house.

I heard it.

A low, humming sound.

I played my light around the room. The humming came from the refrigerator. I stepped over and opened the door. No light came on, but cool air brushed past me. A gallon of milk, a wrapped piece of baklava, and a container of something rested on the shelf. Opening the container, I found applesauce. I closed the door. "Beatrice? Beatrice, sweetheart, can you hear me?"

"You're sure she's here?"

"Yes, but . . ." *Don't say it. Don't even think she's not alive.*

None of the light switches worked. The kitchen led directly into a living room devoid of furniture. A short hall to my left opened to a bathroom directly ahead and doors at either end. The door on my right, which would have faced the front of the house, stood open. The one on the left was held shut with a simple slide bolt. I tried to unlatch it, but my hands were too sweaty. Dan slid it aside. The door opened with a *screech* of rusty hinges.

The earlier slight stench was immediate and overwhelming.

Human waste.

My eyes burned from the acrid odor coming from an overflowing bucket in the corner. A single stained mattress with a sleeping bag was in the center of the room. A ladder-back chair held a tray with an empty paper plate and bowl. Two water bottles, both empty, were on the floor.

"Beatrice?" I took a step into the room. Empty. Had he killed her? Were we too late? "Beatrice, sweetheart, I have someone here for you." My voice warbled. "Come here and see. I have your teddy bear." I put the light on the bear. "Come on, Busy Bee. Please . . ." My voice broke.

A soft sigh.

I spun. In the corner behind the door a tiny girl crouched, arms wrapped around her legs. I pulled the light off her and returned it to her teddy. "Come on, sweetheart. Let's take teddy and leave." I crouched and held the bear out to her.

Slowly she untangled herself and stood. She wore a too-large dress, urine-stained pants, and one sock. Her other foot was bare. Outside of being dirty and smelly, she didn't seem to have any cuts or bruises on her. "Come here, darlin'." I opened my arms and held my breath.

Her thumb went into her mouth. She hesitated.

"Come here, Busy Bee."

She flew into my arms, burying her face in my neck. I tucked the bear under her arm and stood, still holding her. Dan had remained in the doorway. "Let's get her out of here."

We hurried through the house, Dan now holding both lights so I could see. The outside air was pure pleasure to breathe. "Can you call Seth now?" I paused in the yard to clear my lungs. Dan pulled out his phone, then shook his head. "We'll need to be closer to town."

When we reached the SUV, I had Dan open the rear where my luggage and art supplies were. I found a soft pink cashmere sweater I'd purchased at my favorite second-hand store and wrapped the child in it. Placing the little girl in the back seat, I was about to shut the door when she whispered something.

"What's that, sweetheart?" I leaned closer to her.

She whispered it again. "What about the others?"

CHAPTER FORTY-FIVE

I grabbed the car seat to keep from falling. "What others, Beatrice?"

Still holding her bear with one arm, she raised the other and pointed at the house. I turned to Dan. "Did you hear her? There are others in the house."

Dan leaned close to my ear so the child couldn't hear. "Alive or dead?" he whispered.

"I don't know," I whispered back.

"You stay here with the little girl. I'll see if I can find . . . anything." He left.

I crawled onto the back seat next to Beatrice. Her bare foot bothered me. Giving her a hug, I got out and opened the rear cargo area. I found a bag of clean underclothes and pulled out a pair of black wool socks. Nearby was the file with the names of the children. I'd made a point of not knowing their names. Now it might be important. Grabbing the file, I returned to the back seat and pulled the socks on the child. They would have felt really good in the wilderness. *Was that just two days ago?*

Opening the file, I saw the summary of abductions along with the names of the children stapled on the inside. Opposite were the wanted flyers Beth had collected from the year of my parents' deaths. I read the names. The car's overhead light gave me enough illumination to read. *Amanda, Ethyn . . .*

Eric, make that Jacob, had been wrong. We probably would have eventually found the children's bodies, but way too late. The cruelest end of all.

Olivia, Jess . . .

He'd fooled me and covered his tracks well, using the excuse of feeding the homeless to bring food to Beatrice. He was dead now. He'd never hurt another child.

Noah . . .

He got hit on the head. Beth's voice echoed in my brain.

Yeah. Technically, he hit himself on the noggin to stay off my radar.

No, Gwen, remember what Lila said? Beth's voice was insistent.

Beatrice had drifted off to sleep, tucked under my arm. "Lila said a lot of things," I whispered. "What are you talking about?"

Eric baked the baklava on Sunday. He was up the night before because of the knock on the head. That's what Lila told you.

What Beth said was important. I just couldn't figure out why. "Okay. Sunday. Why is that important?"

When did someone try to kill you with arrows in the wilderness?

"Sunday."

But you figured out whoever shot you and Phil had to have been out in that wilderness the night before. So it couldn't have been Jacob.

"Are you saying Jacob *didn't* try to kill me?"

Oh, he tried to kill you all right, but not with arrows. Not in the wilderness. Someone else didn't want you to go to that plane crash.

The sound of crickets grew louder. Crashing doors and footsteps came from the house.

My stomach twisted. "But all that was there was a gun, part of a purse, a tube of lipstick, a chain, and a compact."

What were your parents seeking?

Carefully I withdrew my arm from around the sleeping Beatrice, then stepped from the car. I aimed my flashlight at the wanted flyers.

Wanted by the US Marshals. William Law-

rence Waters. A blurry black-and-white photograph captured a group of Native Americans, all carrying rifles, walking toward the cameraman.

The creak of the back door was followed by footsteps across the wooden porch at the rear of the house.

I held the light closer to the paper, straining to see the faces.

The swishing of disturbed grasses silenced the crickets. The footsteps grew louder.

There were four faces in the photo. One by one, I studied them. *No. No. No. Yes.*

Adrenaline coursed through my body. I wanted to run but remained rooted to the spot.

Someone stepped on a twig. Swiftly I closed the file, then held my light on the path.

Like the Pied Piper, Dan led the children toward the SUV. I counted. Five children. Only the first girl Jacob abducted hadn't made it. *All of them. All but one. Thank you, Lord.*

I kept my eyes on the children, not wanting Dan to see my expression. The children gathered around me. I tried to remember their names. "Amanda?"

A small five-year-old girl with braided hair smiled shyly at me.

"Noah?"

The tallest of the children raised his hand. He'd been with Jacob the longest. Five years.

"Ethyn?"

A black-haired boy nodded.

"Olivia? Jess?"

Two girls between six and eight raised their hands. I wanted to ask them what had happened to them, but I knew better. They would need trained interviewers who specialized in working with children. I just needed to get them to safety. "My name is Gwen."

"Angel Gwen," Noah said.

"No, just Gwen," I managed to say around the lump in my throat. "Hop in the car. Let's get you out of here."

Beatrice woke as the children got in the car. She stared wordlessly at the newcomers, then slid over so Amanda could sit next to her.

Once everyone had settled, I got into the front seat. Dan was already behind the wheel. He turned the SUV around and headed down the road toward civilization.

Soon, very soon, we'd all be safe.

"Gwen." Dan's voice was soft. "What were you reading when we came to the car?"

"Noth . . . nothing. Just looking up the

names of the children."

"Let me see it."

I could say no. Tell him I threw it away.

"Gwen, give me the file." He held out his hand.

The images were faded and extremely difficult to see. And the name was different. I could act stupid and pretend I didn't recognize the face in the photo. "Here." I pulled the file out. "Just names and some of Beth's research."

He snatched the file from me and opened it on the console between us.

Wanted: William Lawrence Waters

Blood drained from my face. Dan let go of the file and reached to his left side. "The Nimi'ipuu name for *water* is *Ku's.*"

He leveled a pistol at me.

CHAPTER FORTY-SIX

"If you try anything, if you so much as move, I'll shoot you. Then I'll shoot the kids." His quiet voice left no room for argument.

I clenched my hands into fists. "What are you doing?" I whispered.

He concentrated on driving, but his aim never wavered from my midsection. "You're a smart lady, Gwen. Even without finding the wanted poster, you had already pretty much figured out your dad was with law enforcement. As my son said to you" — he smiled without showing his teeth — "you would have connected the dots."

"But I didn't —"

"Ah, but you were so close. Once you started looking at law enforcement, that would have led you to who died on the date of the plane crash. Even though working undercover, a federal marshal's death is noted. Federal marshal usually means fugitive."

"Why didn't you kill me at the motel? Or the other times we were alone?"

"I tried killing you twice."

"Twice?"

"Once at the police department when I found out who you were. Once in the wilderness."

We reached the bottom of the hill and turned toward Kamiah. Maybe I could jump out of the car when we stopped for a light. I glanced back at the children. No. I couldn't leave them.

Dan was right. I would have figured out his secret eventually. "You said to keep away from Nick Wolf, who has ties to Pine Ridge. You said you and Nick have a long history — I bet it goes all the way back to the American Indian Movement."

"See? You had all the information."

"But you also said their son, Thomas, was a foster child. If Nick was on the wrong side of the law, he wouldn't have been allowed to be Thomas's foster parent."

"Very good, Gwen. I even told you about the murder of my wife and daughter, yet another Indian slaughter sanctified by the United States government. They were just another set of dead rez Indians." His voice dripped bitterness.

We drove though the small town. The night was quiet, traffic nonexistent. When we reached Highway 12, Dan turned left toward Lewiston.

Maybe he was taking us to a hospital. Or back to my motel.

Fat chance.

"Where are you taking us?"

"I disappeared before. I can do it again. I just need to buy time, put you someplace where you won't be found for a while."

I didn't believe him.

"What about your son? You're so proud of Seth. What's he going to say?"

"Don't worry about him. I'll explain it to him. He knows me. He'll understand."

The children had curled up in the back of the SUV and were sleeping. Sleep was a good defense mechanism. I racked my brain trying to think of some way I could stop Dan, get help, escape. Every time I glanced at him, he seemed to know and gently moved the pistol.

We turned toward Ahsahka — and the reservoir.

"You could just drop us off someplace." I tried to keep my voice level. "I won't say anything. I promise."

He didn't bother to answer.

413

We climbed past the dam, then down to the Big Eddy Marina. "When I stop the car, I expect you to control the kids." He slowed the SUV as we entered the parking area. "We're going on a boat ride. That's all you need to tell them."

He stopped the car and motioned for me to get out. He knew me too well, knew I wouldn't run, wouldn't leave these kids. The night was cool, filled with scents of the lake and the gentle slapping of water on the shore. I opened the rear door and helped the sleepy children out. When all six children were assembled beside me, Dan turned on a flashlight and motioned us to the docks.

I picked up Beatrice and stumbled ahead on numb legs. I didn't want to consider what his plan was.

His boat was moored at the end of the dock. I headed toward it.

"Stop."

I paused.

"Get in the boat."

Looking around, I didn't see a boat.

"I said, get into the boat." He indicated a tiny rowboat tied up behind his boat.

"But . . . but that's not big enough —"

"One more word out of you and I shoot the nearest kid," he whispered.

The rowboat was designed for two adults,

not an adult and six children. The oars were missing and there were no life vests.

The young faces stared at me.

Taking a deep breath, I stepped into the middle of the boat. It wobbled under my weight. "Okay, children, please listen to me. We're going for a boat ride. Noah, you're the oldest. Bring the children over, one at a time, and I'll help them in."

Noah frowned but took Beatrice by the hand and led her to the edge of the dock. I pulled the boat as close as possible and lifted her over, placing her in the front. One by one, the children quietly got into the rowboat. Tears stung my eyes and I bit the inside of my mouth, wondering what all they'd gone through to be so quiet and obedient.

When all the children were aboard, I sat on the floor to make it more stable.

Dan shoved the rowboat away from the dock, keeping hold of the bow line, and walked to his own boat about four feet away. He tied the line to his boat, then started the engine. Slowly we pulled away from the dock. The rowboat twisted and rocked.

Working some spit into my mouth, I said quietly, "Be still. Be very quiet and still."

After a few moments he slowed, then stopped the engine. Something splashed in

415

the water behind me. I carefully turned.

The splash was the slowly sinking bow line.

"You're leaving us out here?"

"Don't worry. You'll be found."

I wanted to say *not if we sink,* but I didn't want to alarm the children.

Our boats were drifting farther apart.

"Dan, wait. It's not too late. I'm not your enemy. I'm *not* the government. These children are innocent. All those things you did before, whatever it was that made you a fugitive, are in the past. You can't paint everyone with the same brush. We are in a different time, a different place, a different people —"

"Haven't you ever heard about the sins of the father passing on?" He started his engine again.

"Yes, but I've also heard we are each responsible for our own actions. Judge me for what *I've* done to you, for what these *children* have done to you."

"Is he going to sink the boat?" Noah asked.

"No." Dan turned the boat toward shore. "I don't have to. I'm going to disappear again, but first I'm finishing the work I started over thirty years ago." He shoved the throttle forward and his boat took off toward shore. The wake rocked the rowboat violently. The girls clutched each other but were silent.

"What's he going to do?" Noah asked. He'd put his arm protectively around Amanda's shoulders.

Complete the work he started thirty years ago?

Thirty years ago, he was going to blow up the dam.

Chapter Forty-Seven

I was glad it was dark. The children wouldn't be able to see my face. Not clearly, that is. "Children, we need to get to shore as fast and as safely as possible."

The children glanced at the distant illumination from the marina. It seemed miles away. The lights from Dan's boat reached the docks. A bouncing flashlight showed his progress from docked boat, across the dock, up the stairs, and to the parking lot. His SUV was the lone vehicle. The sound of his engine carried clearly across the reservoir, and the headlights tracked his exit up the hill.

"Noah, Jess." Noah was in front of me in the middle of the seat, Jess behind me. "You each need to shift so you are sitting on that side of the boat. You can paddle with your hands, no, wait, here." I took off my scarf, opened it, then tore it in half. "Wrap the scarf around your hand. You'll have a larger surface to move water." Still on the floor of the boat, I started to move to the opposite side. The boat tilted and dipped. One of the children gasped.

"Beatrice," I said to the tiny girl sitting beside me. "You'll need to move closer to the other side. We need to balance the boat for my weight." Beatrice scooted away. The rowboat bobbled a little, then settled. "Now, I need Amanda to sit as close to Jess as you can. Ethyn, you move close to Noah. Olivia, sit on the floor next to Beatrice." I removed my sweater and tied it around my hand. "Now paddle with me. Ready? Go."

Jess gasped. The water *was* cold. My sweater was quickly waterlogged and heavy. Noah and Jess did their best, but the boat kept turning with my more-powerful strokes. "Okay, you two paddle two times. I'll go once. We might go straighter."

The splash of our hands and a quiet sniffling were the only sounds. The shore lights became a tiny bit larger.

"Oh!" Jess said.

"What is it, sweetheart?"

"I dropped your scarf."

"That's okay. You're okay. Let's switch sides so we're using our other hands. Children, we're all going to slowly shift to the other side of the boat. No one stand up."

We gradually moved. I was pretty sure the skiff wouldn't tip over, but children could. The water was black. I'd never find anyone who fell overboard and sank.

I tried to keep my mind off of what Dan was doing. He would have reached the dam long before this. Did he have bombs in his SUV? No. My gear took up the rear of the vehicle. He'd have to drive somewhere to get the explosives.

When he blows the dam, we'll be dead. Swept down through the torrents of water.

Very clever. *If* our bodies were ever found, we'd just be another statistic of the catastrophe.

The muscles in my arm ached from the weight of the soggy sweater and exertion. "Let's take a break." I didn't have to repeat myself. Both children slumped in their seats.

Boom! Boom! Boom!

The water around us shivered, growing into waves that rocked the boat.

In the distance, a klaxon horn beat the air. A warning the dam had been breached?

Beatrice and Olivia started crying, clinging to each other.

Almost imperceptibly the boat started to drift left. Toward the dam.

I didn't need to say anything. The two older children resumed paddling as quickly as they could. I did the same on my side. We were making progress, but too little.

The horn was relentless, howling a warning. I envisioned cracks forming. A chunk giving way, water pushing harder, faster through the breach. The rushing water would open the dam wider, deeper —

Don't think about it.

We had to make it to the docks.

The klaxon continued to sound.

I paddled harder, but it just sent us sideways. There was only one thing to do. "Children, listen to me. We have to get to those docks. I'm going to swim and pull the boat."

"But the water's cold," Jess said.

What did Dan tell me? Fifty-eight degrees? I'd have less than an hour before hypothermia would cause exhaustion or unconsciousness. Pulling the rowboat would slow —

By the time you figure this out, it will be too late.

"We need to all move together." I made sure they all heard me over the siren echoing across the reservoir. "We're all going to scoot to the middle of the boat, all but Jess and Amanda. I'm going to crawl between you to the front of the boat to get the rope. Okay?"

Little heads nodded. "Move slow and don't stand up." *Time! We have to go faster.* But the boat was overloaded and I couldn't afford the children falling overboard. Again keeping my weight low, I passed between the girls and pulled in the bow line. Sitting on the tiny transom, I shivered as I tied the icy rope around my waist. Next came my shoes, which I left tucked under the transom. Now came the hard part. Getting into the water. If I jumped standing up, the boat would bounce too much. I'd have to slip over the front of the boat.

Looking at each face, I said, "You are all so brave, the bravest children I've ever met. I'm proud of you. Now I'm going into the water. The boat will wiggle a bit. All of you must promise that you will stay where you are and hang on. Okay?" Six heads gravely nodded.

Standing slightly, I turned my back to them and straddled the bow. The water was black, oily ink. My goal was the lights at the marina.

I pushed off. The icy waters clutched me.

CHAPTER FORTY-EIGHT

The frigid water closed over my head.

I opened my mouth to scream, sucking in the icy liquid.

Surfacing, I treaded water until I could cough the stuff from my throat and lungs. I oriented myself to the marina, then started swimming, chill piercing my body. The boat dragged behind me, but not as much as I'd thought. The current pulling us toward the dam, however, was stronger than I'd anticipated.

Keeping my face forward, staring at the illuminated shore, I pushed my arms and legs as hard as I could. My fingers were already numb, as were my toes. *That will spread.*

Don't think about it.

I whispered through frozen lips, "Please, Lord, give me endurance. Strength. I can't have saved the children from one death only to face another." *Swim. Kick hard.*

"Come on, Angel Gwen!" Noah's small

voice called from behind me.

To keep my mind off the freezing water and the horrors about to happen, I plotted my path. *Stroke, kick.* The two main docks were my goal, starting with the nearest one on the right. *Stroke, kick, kick.* If I couldn't make that landing, there was the second. If we swept past the first two, there was one more dock at the bottom of the boat ramp. *Reach out, grab the water, pull forward. Kick.* After the boat ramp, a small ridge rose between the marina and the dam. If we reached the ridge, there wasn't a beach, just a steep incline. *Swim, kick harder.* One false step getting off the boat, and the deep water would engulf them. The earthen sides were too steep for such small children to climb. *Kick, kick.* No. We had to make it to a dock.

Pumping my arms faster, I swam as fast as I could toward the first dock, now visible in the dim light. My arms grew heavy, my legs slowed.

The boat was no longer being towed behind me. The current was tugging it to the side, and me with it. I made a lunge forward and swallowed water. Coughing, I reached for the edge of the dock. Too far.

I wasn't going to make it.

The skiff was now facing me from the side, the line pulling me sideways and backward into the center of the reservoir.

Renewing my efforts, I focused on the second dock. My breathing was loud in my ears. My lungs worked at getting more air. Arms were lead weights. Legs made of concrete. *Push, kick.* The second dock only a foot away. *Grab it. Grab —*

I missed.

Wanted to cry. *Just stop. Just sink.*

Too noisy. The klaxon wailed, the sound bouncing off the mountains.

"Angel Gwen! Swim, Angel Gwen!" the children chanted.

A tug on the line. Little boy at the bow. Tugging on the line. Mouth moving. "Swim!"

Moving my arms. First one. Then the other. *Swim. Save. The. Children.* Kicking my legs. *Forward.* The cold wasn't bad. *Swim.* Getting warm. *Swim —*

Something banged my arm. I grabbed, slipped, grabbed again. The skiff pulled my waist, tugging me away. I hung on. Looked up. The edge of the third dock.

I reached for the rope. Couldn't feel my hands. Wrapped rope around arm. *Pull. Get boat next to dock.*

Clunk.

More noise. *Don't care.* Blackness lapped around my brain.

Someone pulling my hair. Hard. *Hurts.* I gasped and coughed. Wouldn't let go. "La go mm air!" Moving, pulling. Knees hit hard. Fell forward. *Hurt.*

Gasping, crawling forward, still pulling boat. Water shallower. Forward. Little hands tugging on shirt. Out of the water.

Little children crying. Someone pulling on rope. Darkness.

I opened my eyes. Little squiggles around me. Cold. A blanket, no, sleeping bag was around me, as were the children. Trying to warm me with their bodies. Everyone shivered.

"What happened?" My voice was a croak.

A boy — Ethyn? — spoke. "You pulled the boat to the dock. We got out, but you sank down."

"I tried to pull you up," Noah said, "but you were too heavy."

"You got out of the water," Olivia said. "But you were really cold. I thought you were dead. You just flopped down."

"Did you pull me by my hair?" I asked.

"Yes, but I had to let go," Noah said.

"I thought . . . Never mind." I patted Noah on the knee.

"There's a cabin thing up there." Noah pointed to the marina. "I broke a window and got in. Upstairs was an apartment. I took this sleeping bag. Will I get in trouble?"

"No." I gauged the distance to the marina. Could I walk that far? "But all of you are cold. Let's go up there and get warm." With help, I stood on shaking legs and numb feet.

We were on a boat ramp leading to the parking lot. I held the sleeping bag over my shoulders with one arm, as my hands were useless. Beatrice was beside me, holding on to my frozen fingers. The other children held on to the sleeping bag and moved as one.

Slowly, slowly, we moved up the ramp. The klaxon blared unrelentingly around us. When the ground leveled, I paused.

Headlights appeared on the road, racing toward us.

Thank you, Lord. We could send for help.

The car slammed to a halt, spotlighted us. A car door slammed. I couldn't see the driver.

"I thought you'd be dead by now." Dan Kus stepped into the light.

Chapter Forty-Nine

My legs threatened to give way. I was *not* going to give in. Locking my knees to stay upright, I pulled Beatrice, still holding my hand, behind me under the sleeping bag. I then opened my arms to form a barrier between Dan and the rest of the children. Whatever happened, they wouldn't see it.

The klaxon finally stopped, the sound fading with the last echoes. In the silence, I heard his harsh breathing and the quiet weeping of the children.

"Did you return to see your handiwork?" My voice sounded gravelly and loud. "To make sure we were swept through the collapsed dam? To watch the reservoir empty?"

Dan moved forward until he was in front of one of the lights. I couldn't see his face, only his black outline. "The dam hasn't collapsed yet. I blew the sluice gates and protective barrier around them. I'd hoped that would be enough."

He failed! The dam didn't break.

"I didn't expect to see you, but I should have known." Dan took a step forward. "You stand there, your arms outstretched," he said in a strange, singsong voice. "You are truly the spirit of the bear, strong and courageous, guarding life."

I didn't feel strong and courageous. I felt cold, exhausted, and spitting mad. I took a deep breath. Anger wouldn't help. Reasoning might. "Dan, think of all the people, the death, the destruction you were trying to do. You don't want to do this."

"But I do. Get in the car."

"But —"

"Do you think a sleeping bag will stop a bullet? If you don't get into the car, I will start shooting."

Dropping my arms, I turned and took hold of Beatrice, then gathered the others around me. My back was to Dan. A spot between my shoulder blades tingled where I imagined the bullet would strike. "Children." My voice was surprisingly strong. "Go to the marina building and stay there. Stay together. Promise?"

"Will you come and get us?" Amanda asked.

Will I come and get them? "God willing, sweetheart."

"Promise?" Noah asked.

I hesitated. "I promise."

Noah picked up the sleeping bag. The older children took the hands of the younger and walked toward the marina building.

Turning, I faced Dan. He threw something at me, and it landed at my feet. One of my flex-cuffs.

"Put it on," he said quietly.

I complied. The children were safe.

Dan didn't say anything. He moved to the passenger side and opened the door, then motioned with his gun. As I passed near him, he reached over and tightened the cuffs. With both hands, I pulled myself into the Sequoia.

He slammed the door, got into the driver's seat, and turned the SUV toward the dam.

I pictured the towns downstream. Ahsahka, lying in the shadow of the dam. Once the massive structure collapsed, the escaping water would take out a chunk of Lewiston, still in Idaho, and Clarkston, in Washington state. The torrent would spew into the Snake River. The four dams on the Snake would open to dump as much water as possible, but the sheer volume of the contents of the massive reservoir would overtake them. Then on to the Columbia River, with four more major dams. Portland,

Oregon, would be a memory. Complete catastrophe.

A vein pounded in my forehead. I clenched my teeth together. *How do I stop him?*

"Why, Dan?"

"These are the people who stole my land, my culture. This is the government who murdered my family." Sweat gleamed on his forehead. He seemed to be speaking more to himself than to me. "We were right, and we were righteous, but we faced the leader and his goons. There was the reign of terror, with the highest death toll in the country. They put us in prison. We went into hiding. And nothing changed."

"Dan, are you talking about the American Indian Movement? Wounded Knee and Pine Ridge?"

"Of course."

"But that was in the early 1970s."

"Yes."

A police vehicle with flashing lights sat next to a split in the road. An officer with a flashlight waved us to a stop.

I sucked in air and tightened my muscles to run.

Dan lifted the pistol he'd left in his lap. "Say one wrong word and the first bullet kills him. The second is yours. Do you

431

understand?"

I nodded.

He put the gun down, reached behind him, and brought out two jackets. One he threw over my lap to hide the flex-cuffs, the second he used to cover his pistol. He stopped and the officer approached the driver's side.

Dan rolled down the window. "Oh, hi, Dean, it's me, Dan Kus."

"Dan, hey, good to see ya. Lotta excitement going on." The young officer flashed his light into the car, spotlighting me. "Ma'am."

"What's going on?" Dan asked. "I was way up the lake in my boat and heard the sirens."

"Someone blew up the Tainter gates and barrier. Good thing you're off the water. In a boat and without a good engine, you'd have gotten swept down the spillway." He looked at me. "You look wet."

"She fell in while trying to dock my boat. The current was pretty swift."

"Good thing you were there to help," he said to Dan. "Anyway, just to be safe, they've put the Ahsahka on evacuation notice. It's in the inundation area."

"Do they think the dam's going to collapse?" Dan asked.

"Nah. They're sending out a crew to

check, but the resident structural engineer said the blast wasn't enough to do much damage, except to the gates. The evacuation is just a precaution. Where are you folks headed?"

"I was going to head down 12 to Lewiston. Gwen here is staying there."

"Just be sure you're staying up high in the Orchards." He laughed.

Dan's lips thinned. "Take care now." Before I could react, he'd rolled up the window and put the car in gear.

I kept my voice soft and calm. "You were a young man in the 1970s —"

"I was twenty-two at the protest in Wounded Knee, February 27, 1973. A seventy-one-day standoff. My wife and daughter had been killed. I swore revenge, escaped from the reservation, changed my name. I plotted how to get even."

We'd traveled down the road from the dam. The lights from the town glowed in the distance. "And you decided to blow up the dam."

Dan nodded. "AIM developed a twenty-point list of our issues. I was going to force the government to honor the list . . . or else. I would die a martyr."

We reached Ahsahka, then turned left and crossed a bridge over the North Fork of the

433

Clearwater. The rushing water ran high from the damaged gates. From the center of the bridge, the lights from the dam were clear. Ahead in the distance were more flashing lights. Immediately on the other side of the bridge, Dan turned left again, shut off his headlights, and headed up a small lane paralleling the river.

"But you didn't follow through with your plan to destroy the dam thirty-some years ago. What stopped you?"

"The man sent to find me, to uncover my plans —"

"My father," I whispered.

"Yes, your father, died in a plane crash. I didn't have to look over my shoulder anymore. I changed fate. This time everything would be different. I defeated the enemy."

"I don't know what you mean."

"The cycle of life."

I vaguely remembered Seth telling me Dan believed in reincarnation. "You're talking about the time of Chief Joseph? When the US Army chased your people —"

"The warrior who led his people to defeat the enemy was named Wahlitits. Shore Crossing in English. The name my *Wy ya kin* gave me. I was to finish the war, but this time I would defeat the enemy."

He stopped the car beside the raging river,

checked his watch, and got out. He came around to my side and opened the door, holding the pistol on me. "Get out."

I was afraid my legs wouldn't hold me. Sliding off the seat, I almost crumpled to the ground. Dan caught my elbow and pulled me upright. The moon had risen and I could clearly see his face.

He stared into my eyes. "And now it's time."

CHAPTER FIFTY

Was Dan going to shoot me? Throw my body into the river? Or just push me into the raging rapids? I had no strength. I'd never be able to get to shore. "What do you mean 'it's time'?"

"I didn't think the initial bombs would breach the dam. I'd hoped. But it's always good to have a backup plan. So I packed a bunch of explosives into the diversion tunnel."

"What?"

"The tunnel is forty feet in diameter, used to divert the river when the dam was being built. The ripple effect will open up the cracks and fissures left over from the original construction."

I took another step backward.

"It has water in it, crystal clear. They keep a small boat down there to check on things. I just filled the boat and sent it on its way."

"But why? Why have you gone back to

your plans of over thirty years ago? Why now?"

"I told you. I thought I'd defeated the enemy. Before, General Howard defeated the Nez Perce. This time, I defeated Howard. I didn't need to destroy the dam." He glanced at his watch. "The bomb should go off about . . ." He checked his watch again. "Now."

Boom!

The ground shook under my feet. The klaxon wailed, much louder here downstream of the dam than when we were at the marina. "What have you *done*?"

He tucked the pistol into his pocket and took out a knife.

I turned to run, but he caught my hands. Before I could scream, he sliced the cuffs from my wrists.

"There's no place to run, Gwen. The water will reach this spot before you can get away."

I glanced around. Could I get to the car and drive?

"Once and for all, I've defeated Howard."

The ground rumbled again under our feet.

"How could you defeat Howard? He died over a hundred years ago! You're crazy!"

Dan cocked his head at me. "You don't

know, do you? Your father's name was Howard."

I took a step backward, then shook my
head and moved forward. "You never defeated him. My father died in an accident."
Sirens blared around and above us as law-
enforcement vehicles raced into the doomed
town.

"That was not an accident. The plane
crash that killed your family — I caused it."

The blood drained from my head. I
swayed. *Don't you dare faint now!*

"I killed you, too, Gwen, or tried to. But
your spirit was too strong."

I grabbed my cross.

The earth vibrated. A sharp wind whipped
my hair.

Dan pulled out his gun. "This way, this
time, no one wins. We all die. The land is
washed clean. My wife, my child, my people
are all avenged."

"This doesn't change the past."

Dan moved to the front of his car and
leaned against it, staring at the dam. "What
should I have done?" He stared at my hand
clutching the cross. "Turn the other cheek?"
he asked sarcastically. "Forgive the people
who killed my family? My people?"

"This wasn't the answer."

Cars and trucks, horns blaring, exited

from the direction of the dam. The roads leading from town were clogged.

"Would *you* forgive the person who killed your family?"

My pulse raced. I stared at the pistol for a moment, then looked at Dan. "I would have to. I can't go through life with that burden. As my friend Beth once told me, forgiveness isn't for them, it's for me."

"Prove it." He leveled the gun at me.

I licked my lips, then cleared my throat. I kept having to forgive Robert. He knew how to push my buttons, get under my skin, hurt me. And Robert didn't care.

But with Dan, I would have only this one chance. And Dan wanted absolution.

On shaking legs, I walked over until I was nearly toe-to-toe with the man. "Dan Kus, I forgive you."

Silence. The howling klaxon ceased. Traffic stopped. I tore my gaze from Dan's face, turned around, and looked at the dam. It stood strong.

"You didn't bring it down," I whispered. My vision blurred. I blinked rapidly, then turned back to Dan. "You —"

He put the pistol up to his head and pulled the trigger.

CHAPTER FIFTY-ONE

I'd made a promise that I would keep. Placing one of the jackets over Dan's face, I got into his SUV and turned around. The small lane Dan had driven us on appeared little used. Dan wasn't going anywhere for a time.

The roads were still clogged with emergency vehicles and cars overloaded with families and possessions. Most had stopped in the middle of the street, gotten out of their vehicles, and were staring at the dam.

No one tried to stop me.

I debated telling one of the patrol officers about Dan's body, but that would involve a lengthy explanation, perhaps a trip to the station, and a lot of paperwork.

The road that veered off to the top of the dam was blocked but clear to the marina. I pulled up to the set of buildings holding the offices and apartment of the ranger. No sign of the children.

Stepping from the SUV, I called out,

"Children? I promised I'd return. Time to go."

Six bodies flew out of the darkness of the building.

"Gwen!"

"You came back!"

I picked up a sobbing Beatrice. "What's wrong, sweetheart?"

She threw her arms around my neck. "Mr. Teddy. I lost Mr. Teddy."

"I'll come back and look for him. Let's go now." After loading up the children, making sure seat belts were buckled, and sliding in, I sat for a moment. *Thank you, Lord.*

I drove directly to the Orofino medical hospital. Our arrival launched the staff into overdrive. The children disappeared into different emergency-room cubicles. I had my own curtained bed where a new set of doctors and nurses poked, prodded, took my temperature, tut-tutted, and brought me, finally, an Orofino patrol officer. The officer, a woman, politely started writing down my story as I explained who the children were and the location of Dan's body. I could tell she didn't believe me. "Look, you need to find Dan's body. Then we'll talk again."

She shook her head and left. I knew she, or a whole host of folks, would soon return.

A nurse tucked me into bed. This time a real hospital bed. And I'd been given a real cotton gown, albeit open to the breezes in the back, and in an ugly pink floral pattern.

I had no idea how long I slept, waking only when a nurse would visit on her rounds.

A doctor — at least I assumed he was a doctor — looking to be about eighteen years old checked my vitals the next day. "If you're up to it" — he prodded along my jawline, examined my fingers, and peered into my eyes — "there's a crowd out in the hall waiting to talk to you."

"Okay, but first tell me about the children. Are they . . . okay?"

He smiled briefly. "They tell me you're an angel. Hospital rules prevent me from saying that all the children appear to be healthy and unharmed."

"Did any of them tell you . . . what happened to the little girl whose body we found?"

"The oldest boy said a little girl was very sick when he . . . um . . . arrived. He said she disappeared one day. After that, the man put the new kids into isolation for a few weeks."

I relaxed into my pillow. *Thanks again, Lord.* "Do you think I should freshen up to talk to everyone?"

"Nope. You need to look like you've twice suffered from hypothermia, spent a night in a plane crash fighting off a cougar, faced a madman, rescued six kids, and swam in the freezing reservoir." At my expression, he grinned. "People talk." He raised the head of the bed, stood, and opened the door.

The first one in the room was Seth.

I didn't know what to say.

Seth took a chair, sinking down into it as if his body could no longer hold up his weight. Face pale, eyes sunken and underscored with purple, cheeks more prominent, he looked like he'd aged ten years. "I spoke with the oldest boy. He told me much of what happened. And I saw . . . my dad. I'm sorry."

"Don't be sorry, Seth. None of it was your fault."

"Dad used to say . . . the sins of the father passed on to the son. But he kept saying he could reverse the past." He leaned forward, resting his arms on his knees.

"Your dad and I didn't have the same philosophy." I pushed the button to raise the bed even more. "He had a lot of demons haunting him."

"He didn't share that much with me. All that happened with the AIM, Wounded

Knee, my mom's and sister's murders."

Seth doesn't know that Dan killed my parents. I would never tell him. Some burdens didn't need to be shared.

Seth looked at me. His eyebrows furrowed, his lips pulled down at the corners. "He tried to kill you."

"I forgave him. For everything."

"I don't know that I can, though." He stood and moved toward the door.

"Seth."

He paused but didn't turn around.

"A much wiser person than I said there would be seasons in our lives. A season doesn't last forever."

He glanced over. "And when that season is over?"

"We're friends. Call me."

He left, closing the door quietly behind him.

I stared at the closed door for a long time.

The hospital released me that afternoon, only so I could be whisked away by first the Lewiston police, then the Clearwater County Sheriff's Department, then the Nez Perce Tribal Police. I was plied with greasy hamburgers, bad coffee, and soggy french fries. Midnight came and went before someone offered to drive me back to the

444

motel. Someone had found my gear in the back of Dan's SUV and unloaded everything into the room. I was too tired to see if anything was missing. I was too tired even to care.

I woke to the bang of a nearby car door. My mouth felt like it had been stuffed with dirty socks, and I hadn't bothered to undress from the night before. I found the same tiny coffeepot and heated up one bad cup.

A quick check of my belongings showed everything intact. I found some clean clothes and put them in the bathroom to change into after my shower. Holly's jewelry box went on the bedside table.

Someone pounded on my door. I peered through the window. Beth spotted me and gave a small wave. Winston merely stared intently at the door. I let them in.

"Oh, you look awful. Did you really save all those kids? You won't believe all that's happened. You'll have to guess. You'll never guess, though. And Winston's much better."

Winston shoved me backward until my knees hit the bed, then he jumped up and lay across my stomach.

"Thank you. Yes. I won't. I don't want to. You're right. That's good."

Beth gave a delighted laugh. "You're fixed!"

"I didn't know I was broken. Can you get this dog off me?"

Beth grabbed his collar and pulled. I slid from underneath him and stood. Winston stayed on the bed, eyeballing a pillow.

"Seth called and said I could pick you up. But you simply won't believe what's happened. I can't even believe it. It's wonderful news."

I *was* fixed. I wanted to throw a pencil at her head. "Beth, just tell me."

"I will, but I almost forgot. Seth told me to bring you some food."

Before I could speak, she'd opened the door, flipped the metal security latch so it wouldn't lock behind her, and left.

Winston watched her exit from the bed, then flopped over onto the nearest pillow.

"You're a whole lot calmer than the last time I saw you," I said to the dog. "Looks like you were fixed as well."

He lifted his head.

"In a manner of speaking. Nothing personal, ol' buddy."

Beth returned with a large cooler. "First course is black-olive tapenade with figs. Then tomato, cucumber, and sweet onion salad with cumin salt, and fried chicken

446

with spicy raspberry honey." She dumped the cooler on the desk, opened it, and pulled out a loaf of bread. "And artisan bread."

"No dessert?" I muttered as I filled the paper plate she brought. "So? What's new?"

"Well." She moved Winston's legs over so she could sit on the bed. "The guy who was the head of the Interagency Major Crimes Unit —"

"Commander Gary James." I took a second helping of salad and grabbed a hunk of bread.

"Yes. He took a job as chief of police at some big department, and guess who is taking his place?"

I was going to throw that pencil at her head just as soon as I finished eating. "Who?"

"Dave Moore. Your buddy, Sheriff Dave! And he's going to hire you as the forensic artist. And the best news of all?"

I put down the chicken leg. *I have a job? I have a job!* "What's the best news of all?"

"Dave said I could work as support staff. Logistics, computer work, you name it!" She did an arm-waving jig around the room. "I get to wear a *badge*. We'll officially be working together. Don't you love it?"

"I do. I can't wait." Placing the chicken leg on the paper plate, I wiped my fingers and gave Beth a hug. "Can I borrow your phone?"

"Sure." She handed me her cell.

I dialed. "Hi, Robert? I'm coming home. My *job* is waiting for me. You can bring all of Aynslee's things back to the house when you drop her off."

"But —"

"And I'll see you in court." *Click.* I handed Beth her phone and grinned. "That felt really good." She gave me a high five.

Winston jumped off the bed and headed for my abandoned chicken leg, flipping the jewelry box off the table with his tail. It crashed against the floor and broke into two pieces.

"Oh no!" I picked up the top and bottom.

Beth took the pieces from my hands. "Why don't you take a shower and get dressed. I'll see if I can put the box together."

"Thank you. And thanks for the great food."

A half hour later, showered and fluffed, with a hint of perfume and fresh makeup, I exited the bathroom. Beth had replaced the food into the cooler and was in the only chair, holding something. She looked up as I entered. "You clean up well."

"What do you have?" I indicated her hand.

448

"It was in the box's lining. Some photos." She handed me the top one, a faded photograph of a far younger Holly.

I had a funny, hollow feeling in my stomach.

"What are you thinking, Gwen?"

"I don't know what to think just yet. I need time to process all that happened."

She handed me a second photo. I was standing in front of a white picket fence in what was probably an Easter outfit. I looked about five. The third photo, the most faded, was of a man and woman. They appeared to be in their thirties. I turned it over. Someone had written in faded blue ink *John and Mary Evelyn Howard.* Moving to the window, I tilted it until I could more clearly see the faces. "Mom and Dad," I whispered.

Beth moved over to see. "Your parents?" She took the photograph and read the back. "You're Gwen Howard Marcey!"

I grinned at her through my tears. "So I am. My season of searching is over."

"I'll start looking for their graves. Oh, that reminds me of a couple of things. They finally recovered Phil's body." She picked up her purse and pulled out my cell. "And Officer Attao's had your phone since he located it in the saddlebags of Phil's horses. Seth said everyone kept forgetting to give it back to you."

She handed the cell to me. It showed eleven messages, all from Blake. I clicked on the first message.

"Hi, Gwen. I've been a jerk. I realize a missing child can't wait, but I can. Please call me. I'd . . . I'd like to try again."

Beth touched me on the shoulder. "Is everything okay?"

I grinned. "Oh yeah."

ACKNOWLEDGMENTS

This story, like several of my previous books, came from a simple comment by my husband, Rick. "I find the Nez Perce tribe fascinating. Why don't you write about them?" I, too, found the story of the Nez Perce, Chief Joseph, Lewis and Clark, and Sacajawea formed a rich tapestry backdrop for a novel. As in all my books, I threaded actual cases and history into the story line. Rick's FBI former boss, hero, and mentor, Horace Hefner, worked on the Leonard Peltier, Pine Ridge case. In addition, I used a murder I'd worked on for the details of the homicides.

Much of the legwork and research came from Marcus and Molly Smith, dear friends who lived in the north central part of Idaho for many years. Marcus and Rick, banjo-picking buddies, drove around the various locations, took photos, and made notes. They met with Matt Young and toured the visitor center at the dam. They also ate their weight in pork products. Molly provided much feedback both as a beta reader and with her lyrical notes on the Clearwater valley.

Dave Pfieffer provided a lovely description of a plane crash . . . well, okay, maybe "lovely" isn't the right word. Karen Fisher, Dreamer Horse Farm on Lopez Island, Washington, provided insight on Nez Perce and Akhal Teke horses. Thank you to Jordyn Redwood, author and editor. My gratitude goes to David Turk at the US Marshals Service.

Richness and depth came from a brainstorming retreat at the home of bestselling author Colleen Coble, along with Robin Caroll, Ronie Kendig, and Michelle Lim. I thank them so much for a wonderful experience.

My beta readers, Kerry Woods, Lorrie Jenicek, and Michelle Garlock, are greatly appreciated blessings.

A special thank you to Phil Cicero, Tennessee Bureau of Investigations, for telling me that dying in my book was a bucket list item for him. I hope it was sufficiently gruesome.

My awesome agent, Karen Solem, provided me with inspiration, advice, and guidance. I am indebted to her for so much.

Amanda Bostic, editor extraordinaire, is a rock! And she rocks! Her insight encourages me to do more and better. My first experience working with author and editor Erin Healy was fantastic. I hope to work with her again in the future. A lot.

To the fabulous folks at Thomas Nelson, thank you. Daisy Hutton, your faith in me makes me humble and grateful. Jodi Hughes, thank you for shepherding all my books through typesetting and proofreading. To the marketing team headed by Paul Fisher, with Allison Carter and Meghan O'Brien, thanks for your work on marketing and publicity so *someone* could find and read my books. And Kristen Ingebretson, thank you for the artistic design on the cover for the original publisher's edition. It looks like one of my paintings.

I'm infinitely thankful for the caring, encouragement, teaching, sharing, patience, and love from my mentor, Frank Peretti, and his dear wife, Barb.

And best for last, I'm forever grateful to my Lord and Savior, Jesus Christ, to whom goes all the glory.

DISCUSSION QUESTIONS

1. If you've read other Gwen Marcey novels, how did this look into her childhood influence your view of her? How do you think you'd respond if you learned key facts of your life weren't factual at all?
2. Gwen Marcey has people in her life who represent parts of her personality. What part do you think Beth plays? Robert? Do you have people in your life who seem to do the same?
3. After reading this book, are you more aware of signs of deception in others? Have you seen it in any places that surprised you?
4. At one point, Gwen knocks over a vase. What do you think the vase represented?
5. Beth reminds Gwen that her adversity and trials helped her to grow and turn into the person she is today. Are there scripture verses that say the same thing?
6. One of the themes of the book is that

some events of the past are of a different time, a different place, and a different people. Reflect on this.

7. Another theme is from Ecclesiastes 3:1–8, that there are seasons in our lives. Do you find this to be true in your life?

8. Gwen makes the comment that love is like tissue, easily torn, unrepairable when damaged. Do you agree with this?

9. Winston is truly an ally and a companion for Gwen, not just a pet. Have you ever had a dog like Winston in your life?

ABOUT THE AUTHOR

Carrie Stuart Parks is an award-winning fine artist and internationally known forensic artist. She teaches forensic art courses to law enforcement professionals and is the author/illustrator of numerous books on drawing. Carrie began to write fiction while battling breast cancer and was mentored by *New York Times* bestselling author Frank Peretti. Now in remission, she continues to encourage other women struggling with cancer.

CarrieStuartParks.com
Facebook: CarrieStuartParksAuthor
Twitter: @CarrieParks

DATE DUE

APR 2 0 2018	